17-

Summer at Meadow Wood

Summer at Meadow Wood

Amy Rebecca Tan

HARPER
An Imprint of HarperCollinsPublishers

Summer at Meadow Wood
Copyright © 2020 by Amy Rebecca Tan
www.harpercollinschildrens.com

ISBN 978-0-06-279545-8

Typography by ebb-n-flo and Catherine San Juan
20 21 22 23 24   PC/LSC   10 9 8 7 6 5 4 3 2 1
❖
First Edition

For Jan and Gayle, the best camp sisters of all

Meadow Wood Cabins

JUNIOR CAMP

Chicory—six- and seven-year-olds

Daisy—eight-year-olds

Violet—nine-year-olds

INTERMEDIATE CAMP

Goldenrod—ten-year-olds

Dandelion—eleven-year-olds

Clover—twelve-year-olds

SENIOR CAMP

Yarrow—thirteen-year-olds

Marigold—fourteen-year-olds

Aster—fifteen-year-olds

Day 1—Saturday

→>>·<<<-

We realized the frog didn't make it somewhere near the Massachusetts/New Hampshire border.

The smell was what gave it away.

I could only describe it as the smell of a decaying frog in a cardboard box on a hot bus moving north at sixty-five miles per hour.

It was a unique odor.

Poor Vera Simon. She took the seat in the first row as soon as we boarded the bus and clutched that shoebox on her lap as if it contained Cinderella's glass slipper. Her two blond braids were pulled so tight on either side of her head you could practically see her mom working on her hair earlier that morning, combing and twisting and locking them in place like her life depended on it.

It had worked, though, because her braids still looked perfect.

Little Vera.

Someone had to tell her about the frog.

And because I was her designated camp sister, it was going to have to be me.

Every junior camper was assigned a senior camper to be their "sister" for the entire eight weeks at Meadow Wood. This gave the juniors a safe person to go to any time they felt homesick or had a problem in their cabin or had questions about evening activity or mail or canteen.

If you had a good camp sister, it made all the difference in the world.

If you had a bad one, well, it could get pretty ugly. I should know.

When I was nine years old, starting my first summer at Meadow Wood, my camp sister was Jennifer Maskers. Jennifer was fifteen, wore sparkly eye makeup, and had hair so long she could sit on it. She was also a Meadow Wood lifer. She had started camp in Chicory, the youngest bunk, and had returned every summer until reaching the oldest one, Aster.

The Aster girls were the queens of Meadow Wood. If an Aster knew you, you got popularity points immediately. If an Aster hugged you or gave you a piggyback ride to the dining hall or bragged about how cute you were, you were golden. Jennifer Maskers did all that for nine-year-old me. I thought I'd hit the jackpot.

Until the Byars Beach field trip in July.

Only senior campers went on that trip, but Jennifer brought a gift back for me: a gigantic rainbow-swirl lollipop the size of my head. It was almost an inch thick and weighed way too much for a piece of candy, but I wanted Jennifer to keep thinking I was adorable and someone worth spending money on, so I put on a show and bit greedily into it.

I just meant to bite off a small piece to suck on while she showed me the other treasures in her shopping bag.

Instead, a solid chunk of my top front right tooth snapped off with a crack as loud as a campfire twig popping.

Jennifer's face went from shocked to horrified to hysterical laughter so quickly I didn't even have time to react to the pain. I was focused on her face—her glamorous fifteen-year-old face—to figure out how I should feel about the jagged piece of tooth in my hand and the sharp edge my tongue kept running over inside my mouth.

After an uncomfortable drive in the camp director's car to the closest town (twenty-five minutes away) for an emergency dentist appointment, I had a repaired front tooth. I also had new feelings about my camp sister.

Not good ones.

And that's why I always told myself that I would be the best camp sister ever, when my time came.

And that time was now.

On this bus.

With that smell.

I was sure Vera had no idea she was cradling the corpse of her pet frog. She was only seven years old, after all.

I had just met Vera minutes before boarding the bus when one of the counselors paired up all the camp sisters for a photo. I didn't know if she was the kid who cannonballed straight into the pool without testing the water first or if she was the kid who eased in slowly, an inch at a time, letting each new bit of skin adjust to the temperature. So I didn't know if I should just blurt out the bad news or approach carefully.

I unbuckled my seat belt, walked up the aisle, and stopped at the first row on the bus where Vera was seated alone, next to the window.

"Mind if I sit here?" I asked.

Vera gazed up at me with big brown eyes that looked one size too large for her head.

"Sit down!" she practically ordered me. "It's dangerous to stand in the aisle at this speed. And buckle up—it's the law."

I quickly sat and clicked my seat belt across my hips. Vera looked relieved.

"So, how are you doing?" I asked her.

"I'm fine," she said, turning her head to look out the window, away from me.

"Are you excited? To get there and see your cabin and meet your counselors?" I tried to make my voice sound enthusiastic, which took effort, as I was mildly carsick. The dead frog smell wasn't helping.

"Excited? Not at the moment, no."

"Oh. Well, maybe once we get closer," I suggested.

Vera looked at me the way my mom looks at my little brother sometimes, with extra patience. "Maybe," she said.

"So." I shifted in my seat, turning toward her. "I'm concerned about your frog, Vera."

"There's no need," she replied without pause.

"Well . . . I think this trip might have been too much for him."

Vera's eyes opened wide—they seemed to take up half her face. She looked at the box on her lap, then turned her huge brown eyes up at me again.

"I'm sorry, but that smell," I said. "I think he's . . . no longer with us."

Vera blinked slowly.

"I'm sorry," I said again gently.

"I know she's gone," she replied.

"You know?"

"Of course I know. That smell is a dead giveaway." Her eyes twinkled at me.

"O-okay," I stuttered. "Well, are you upset? You must be upset," I said, even though I couldn't read her face.

"I'm fine. I knew it was a risk bringing her. I just rescued her from my neighbor's pool this morning. I don't know how long she was stuck in there, but I know chlorine penetrated her skin. Frogs breathe through their skin, you know."

"Yeah, I know," I said.

"She's a green frog, *Lithobates clamitans*, very common in Pennsylvania."

"How do you know she's a she?"

"Her tympana, the circular patch of skin behind the eyes, are smaller in size than her eyes, which means she's a female. If the tympana were the same size as the eyes or larger, she would be a male."

"Oh. Cool." Vera would probably love the nature hut at camp, with all its pressed flowers, boxes of seeds, bark samples, and posters about indigenous New Hampshire species. In junior camp, nature hut was a daily activity.

"Anyway, I know she's deceased. The odds were stacked against her."

"Guess so," I agreed.

Vera hugged the box closer to her body. There were air holes punched on four sides. You could practically see the dead-frog fumes wafting out of them.

Vera didn't look sad, but she didn't look not sad, either. I tried to figure out what a good camp sister would do.

"What was her name?" I decided to ask.

"Happy."

I stifled a laugh. It was hard not to laugh at a dead frog named Happy.

"I'm aware of the irony in her name," Vera clarified.

Irony? Did she really just say *irony?*

"This is how you think, Vera? Aren't you seven? Aren't you in Chicory?"

"I'm gifted." Vera sighed, as though she were tired of explaining it to people.

"Oh." I bit my lip. It figured—my first shot at being a camp sister and I got the one safety-focused, amphibian-loving, gifted kid in the whole junior camp.

"I've been advanced since the day I was born, according to my mom. She calls me her sponge because I absorb everything. It's just the two of us, so I'm always with her and her adult friends, which has done wonders for my vocabulary. After only two months in kindergarten, they moved me right to second grade." Vera paused to catch her breath, and then her tone changed completely. "Don't tell anyone, though, in my cabin." Her face was serious as a heart attack. Serious as a dead frog. "I don't want to seem obnoxious about it."

"My lips are sealed," I told her, and acted out zipping my mouth shut and tossing the key. "I'm sure they'll never figure it out."

She squinted her eyes at me.

"What?" I asked.

"I hear your sarcasm," she scolded.

How was I feeling like the younger one here? I was thirteen! I was almost twice Vera's age. I was in Yarrow, in senior camp, *finally*.

"Easy, Vera. I'm just making a joke," I explained.

She turned away from me and looked back out the window.

"We really should get rid of that box, though," I told her.

Vera took a deep breath and released it slowly. "Okay," she agreed.

"Maybe at the next rest stop?" I proposed.

She nodded.

We sat in silence for a minute. I stared at the unbending road ahead of us, but Vera could only stare at the back of the safety barrier in front of her. She was too short to see over it.

Then she asked, "Will you do it for me?"

She all of a sudden sounded her age, her voice matching her size, her butterfly hair ribbons tied around each braid, and her glitter shoelaces, which had a strawberry-daisy-strawberry pattern on them.

"Sure, Vera," I told her. "I'll take care of her."

Vera smiled at me then, for the first time.

"I'm your camp sister. I'll always help you when you need it," I reassured her. "Us *V*s gotta stick together, you know. Vic and Vera. We're the *V* team."

Her smile grew and she let her dangling legs swing back and forth a few times. They didn't reach the floor. Even for seven, Vera was small. I was glad she'd be in a cabin with other seven-year-olds. She might have been able to fit in easily with kids two years older than her at school, but camp was not school. At camp, she'd stick out like a snowflake in July if she were placed in a cabin with the older girls who matched her school grade.

Vera took one hand off her box then, reached over to my seat, and placed her hand in mine.

Her hand was clammy from pressing against the cardboard, but her grip was tight and I felt her whole body relax next to me. It was funny how you could go from not knowing a person at all to holding their hand and making them feel safe in just a matter of minutes.

Or maybe not funny. Maybe amazing was what it was.

I held Vera's hand in my lap and looked out the flat glass windshield in front of me. There was nothing but gray road and blue sky, trees leaving a blur of green on either side. We'd been on the bus for hours, so the chatter and cheering and tone-deaf singing had died off a while ago. Girls in every row were either asleep or completely zoned out, rocked into a trancelike state by the purring motor of the bus.

I held on to the silence, just the sound of tires whirring and air rushing past, because I knew it was the last time I'd hear this kind of quiet for weeks.

And I tried not to breathe through my nose.

Day 1—Saturday evening

—>>>·<<<—

"It looks like a pharmacy threw up in here."

Chieko stood in the doorway that separated the camper room from the counselor room in our cabin, her hands on her hips, her dark brown eyes narrowed as she scanned the space.

We were unpacking. Badly.

An explosion of hairbrushes and headbands, shampoo bottles and plastic razors, Q-tips and packages of gum (not technically permitted), bug spray and balled-up socks covered the worn wooden floor.

"You've been at it for almost an hour," Chieko told us, looking at the oversize black watch that was fastened around her slim wrist. "I find your lack of progress disturbing. Also, somewhat impressive." She disappeared back to her room, and

I heard the springs of her cot screech as she settled onto it.

Chieko was the only one in Yarrow new to Meadow Wood.

And she was our counselor.

The bugle for dinner was going to blow soon, and none of us were ready to go. Jordana was hanging a *Hamilton* poster on the front of her cubby door with so much duct tape she'd probably never get it off again. Carly was sitting on a mound of her own thick hoodie sweatshirts while trying to open a container of red rope licorice (also not technically permitted). Jaida A and Jaida C were in the bathroom organizing toiletries together. I was trying to wrestle my pillow from home into a Meadow Wood pillowcase. It was like trying to slip a whole baked potato into a piece of pita bread. But I wasn't giving up. Yet.

Chieko stuck her head back in our room and said, with no enthusiasm at all, "Time for forced bunk bonding, also known as Roses and Thorns. Move it, campers."

She turned on her heel and walked back to her room, muttering, "Good God, what did I get myself into?" loud enough for us to hear.

"Did she just call us *campers*?" Jordana asked, already chomping away on the gum she had packed. It was Big Red. I could smell the spicy cinnamon of it from six feet away.

"This is *senior* camp," Carly joined in, shaking her head. "I will not be referred to as a *camper*, for Jake's sake."

"Ooh, who's Jake?" Jordana said, thrusting her hip out in an exaggerated flirty pose. "Is he hot?"

Carly looked at her like she couldn't believe this was starting already.

"Yes, Jordana," I answered for Carly. "The fictional Jake from Carly's rhyme is hot. Smokin' hot. Edge-of-the-sun hot."

"Woot-woot!" Jordana hooted. She flipped her mane of amber-brown hair upside down and then whipped it back up, gathering it into a high ponytail. Her skin already had a sun-kissed look from time spent at the pool before camp started, the light sprinkle of freckles on her nose more pronounced from her tan. She cackled like a wild animal and then, in a motherly tone, said, "Time for Roses and Thorns, campers!"

She sashayed over to me, linked her arm through mine, breathed her hot gum breath on me, and pulled me out to the counselor room.

Carly and the two Jaidas dropped what they were doing and followed.

"I'm told you've all been here since junior camp, so you know the drill," Chieko started. "Share one rose and one thorn each and this will instantly make us lifelong friends." She said this like she was reading the instructions from a board game.

"Way to sell it, counselor," I said, crossing my legs pretzel-style as I sat.

Chieko looked at me, a sparkle in her eye. "Why thank you, young one."

We were sitting on the floor in a circle in the front room of the cabin, also known as the counselor room, also known as the meeting room. Only one of the three counselor cots was made up. We only needed one counselor because there were only five of us *campers* in Yarrow this year, even though the bunk was built to hold up to twelve.

Jordana, Carly, the two Jaidas, and me. That was it.

Meadow Wood had seen better days.

Meadow Wood was a real back-to-nature kind of camp—rustic wooden cabins with only screen doors, campfires by the lakefront, clay tennis and bocce courts, hiking trips with butterfly nets and magnifying lenses, an arts-and-crafts shack to draw native flora and fauna. There were no rock walls, no zip lines, no paintball fields like all the other camps had. Meadow Wood was the fossil of summer camps, so attendance was slowly shrinking, the way a shadow does as the sun rises higher in the sky. What really sealed our fate, though, was the *No Devices* rule.

No cell phones.

No tablets.

No laptops.

No smartwatches.

Nothing.

Or almost nothing.

We all knew Jordana had something hidden somewhere.

She always tried, every year, to sneak a device in. We made a bet each summer, Carly and me, about how many days she'd last before getting busted. The winner got to claim two canteen items from the loser. Last summer I won. I got a grape soda and a Kit Kat Big Kat bar from Carly. But then I shared them both with her anyway.

"All right," Chieko said, sounding as bored as humanly possible. "Who wants to go first?"

Chieko, I realized, was also chewing gum. Her dark black bangs cut across her forehead straight as an arrow, and one small section over her right eye was dyed an electric blue. She was thin and fair-skinned and looked like she would be stunningly beautiful if she smiled.

But she didn't smile.

"I'll go." Jordana jumped at the chance to be first.

Chieko leaned back and stretched her legs out in front of her into the middle of our small circle. The tip of a tattoo peeked out from under her sock on one ankle, but I couldn't tell what it was.

"We're doing from the whole last year, right?" Jordana clarified, and then started without waiting for an answer. "My rose is that I got the lead in the middle school play this year, even though I was only a seventh grader. I was Annie, and it was the most amazing show ever!"

"Drama. Fantastic," Chieko said, her voice flat as roadkill.

Carly laughed quietly while Jordana completely missed the dig.

"The girl can seriously sing," I told Chieko, because Jordana really was talented. Her mom was a singer. Her dad was a singer. Jordana was not even the tiniest bit modest about her talent.

"And my thorn," Jordana continued, "is that my farty older brother decided to be a counselor at Forest Lake this year, even though he promised me he wouldn't. So now he'll be at all of our socials." Jordana glared at the space between me and Carly, as if her brother was sitting right there with us. "I want to kill him."

Forest Lake was our unofficial brother camp. It was a few miles down the road, or straight across the lake if you could travel the way a bird flies. Our senior camp had several socials with Forest Lake's senior camp every summer.

"It epically sucks," Jordana said, all eyes wide and mouth

open and hands gesturing for dramatic effect. "I will get no action at all this summer."

"Eww." Carly grimaced. "Gross."

"It's true. No one will go for a counselor's little sister. It's like an unwritten rule." Jordana said this like she might as well pack up now and head back home. "Worst. Thorn. Ever."

"It's definitely *not* the worst thorn ever," Carly responded. "There are a lot of worse things than a brother at some socials."

"Yes, very true," Jaida A piped up.

Jaida A was Jaida Acevedo. We called her Jaida A because there was also a Jaida C: Jaida Cohen. I had never met a Jaida in my whole entire life and then—wham!—four years ago there were two of them right there, sharing a bunk bed, brushing their teeth in the same sink, and folding laundry with me every Sunday afternoon. Even the two Jaidas had never met another Jaida before that summer when we were all thrown together in Violet, the oldest bunk in junior camp. The Jaidas pretended they were twins even though they looked nothing alike—Jaida A had straight dark hair, dark eyes, and olive skin, and Jaida C had light brown curls, blue eyes, and fair skin that managed to turn a creamy tan every summer even though it looked like it should burn after just six seconds in the sun. The Jaidas became inseparable in half a heartbeat.

"Take SeaWorld," Jaida A began. "Another orca *died* there this year!"

"What the butt is an orca?" Jordana asked, flipping her hair and rolling her eyes.

"It's a killer whale, right?" Carly asked.

"It's a kind of dolphin," Jaida C answered, then added more quietly, "I think."

Chieko leaned in and folded her arms across her chest, watching us like she was watching TV. She almost looked amused.

"Dolphin, yes." Jaida A continued, "This poor orca was kidnapped from his family in the ocean—"

"You mean orca-napped," I said.

Carly chuckled and high-fived me.

"Orca-napped, yes. Stolen!" Jaida A insisted, her voice urgent. "And they locked him up in a tiny pool and forced him to do tricks every single day for a crowd of screaming people until he died, and that was his whole entire miserable life. That is *way* worse than your thorn."

Jordana huffed a strand of hair out of her face. "Maybe," she allowed. "Okay, fine. Orca-napping and death is worse."

Jaida A was our resident activist. Last summer it was all about fracking. The year before that it was about saving the bees. It looked like this year might be SeaWorld. Or maybe animal rights in general. It was too early to tell.

"So that's your thorn then, Jaida?" Chieko asked, trying to move us along. She was looking at her giant watch again.

"She's Jaida *A*. You have to call her that," Jordana said.

"Got it," Chieko said with an eye roll, "'cause it's so confusing who I'm talking to right now."

"I knew who you were talking to," Jaida C chimed in, "but she's still Jaida A."

"She is always and forever Jaida A," Jordana sang, wrapping her arms around Jaida A and giving her a big noisy smooch on her cheek.

Jaida A smooched Jordana's cheek back.

"So, Jaida *A*," Chieko said, "got a rose to throw on the pile?"

"Not really. The world's a mess."

"Think of one good thing that happened over the last year," Carly encouraged her. "Just one."

You could practically see Jaida A scrolling through all the environmental sadness and despair she'd learned about over the last ten months. But then she stopped scrolling and said, "My middle school started an Animal Welfare Club, and we did a food drive for a dog shelter and a letter campaign to a dumb company that sells fur. That was kind of rosy."

"Absolutely rosy. Terrifically rosy. Thank you, Jaida A," Chieko acknowledged. "Who's next? And is anyone else starving?"

"I am." Jordana clutched her stomach dramatically and fell onto Jaida A's lap.

"Eat your gum," Jaida A ordered.

We all cracked up.

"Why is that funny?" Chieko asked, looking at us like we were nuts.

"It's an inside joke," Jaida C answered, still giggling.

"Back in Violet," Carly explained, "Jordana claimed her gum was like the gum from Willy Wonka and had a three-course meal in it."

"And that she could just chew her gum instead of eating meals in the dining hall, because her gum food was so much better," Jaida A added. "For the entire summer, just gum!"

"You didn't even last one morning!" Jaida C reminded her. "You jumped that tray of grilled cheese at lunch like a starving zombie."

"I was *nine*!" Jordana defended herself.

"You're not helping yourself, Jordana." I couldn't stop laughing. "Nine is really old to believe in magic gum."

"I had a vivid imagination, okay?" Jordana claimed, smiling

now, loving all the attention. "It's a *good* thing. It helps with my acting."

"Then act like you're not hungry right now," Carly challenged her.

Jordana put her hands to her throat and mimed chewing and swallowing. "There," she said. "I just ate two pieces of gum. I'm stuffed."

"Are all campers at Meadow Wood like you guys?" Chieko asked.

"Of course not," Jordana answered immediately. "We are superior Meadow Wooders."

Chieko looked unsure. "Whose turn is it? We need to finish up."

"I'll go," Carly volunteered.

Carly was my closest friend at Meadow Wood. Carly was short and thin and had perfect teeth without ever wearing braces. Her skin was a lot darker than mine because she was biracial—her dad was black and her mom was white—but our eyes were practically the exact same shade of deep dark brown. Carly and I never saw each other during the school year because I lived in Pennsylvania and she lived in Connecticut, but we wrote letters to each other—actual snail-mail letters. And we tried to find the most horrible stationery in existence to write on. So far, I was the champion. My last letter was on stationery that had a unicorn roasting marshmallows on his horn over a campfire, but the marshmallows were dripping into the fire and the unicorn had a crazed expression on his face so it looked like he was actually cooking his horn. The caption across the top read *Warm Greetings to You*.

It was awful.

And hilarious.

"My rose is that I had a steady job all year. I babysat for my neighbor Lola every weekend and made so much money I had to open a savings account."

"Ooh, Carly." Jordana rubbed her fingers against her thumb in that money way. "Sharing is caring."

"You can donate to the Orca Project!" Jaida A shouted.

"I didn't bring the money," Carly explained. "It's all in the bank."

Jordana stuck her tongue out at Carly and let out a *humph*.

"Except for what I spent on books," Carly added shyly.

Jordana turned to Chieko then. "In case you didn't know, Carly is *obsessed* with books. She *like* likes them, the way you *like* a crush. If you ever can't find Carly, it's because she's off somewhere, alone, making out with a book."

Carly didn't argue, even though she definitely didn't make

out with books. She just read them, new ones and old favorites, constantly.

"Books are my life," Chieko declared, sharing something about herself for the first time. She twisted herself around then to reveal a red paperback sticking out of the back pocket of her shorts. It was pretty beat up, the corners rounded and splayed like a paper fan. "I always have one with me."

Carly did a seated bow at Chieko, as if she were paying respects to royalty. It made me think immediately of the charades game we had to play every summer for evening activity. I hated it. Jordana loved it.

"I saw your cubby," Jaida C said, addressing Chieko. "It looks like you brought more books than clothes."

"I did," Chieko said.

"You've got to be kidding," Jordana said in total disbelief.

"And if we could wrap up this delightful mandatory activity, I might get a chance to read one before the dinner bugle goes off," Chieko added.

Carly's face became serious then and she quickly shared, "My thorn is that my grandmom died in January, and that was the worst thing that happened all year"—she glanced quickly at Jordana when she said it—"and probably the worst thing in my whole life so far."

"I'm sorry, Carly," Jaida C was the first to say.

"Me too," Jaida A said next.

I already knew about her grandmom, because of our letters, so I just pushed my knee against her knee lightly, and she pushed hers back.

"It's okay," Carly said. "I'm okay."

Chieko turned toward me. "Victoria, it's your go."

"Vic," I corrected her.

"My apologies. Vic," she repeated.

"My rose is easy. My rose is today, coming here, back to Meadow Wood."

"Woot-woot, Meadow Woot!" Jordana cheered, rocking her head up and down so her ponytail bounced.

"And," I continued quickly, "my thorn was bouncing around on a bus for seven hours inhaling the mind-numbing fumes of a dying amphibian."

Saying this out loud reminded me to check on Vera after dinner.

"A dying amphibian?" Jaida A asked, her face softening with concern.

"Fumes? Ewww." Jordana grimaced.

"That's awful." Carly took my hand.

Chieko leaned forward and tipped an invisible hat to me. "Excellent sentence, Vic. By far the most entertaining thorn

I've heard so far." Then she stood and looked down at the five of us still on the floor. "Now, for the love of God, go finish unpacking your junk."

"I want a maid," Jordana whined.

"We *are* the maids," Jaida C said, "for the next eight weeks of Meadow Wood, at least."

"Welcome to Meadow *Work*!" Jordana said.

Chieko smiled at that, her eyes crinkling up under the shock of blue and black bangs covering her forehead.

And she *was* really beautiful when she smiled.

Day 1—Saturday evening

-»»·«««-

Here's the thing, though: I lied about my thorn.

My thorn wasn't the frog smell on the bus, although it was no exaggeration to put it on my top-ten list of awful experiences. But my thorn, my honest and true thorn, was way worse.

My thorn was that I wasn't at Meadow Wood this summer because I loved camp so much and I had been looking forward to it all year and I couldn't wait to see my friends again for a fun two months in the woods of New Hampshire.

My thorn was that I was at Meadow Wood this summer because my mom dumped me here. I was at Meadow Wood because my mom wanted to get rid of me.

I was thirteen, and even though I loved my summer friends, I didn't want to go to camp anymore. I didn't want to wake up at the crack of dawn every morning to the sound of a blaring bugle and shuffle from one activity to another all day long. I wanted to be home riding my bike every day to the pool. I wanted to be drinking blue slushies so fast the cold made my teeth hurt and my head tingle. I wanted to be watching videos of bad lip syncs and cute snoring baby animals until my butt fell asleep in the chair. I wanted to read magazines and watch old movies and redecorate my room. *I* wanted to find a babysitting job that would earn me enough money to need a bank account.

And I wanted to be home for Jamie, my best friend, who had made the biggest mistake of her life and was a complete mess because of it. I wanted to be home for *her*, to help her and cheer her up, the way a best friend should.

But my mom used Jamie against me. She said I had to go away for the summer because Jamie was a bad influence on me, which was truly the lamest excuse she could have come up with. My mom *loved* Jamie. My mom had spent the last six years praising Jamie and pushing me to be more like her. Jamie was a quiet, polite, artistic book nerd who spent every waking moment that she wasn't with me with her own mom and aunt. Jamie always did her homework. Jamie never called out in class. Jamie was respectful and responsible.

So my mom did *not* send me to camp to get me away from Jamie.

She sent me to camp to get me away from *her*.

And I knew why.

I saw the email.

I saw it by accident, when she left her computer suddenly, frantically, because the oven caught fire. One second she was typing at her desk and the next the fire alarm was shrieking loud enough to raise the dead. She ran to the kitchen to find billows of dark smoke swirling out of the oven like clouds of ugly lies.

I read the email.

It was all there, in black and white.

That was why she wanted me gone.

And my eight-year-old brother, Freddy, too, who she sent off to Forest Lake for his first time ever away from home.

Once she opened all the windows and fanned the house clear and got the alarm to stop shrieking, she pulled the blackened cookies from the oven and tossed them into the sink, pan and all, with a clatter that was more jarring than the fire alarm. By the time she got back to her computer, I was tying my second sneaker, a sick heat flaring inside my body, prickling every inch of my skin from the inside out.

"What are you doing?" she asked me, a little panic in her voice as she looked at what she'd left up on her screen. "What were you doing?"

"Getting my shoes," I said, quick and curt, my breathing short and shallow.

Then I stood up and pushed the screen door open, stepped out, and let it bang closed behind me in that way I knew she hated.

And then I just ran.

So that means I lied about my rose, too. Coming back to camp wasn't my rose.

I didn't have any rose at all.

Day 2—Sunday

→>>·<<←

The bugle blared at seven o'clock the next morning and I woke up unsure of where I was, but the wire springs jabbing my back through my mattress accompanied by Jordana's monologue of curse words about how early it was reminded me pretty quickly.

Every morning would start this way. The bugle, then resentment at hearing the bugle, then Jordana's cursing, then an attempt to hunker deeper down beneath my soft, cozy comforter from home to drown out all those sounds. Next, Jaida C would pop up and encourage us all to get out of bed, stretching while she circled the room, giving each of us a gentle shake to help us wake up. Jaida C was the only one who didn't seem to mind waking up early. She was also the first one to pass out every night, which might have had something to do with it.

After bugle we had flag, where every camper stood on a bald piece of ground circling the pole while we raised four flags in a row—first the American flag, then the New Hampshire flag, then the Meadow Wood flag, then a homemade burlap flag with the words *Nature Nurtures Life* surrounded by leaves and flowers.

Four flags.

"The raising of the flags gets old by number three, don't you think?" I muttered to Carly and Jordana, both standing beside me, both yawning.

"We might as well put a flag up there for world peace while we're at it," Carly whispered back, rubbing sleep sand out of the corner of her eye.

"Or a flag for the orcas?" Jaida A said, clearly missing the sarcasm.

"We could make one at arts and crafts," Jaida C said.

A counselor from the next bunk shushed us, then turned her attention back to Brenda.

Brenda, the camp director, was wearing her usual white collared shirt tucked into khaki shorts with an old-fashioned black walkie-talkie clipped to the waistband. Her husband, Earl, had the other walkie-talkie. Earl spent his days fixing plumbing, patching screens, mowing fields, and doing every other possible maintenance job that could come up at camp.

Earl was quieter than Brenda, but we all knew him and we all wanted a turn driving the golf cart he used to get himself and his equipment wherever he needed to be.

None of us ever got to drive it.

Brenda was a retired second-grade teacher who loved the outdoors, loved kids, and loved running camp, which she had been doing for the last thirteen years. She always wore her hair pulled back in a tight bun, and the pale blond showed more streaks of gray now than I remembered from last summer. She was talking about the special blueberry pancakes we were about to enjoy at our first breakfast of the season and how the blueberries were grown right on Meadow Wood property. Then she went on to explain the farm-to-table program the camp was embracing this year, but I zoned out. It was too early and I was still half-asleep.

At the end of flag, Brenda counted to three and we all shouted, "Meadow Wood!" as loud as we could. After that, we were dismissed to the dining hall.

It probably wasn't the worst way in the world to start a summer day, but it definitely wasn't the best way, either.

The dining hall was like a giant wood cave—high ceilings with wooden beams running the width of the place, wood floors, wood walls made up of horizontally hung planks, windows with wood trim, so warped they were nearly impossible to slide up or pull down.

They mostly always stayed up.

The tables were heavy and older than dirt, with previous campers' names and years carved into the surfaces, like *Gayle Robin '87* and *Janel B 1992*. We knew exactly which table was ours—it was where Yarrow sat year after year after year. At camp, things like that didn't change. If Yarrow was the table in the right back corner, Yarrow would always be the table in the right back corner.

Our table fit the six of us easily. But only five of us were there.

"Uh, we're missing a counselor," Jaida C noted.

"She should be here by now," Jaida A said. "I thought she was just skipping flag."

"We are not properly supervised!" Jordana exclaimed. Then she yawned again and grimaced. "Where is the coffee? How are we supposed to function at this hour without coffee?"

"You drink coffee?" Jaida A asked.

"You're only thirteen," Jaida C reminded her.

"How did you get up for school every day?" Carly challenged. "I bet it was earlier than this."

"Yes, it was," Jordana conceded, "but I had COFFEE!"

Brenda appeared suddenly. She was a large woman—tall and thick and solid muscle—but she somehow still managed to not be there and then be there in a flash, without any warning.

"It's a bit early for hysteria, Miss Jordana. What seems to be the problem?" Brenda smiled at Jordana from her towering height of six feet two inches.

And that was when Chieko showed up. She stumbled to our table with her eyes half-closed, pulled out a chair, plopped herself down into it, and said in her scratchy morning voice, "What do you have to do around here to get a cup of coffee?"

We held our breath.

Literally.

Like if you were a scientist trying to measure inhales and exhales of oxygen and carbon dioxide in our exact table space, you would have come up with nothing.

Nada.

Zilch.

"Water, Chieko. Proper hydration is the best stimulant," Brenda answered. She leaned over the table, poured a tall glass of water from the metal pitcher, and placed it in front of Chieko. "We don't provide coffee at camp, as you know from counselor orientation. The sun and sky and spring water are stimulants enough."

Chieko stared at the glass of water as if she were trying to cast a spell on it and magically turn it into coffee.

Brenda switched topics to say, "You seem to be just catching up with Yarrow. You are required to attend flag and escort your cabin here every morning."

"There was a problem. With the sink. In the cabin." Chieko sat up a little straighter in her chair, but her eyes were still puffy and half-closed. "I fixed it."

"Completely? Do you need Earl to take a look?" Brenda offered.

"No, it's all good," Chieko answered. "But thanks anyway."

Brenda put her hands on her hips and took a good long look at the six of us. It seemed like she was trying to figure out if we were going to be the pain-in-the-butt cabin this year. There was always one, and it was almost always a cabin in senior camp.

"Enjoy your pancakes," Brenda said, distracted now by a table where napkins were being scrunched up and thrown like balls. "Earl grew those blueberries himself." She said this with pride, then marched off.

"Was there really something wrong with the sink?" Jaida C asked the moment Brenda was out of earshot.

"As far as you know," Chieko answered. Then she picked up a different glass, filled it with orange juice from the clear plastic pitcher, and chugged every drop. She slammed the empty cup down on the table, let out a giant breath, and announced, "Like drinking the sun."

Carly and I exchanged smiles while Jaida C passed napkins around the table.

And then the two Clover tables burst into cheer: "We've got spirit, yes we do! We've got spirit, how 'bout you?" And they all stood on the last word and pointed to the two Dandelion tables next to them.

All the Dandelion girls hopped onto their feet and cheered, "We've got spirit, yes we do! We've got spirit, how 'bout you?"

The Clover girls immediately shouted back, "We've got more! We've got more! We've got more! We've got more!"

Then Dandelion cheered, even louder, "No you don't! No you don't! No you don't! No you don't!"

Clover answered, at full volume now and with stamping feet, "Yes we do! Yes we do! Yes we do! Yes we do!"

"What in God's good name is happening?" Chieko asked me, a look of horror on her face.

"Cheering," I said, pouring my own glass of orange juice and spilling a little on the table.

"But it's barely eight o'clock in the morning," Chieko protested. "Is it even eight o'clock in the morning?"

"This is normal," Jaida C assured her.

"This is at every meal," Jaida A added.

"This is barbaric," Chieko said, covering her ears with both hands and slumping down in her chair.

At that point, junior camp caught on and all the Daisy campers started their own challenge by jabbing their fingers at the table of Violets next to them and cheering, "We've got spirit, yes we do! We've got spirit, how 'bout you?"

The Violets popped up out of their seats and answered, "We've got more! We've got more! We've got more! We've got more!"

As the Daisies yelled back their *No you don't*s, Chieko leaned in to me to ask, "Why does one want to have more spirit anyway? Can't we just share the spirit evenly? And quietly?"

"Uh-uh." I shook my head at her. "We can't. Welcome to camp, Chieko."

When the Violets screamed their round of *Yes we do*s, you could already hear voices cracking. There was always a fair amount of laryngitis by the second week of camp.

"At least the lyrics were thoughtfully composed," Chieko said to me, sarcasm heavy as a canoe.

It was the first time I had really listened to the words in the cheer. When you were screaming them, you were caught up in the moment so the words didn't register, but when you were just listening, well, it was easier to notice how dumb it all sounded.

Chieko shook her head like she was trying to get water out of her ear. Then she pulled out that same red book she'd shown us the night before and disappeared into it. I saw that the cover had a drawing of a woman's face on it, and underneath were the words: *You Learn by Living, Eleanor Roosevelt*.

The cheering only stopped when the pancakes were served. The Aster girls were the waitresses.

Chieko drank more orange juice and read while we slurped up way more syrup than our pancakes called for and did our best to keep it out of our hair.

I had to admit that the blueberries Earl grew were so sweet and juicy that they were almost worth getting up early for.

Almost.

Day 3—Monday

→→→·←←←

It was rest hour, which was exactly what it sounded like: one hour of quiet cabin time after lunch to rest, write letters, play cards or jacks, or do some other non-noisy activity with your counselors and bunkmates.

Carly was reading on her bed, which was the top bunk directly above mine, and Jaida A and Jaida C got permission to visit their camp sisters in Daisy. Their camp sisters were identical twins, so the Jaidas were competing to see who could master telling them apart first. Jordana was busy applying a cleansing charcoal face mask in the bathroom, and Chieko was on her bed in the counselor room, also reading.

I was about to write my first letter of the summer to Jamie when Carly popped her head down over the side of her bunk.

"Wanna make a bed tent?"

"Do you even need to ask?" I jumped off my cot to stuff my stationery back into my cubby as Carly climbed down from her bunk. We pulled out the extra-long sheet and blanket from her bed so they hung down like walls around my bottom bunk, and then we tucked them under my mattress to hold them in place. We crawled in through the short end where my pillow went, then propped my pillow and hers in that space to make another wall.

"Perfect!" Carly decided.

"Super cozy," I agreed, looking at the walls of white sheet and blue blanket wrapped around us like a hug.

"Do you remember our first bed tent?" Carly asked, her eyes twinkling the way they did that day we met four years ago in Violet.

"Dori called us out for 'excluding others,'" I mimicked our old counselor.

"But then everyone copied, so every bunk bed in the cabin turned into a bed tent!"

"It was pretty awesome," I admitted. "How did we even think of it? Was it my genius mind at work?"

Carly rolled her eyes and explained, "I was telling you about that book I loved, *The Maggie B.*, about the girl and her little brother alone on a boat at sea, and you said you could turn our bunk bed into a boat."

"Yep, I was a nine-year-old genius," I bragged.

"Yeah," Carly agreed, then crinkled her eyes at me. "What happened?"

I shoved her and she fell into the sheet, knocking it out of place.

"Hey, you butt-butt!" Carly righted herself and shoved me back.

"Oh my God—butt-butt! Who could forget Mean Melanie?"

Melanie was a counselor for one of the intermediate cabins, but she was also a swim instructor, so we saw her every day that first summer. We had third-period swim. The early morning cold was usually gone by then, but there was one random day in the first week of July when the bite in the air made it impossible for Carly and me to drop our towels and plunk ourselves into the lake with everyone else.

"Let's go, girls. You're holding us up," Melanie scolded us. She turned to the rest of our Violet bunkmates, all ten girls frantically bobbing up and down in the water to warm up, and ordered, "Everyone grab a kickboard."

Carly and I shuffled closer to the edge of the dock. I dipped my toe in and shuddered at the icy spark it sent up my leg. Carly hadn't even touched the water but was already shivering in her bathing suit.

"I can't," she whispered to me. "It's so cold. I just can't."

"It's too cold to swim," I declared, speaking up for both of us.

"It's not too cold for them." Melanie pointed at the girls in the water.

"Jaida C's lips are blue," I said.

"Which one is Jaida C?" Melanie asked, scanning the group.

"The one with the blue lips," I answered. I never would have answered a teacher at school like that, but this wasn't school. This was camp. The counselors were technically adults, but they were *young* adults. They were all college students. Only Brenda and Earl and Steven, the head chef in the dining hall, were *real* adults.

"Don't be sassy," Melanie snapped at me.

"But I *am* sassy," I replied immediately, feeling less cold the bolder I got. "I've always been sassy. Are you telling me not to be myself?"

"That's enough out of you," Melanie barked at me. "Get in the water like everyone else. Now!" She turned away from us and blew her whistle at my shivering bunkmates in the lake.

"But . . . but," Carly stammered, panic clouding her eyes.

Melanie swung back around. "Did you just call me a butt-butt?"

"No!" Carly shook her head with all the energy her small body could muster. Melanie glared like she didn't believe her, so I came to Carly's defense again.

"She didn't. I don't think anyone has ever called anyone a butt-butt in the whole history of the world."

"Get into the water or go to Brenda's office. Those are your choices," Melanie practically spit at us.

"Can I go to Brenda's office?" Jordana pleaded from the lake.

"Me too?" Jaida A echoed. "Can I go?"

Jaida C just hugged herself, her blue lips clamped together, the tops of her shoulders shaking violently above the gray-blue water.

Melanie ignored them, blew her whistle again, and instructed, "Pick a lane and line up for backstroke."

Jordana crossed her arms over her chest and pouted.

"So . . . office?" I asked Carly.

"Will we get in trouble?" she asked back.

"I don't know. Maybe. But we'll be warm. And dry." I raised my eyebrows at her.

Carly smiled, then nodded. "Okay. Office."

We linked arms and marched in sync the whole way there.

* * *

"She really was mean," Carly remembered.

"Not counselor material at all," I said. "I know for a fact Brenda didn't invite her back."

"But the whole camp schedule changed because of her," Carly declared.

"It changed because of *us*," I corrected her. "You and me."

Carly smiled wide. "And we didn't even get in trouble."

Since junior campers were the youngest and smallest, Brenda decided they should only have to face the lake during the warmest part of the day, which was the afternoon. It fixed the rest of that summer for us.

But it was killing us now that we were in senior camp. There were three periods each morning between breakfast and lunch, and Brenda thought senior campers were the ones hardy enough to handle water activities in the morning. So our schedule as Yarrows this year was:

First period: swim
Second period: boating (canoe, kayak, sail, paddleboard)
Third period: tennis

Every single day.

The afternoons had three periods also, filling the time between rest hour and dinner, but those periods changed daily. Fourth, fifth, and sixth period were a random mix of arts and crafts, nature hut, water-ski, soccer, archery, volleyball, basketball, bocce, canoe, dance/aerobics, and drama. As senior campers, we could sign up for electives for fifth period on Wednesdays, Thursdays, and Fridays each week, but that hardly made up for first-period swim.

Brenda was right, though—you sure didn't need coffee to wake up in the morning when you had the brisk lake water of New Hampshire waiting for you. One dunk and every cell in your body jumped to attention.

"Our morning schedule this summer is the worst," Carly complained.

"It's the spirit of Mean Melanie getting us back," I said.

"Go away, Mean Melanie!" Carly yelled, and she pounded her fist into my mattress. "Ouch," she said, pulling her fist back up and cradling it in her other hand. Our mattresses were so thin that she pretty much just punched a metal coil.

"Well, we do have Mean Melanie to thank for your personal swear word," I said. And then in unison we cried, "Long live butt-butt!"

"You guys are so weird," Jordana's voice answered us.

We peeled back one of our sheet walls to find her standing there looking at our tent. She had just come out of the bathroom, her face covered in a dark gray paste, thin lines cracking around her eyes and mouth like tiny roads on a map.

"Would you like to enter our bed tent?" Carly invited her.

"Nah," Jordana answered, then changed her mind and said, "Sure," as she sprinted at us at full speed. She dove onto my cot in one swift motion, ripping the sheet down with her by accident.

"Hey!" Carly yelled.

"What a delicate flower you are, Jordana," I said as we all climbed out together to reassemble the sheet wall.

"A delicate butt-butt," Carly mouthed at me with a smile.

Day 5—Wednesday

->>>·<<<-

By the time Wednesday rolled around, we all needed rest hour for actual rest. Four mornings in a row of ripping ourselves out of bed to run from flag to breakfast to bunk cleaning to swim to boating to the cabin to change out of wet clothes to tennis and to the cabin again to clean up for lunch really wiped us out, even though Brenda built in a lot of time between periods to get where we needed to go. It definitely wasn't like school, where you had to plot the shortest possible route and then race like a maniac to get to your next class before the bell rang, or face an after-school detention if you didn't make it. We never got in trouble at camp if we were late. That was the cool thing about Brenda—she was totally on our side. I wished my middle school had more teachers like her.

Carly was half reading, half napping on her bed, and

Jaida A was writing letters of protest to SeaWorld while Jaida C practiced French-braiding her own hair. Jaida C was amazing at hair, which made sense since her mom owned a salon in New York City, where they lived. Jordana was painting her toenails while wearing earbuds that plugged into nothing, the cord hanging like a long loose thread. Her device had been confiscated that morning when Brenda showed up unexpectedly for inspection. Fortunately, all our beds were made and the bathroom wasn't a complete disaster, so we got a good cabin score, but Jordana hadn't hidden her iPod well and it took just one quick glance inside her cubby for Brenda to spot it. Jordana was now singing every song from the *Hamilton* soundtrack from memory.

Carly won the bet. I hadn't thought Jordana would make it past the first day.

I looked at the stationery in my lap, lemon-yellow lined paper with gold and silver stars in three of the four corners. Just as I was about to write *Dear Jamie*, the loudspeaker turned on with a high-pitched squeal and Brenda's voice announced, "Vic Brown, please report to Chicory. Vic to Chicory."

Carly lifted her head off her pillow long enough to say, "Camp sister alert," and then rolled over on her side and shut her eyes, her book cradled to her chest like a favorite stuffed animal.

* * *

The moment I stepped outside Yarrow, a familiar stillness washed over me. Earl's golf cart was parked in front of his cabin in its usual spot, reliable as a compass pointing north, and the air held the lingering smell of the yeasty baked rolls and chicken noodle soup served at lunch. Everyone was tucked away in their cabins—even Brenda and Earl were out of sight, probably working in the office. It was easy to feel like I had the whole place to myself. I crossed the soccer field and headed up the hill to junior camp.

As I walked, the ground evolved from lush grass to packed-down dirt to old tree roots bumping out of the ground like a nature-made obstacle course. Birds flapped from branch to branch high in the trees and chipmunks scrambled around tree stumps, stopping to chew furiously before scurrying off again. The sun was high and the sky was blue, and I started to wonder why I hadn't wanted to spend my summer in such a perfect place.

But then I remembered why I was here.

The laptop on my mom's desk, the email she was writing, the words on the screen carved into my memory like a scar that wouldn't fade.

I shook my head side to side to knock it away, at least for now. Vera needed me, and I was on my way.

* * *

I stepped into Chicory's camper room to find Vera sitting on her cot, her blanket smoothed pancake-flat and tucked in tight enough to bounce a dime on. The other cots in the room had blankets with images of Disney characters or big-eyed kittens or butterflies swirling over rainbows, but Vera's blanket had a picture of a large frog and the words *Museum of Science* printed smack in the middle of it.

"Vic, you're here! Thank you for coming." Her braids were lopsided and there were small tufts of blond hair sticking out of them, as if she had slept on them overnight.

"I'll always come when you need me, Vera. How's everything going?"

"Fine, and also not so great."

Eleven pairs of six- and seven-year-old eyes looked at Vera and then landed on me.

Vera barreled ahead. "I like my cabin and I like my bunk-mates and I like my bed even though it's not very comfortable, but I'm still feeling homesick. Sometimes I want to cry, but I'm trying not to because I haven't seen anyone else cry yet and I don't want anyone to think I'm a baby. Because I'm not a baby. I'm just experiencing feelings of nostalgia in the amygdala part of my brain, which is the area responsible for strong emotions." She lowered her voice and finished, "Which can lead to crying."

"Umm, do you want to go outside, Vera?" I asked. "To talk? Privately?"

"All right," she agreed, but then continued, "I also think I have a dermatitis starting on my ankles, and I forgot to pack a pencil sharpener, which is a problem because I also forgot to pack my mechanical pencils. I just have the regular kind, and I write *a lot*."

"Of course you do." I took a deep breath and smiled at the other campers. "Come on, Vera."

Vera got off her bed, walked past me out of the camper room, through the counselor room, and out the screen door without looking back.

I followed her.

We sat side by side on the bottom step of her cabin, our legs stretched out in front of us on a patch of worn earth. Vera's ankles had a weird pink color crawling up both of them.

"So, which thing do you want to address first?" Vera asked.

"Well, for starters, I wouldn't announce all your problems right in front of the other kids," I began.

"Why not?"

"Why *would* you?" I answered back.

"To fix a problem, you have to name it. That's a fact." Vera sounded so sure of herself that I couldn't think of any way to argue it.

An image flashed in my mind then of my mom sitting at our kitchen table, her hands cupped around a mug of tea, steam floating up in a misty cloud in front of her face. Her tea bags had small square labels attached to the strings with sayings printed on them, like fortune cookies. I could imagine one saying this: *To fix a problem, you have to name it.*

Vera was seven and had no trouble naming her problems in front of a whole room of strangers. I was thirteen and I hadn't named my problem to anyone, not to Jamie at home, not to Carly here, and certainly not to my mom, even though it was all her fault and I should have confronted her the moment I saw her email.

I bet Vera would have.

But I didn't.

"Hello, Vic! Earth to Vic!" Vera waved her hands in front of my face.

"Sorry." I gathered myself. "First of all, there's no way you're the only kid in there who's homesick. I can guarantee you that. And I get why you might not want to cry in front of the other girls, but trust me, it's really okay if you do. You definitely won't be the only one to cry this summer—I can guarantee that, too."

Vera's face relaxed immediately.

"Now, to deal with the homesick bit, it helps a lot if you

stay busy. And it's great if you can find a good friend, like a best friend. Start by finding someone you have something in common with. Like, if you love arts and crafts, find out who else loves arts and crafts, or if you love canoeing, find out who else loves canoeing. And then try to do that thing with them. You have to go out in pairs in the canoes anyway, so that would be a good time to talk and get to know each other."

"But I don't love canoeing."

"That was just an example." I sighed.

"Okay." She nodded.

"Okay. So what do you love to do?"

"I love to research."

"Research?" I expected a teasing grin on Vera's face. But no—her face was serious. "For real?"

"For real."

"What kind of research? Because I think that might be hard to do at an outdoorsy camp with no computers."

"Any kind. If I don't know something, I like to research it. For example, did you know chicory is a perennial wildflower with blue or purple flowers, and that you can eat the leaves and the root *and* the flowers?"

"No, Vera, that's all news to me," I admitted.

"The leaves are very bitter, so people blanch them first in boiling water. And the flowers only open on sunny days. When it's cloudy out, they don't open at all, which is kind of symbolic for human behavior, like not wanting to get out of bed on a rainy day but popping right up when the sun is out and the sky is bright and shiny."

"That might not be symbolic, Vera," I said. "That might just be science."

"And did you know you can dry chicory roots, grind them up, and then roast them to make coffee?" Vera shook her head in total exasperation at this fact. "Coffee is an adult drink, so I don't understand why they would give a coffee plant name to the youngest bunk in junior camp. We are the last people who would drink coffee."

"I don't know, Vera." I sighed heavily. "I just know the youngest cabin has always been Chicory because that's the name the owner gave it a gazillion years ago when she opened this place. Every cabin is some kind of wildflower that grows around here, and that's all there is to it."

"You're in Yarrow."

"I know I'm in Yarrow."

"Did you know yarrow is one of the most medicinal wild-flowers known? It can heal wounds and relieve pain. It's good for treating fever, the common cold, hay fever, and diarrhea. It's especially powerful as an herb for menstrual cycles and cramping. But it's full of contradictions, too, because yarrow can *cure* nosebleeds but it can also *cause* nosebleeds."

"Where do you get all this, Vera?"

"I told you—research. I tapped resources before camp started," she said in a very matter-of-fact way. "It's *very important* to have resources. It makes all the difference."

"In what?" I asked.

"In life," she answered slowly, somewhat irritated that she had to explain it to me.

"Oh," I said.

"Plus, my mom's a shrink, so I know a lot about psychology and human development."

"Which is why you can name the emotional center of the brain?" I asked.

"Yep," she conceded, and she kicked at the ground until a puff of dust rose, then landed back on her shoe like a fine brown powder. "I sound like a know-it-all sometimes. I'm aware of that."

"I think it's cool that you know so much. School must be a breeze for you." She started nodding before I even finished the sentence. "But I also think you need to get in a canoe with someone and spend some time listening."

Vera took a deep breath and let it out slowly, doubt on her face.

"Just try it," I urged.

"Okay," she gave in. "I'll try it. I'll canoe."

"And after dinner tonight you should go to clinic and get your ankles looked at. They can give you a cream for that."

"Okay."

"And did you mention the pencil thing to Brenda? I know she has a sharpener in her office, and I bet she'll let you use it whenever you want. Or maybe she'll even let your mom mail up your mechanical pencils."

"Duh. I forgot about the office," Vera said, rolling her eyes at herself.

"Wait—so you just used the words 'amygdala' and 'duh' in the same ten minutes," I observed.

"What? Lots of kids say 'duh.' I'm only seven, you know."

"Exactly, Miss *Amygdala*. You're only seven."

"Oh. Ha." Vera smiled, then leaned into me and rested her head against my arm. "You said I can see you, right, whenever I want?"

I thought of my little brother, Freddy, then, new at Forest Lake, maybe sitting alone on his own junky cot this very minute, wishing for the friends he had back home. I hoped he had nice counselors, someone he could go to who would help brush the loneliness away.

"Yeah, Vera. I'm here for you. Whenever you want."

And then the bugle rang again, announcing the end of rest hour like a kick to the head.

"You missed elective sign-up!" Jordana shouted gleefully at me the moment I walked through the door.

"Where's the board?" I asked, panic filling my chest.

"It's by the door—you just walked past it," Jaida A said.

Only senior campers had the privilege of signing up for a fifth-period activity on Wednesdays, Thursdays, and Fridays. There was a short list of choices and a number limit for each, and it was a first-come, first-serve system.

A system that was about to bite me in the butt.

I scanned down the list to find my name.

"Who put me in farm?" I read out loud. "And what the heck is farm?"

"Sorry, Vic." Carly walked over to explain. "I tried to sign you up for volleyball with me, but Brenda was here and she said we could only sign ourselves up. And Aster and Marigold got to pick before us, so there were hardly any spots left."

"Am I the only one who got farm?" I asked, skimming over the chart.

"My first choice was riding, but that was full, so I didn't get what I wanted, either." Carly tried to make me feel better.

"But you already rode this morning. First period. You missed swim to ride."

"Well, I wanted to ride again," she explained, "and I won't get to."

"But I got farm!" I couldn't process. "We don't even have a farm."

"I think it's new," Carly said.

"It's part of that farm-to-table thingie they're starting," Jaida C explained. "I asked Brenda."

"Switch to farm with me," I begged Carly.

"I can't. Brenda said we can't. The numbers are all worked out the way it is."

"Brenda is displaying dictator tendencies," Chieko said as she strolled past us to the bathroom.

Carly shrugged and squeezed my arm in sympathy.

"Thanks," I told her, "for trying."

"And it's for three days in a row," Carly said, regret in her voice.

"Are you kidding me? Since when do we sign up in bulk?" It was getting worse by the second.

"Since today," Jaida A said.

"That's not how it worked last year! It's supposed to be three days, three different choices."

"It's been streamlined, baby," Chieko called from a

bathroom stall. "Now it's three days, one choice. Love it or leave it."

"Can I leave it? Please?" I asked.

"Not a chance." Chieko let out an evil cackle and followed it with the sound of a toilet flushing.

Jordana slid a pair of mirrored sunglasses onto her face and announced, "I'll be thinking of you all later when I'm at water-ski, suckers!" She threw a towel over her shoulders and sauntered out the door.

I saw my reflection in her glasses as she passed—dark brown hair frizzing out of my ponytail, sad brown eyes, cheeks and forehead tinted pink, a shade that would soon turn tan. But mostly the reflection I saw was the face of someone who had to spend fifth-period elective without a friend at farm.

"Don't let the door hit you on the way out," I called after Jordana, a sneer in my voice. But I doubt she heard.

Day 5—Wednesday

->>>·<<<-

I had to ask three different counselors to find out where I was supposed to go for farm, so I was five minutes late by the time I arrived at the yard behind Brenda and Earl's cabin.

I never even knew there was a yard back there.

And "yard" probably wasn't the right word to describe it. It was more like a small field closed in with chicken-wire fencing, part of it covered with raised planting beds and the other part with long parallel rows of small hills, green stalks and leaves fanning out of them.

Everything was green.

Taller bushes lined the back of the fenced-in area, and a long hose stretched between two rows of plants like an extra-long snakeskin drying in the sun. The sun was still high and bright, but a breeze kept it from feeling too hot. There wasn't a counselor or any other campers in sight. The hum of insects buzzing and flitting around was the only sound I could hear.

"Hello?" I called. "Anyone here?"

A head of gray hair, thinner on top than it was on the sides, rose up slowly from behind a raised plant bed. Earl was wearing the white T-shirt and denim jeans he wore every day of the summer, his braided cloth belt strapped so loose around his waist it was hard to understand why he bothered to put it on in the first place. He was only a few inches taller than me and resembled the robot Freddy drew for me on my birthday card in April, all boxy chest and torso, with stick-thin arms and legs poking out on the sides.

"You signed up, or got stuck with it?" Those were the first words out of his mouth.

I just stared at him, shocked by the question.

"Tell me the truth," he directed, his voice easing up as if he were talking to a stray animal.

"Got stuck with it," I admitted.

Then he surprised me. He laughed, just once, quickly and quietly, but it left a grin on his face when he was done.

"I never knew this was back here," I told him.

"Didn't look like this last summer. Only had a bit growing

before." He looked around him as if taking it all in for the first time, like I was. "I started in early spring, got a lot going on now."

"Well, I don't know anything about farming."

"It's not a farm. Brenda wanted to call it farm, but it's not a farm." Earl shook his head. "Just growing some plants, that's all."

"Why?" I asked.

He fixed his eyes on me like he was trying to figure out if my question was serious or not.

"For food," he finally answered. He picked up the hose and coiled it around his arm as he walked toward me, then rested it on a metal bar attached to the back of his cabin. "Most of this goes right to our dining hall for Steven to serve up. Farm"—he used both arms to motion at the plants growing around him—"to table." He pointed in the direction of the dining hall. "Get it?"

"Ah." I raised my eyebrows as I looked around, pretending to be interested.

"I'll start you on the blueberries."

"I don't know anything about blueberries, except how to eat them."

Earl just said, "You couldn't mess this up if you tried."

"I found it! Finally!" came a voice from behind us.

Earl and I turned at the same time to see Bella, an Aster,

walking quickly toward us, her flip-flops smacking with each step.

"Hello there," Earl greeted her. "You're here for the farm elective?"

"Unfortunately, yes," she answered, not even trying to be polite about it. "I'm late because I had to change."

She was wearing denim short overalls on top of a white ribbed tank top. She had only hooked one of the two suspenders, so the bib of the overalls flapped open on one side of her chest. Her hair was parted down the middle, and she wore two long braids with red ribbon threaded through them. A gold ankle bracelet glittered in the sun at the bottom of her left leg above toenails that were painted the same candy-apple red as her hair ribbons.

Bella didn't look like she had dressed for farmwork. She looked like she had dressed for a photo shoot next to *other* people doing farmwork. If she put this much effort into dressing for one lousy elective at camp, I couldn't begin to imagine how much went into her primping for school each day.

"*Thank God* I packed these overalls at the last minute," Bella said, looking down at herself and smoothing out the denim cloth against her stomach.

"Thank God," I muttered quietly.

The side of Earl's mouth twitched up in a quick grin, which

let me know I was louder than I'd meant to be.

"We're happy to have your help, Bella. I was just about to show Vic here what to do. Follow me."

I noticed Bella check me out as we walked behind Earl, although there wasn't much to look at, since I *was* dressed for farmwork. Her gaze moved from my worn sneakers to my blue athletic shorts and Snoopy T-shirt, over my no-makeup face all the way to my ponytail, my hair frizzing out in every direction even though there wasn't a drop of humidity in the air. She lifted her hands to each of her braids then, patted them in place from top to bottom, and smiled to herself.

Earl was far enough away now for me to ask, "You signed up for farm?"

Bella rolled her eyes. "Yeah, right."

"Then why are you here?"

"Because during sign-ups I was stuck in the office getting a lecture from Brenda about sneaking my cell phone into camp. I swear she called me in exactly then so I'd get last pick." Bella glared to the side as if Brenda were standing right there. "There's no reception up here anyway, so I don't know why she even cares."

"That's two today for Brenda."

"What?"

"She found Jordana's iPod this morning," I explained.

I though Bella might ask what I was doing at farm, if I signed up or just got stuck with it like her, but she didn't. She just kept walking after Earl, lifting her feet high as she stepped through the dusty rows, probably trying to keep any dirt from landing on her polished toenails.

Earl stopped at the back of the field, right by a long row of bushes that stood as tall as my chest. They were boring-looking bushes, as wide as they were tall, with small, dull green leaves. As I got closer, I spotted thick clumps of berries pulling on the branches. The blueberries were plump and round, some of them such a deep blue they were almost black.

"Blueberries are a nutrient-dense food. They're high in antioxidants and, luckily for us, in season the first several weeks of camp. Steven has already served them up in pancakes and muffins."

"Those muffins were *so* good." Bella licked her lips. "Can he bake them again?"

"If we grow 'em, he'll bake 'em. That's the point of the program—organic food grown right here by us, for us. Skills for you to take with you once you leave camp. This is our first year trying it out, which makes some of you senior campers our guinea pigs."

"I'll be a guinea pig. Guinea pigs are cute," Bella said.

I peered more closely at the blueberry bushes. They looked

more interesting to me now, important even, but still not as much fun as being on a volleyball court with Carly.

"There are two jobs," Earl explained. "First we gotta pick the ripe ones. All of them. Then we gotta cover the bushes with that." He pointed to a cardboard box on the ground full of pale white netting. "The birds got to pick for a few days, but I'm shutting the buffet down now. We gotta cover up every bit so they can't take any more."

"How do you know if they're ripe?" Bella asked. I saw a flash of pink in her mouth as she spoke. It was one thing to chew gum in your cabin at rest hour when no one was watching, but to chew it out in the open, and while you were working with one of the actual camp directors, was a whole new level of bold.

Earl looked at her with the patience of a saint.

"You like to eat blueberries, right?" he asked.

"Yeah. Of course," Bella answered, the piece of gum moving from the right side of her mouth to the left.

"Well, if it looks like a berry you'd like to eat, it's ripe. Pick it, and drop it in here." He handed each of us a metal pail. There was a white line painted horizontally around the inside of the bucket. "Don't go past this line, or they'll start to crush themselves."

I took the pail and peered inside at the line. Bella took the pail, held it up high in front of her face, and squinted to catch her reflection in it.

"I'll start you on opposite ends so you have room to work. Vic, you stay here. Bella, come with me down this way."

I stood there, my ponytail sagging onto my neck, studying that very full blueberry bush like it might be an enemy. But then my mind jumped to my real enemy—my mom—because she was the reason I was stuck on a plot of mini-farm behind Brenda and Earl's cabin in New Hampshire with a metal pail in my hand like some kid from the Little House on the Prairie series.

"There's no starting bugle, dear," Earl called out from the other end of the bushes. "Just begin."

I stepped closer to the first bush and leaned into it, searching for berries that looked perfect enough to mix into pancake batter or toss on a bowl of ice cream. There were a ton of them, and I filled the bucket before I made it even halfway through the first bush. I turned to look for Earl, but he was already headed my way, holding a tray in front of him stacked with those green cardboard berry containers you always see at roadside stands.

"Next we'll fill these." He leveled the tray of containers on top of the box of netting and started to work on the bush next to mine. "These are gonna be the ones we sell," he explained before I had the chance to ask him.

"Sell?"

"There's a farmers' market in town every Saturday at eight a.m. Got enough berries here to turn all you campers blue, which I doubt your folks would appreciate, so I sell some. Already been to the market three Saturdays, got a tent and the same space reserved for the whole summer."

Selling blueberries out of a tent at eight o'clock on a Saturday morning sounded even worse than the bugle and flag morning routine I was already stuck with until the end of August.

I glanced at Bella at the far end of the field. She was sitting next to the last blueberry bush, her half-full pail tipped over on the ground beside her while she picked dirt out from under her fingernails. Earl followed my gaze, sighed, then looked back at me.

"It's my first summer at the market. A lot of work for one person, but I enjoy it."

He had to be kidding.

"I can't handle mornings," I admitted, "so that sounds like sheer torture to me."

"Well, you never know. . . ." Earl's words trailed off.

"You never know what?"

"You never know what you can handle until you try to handle it."

"Right," I said as nicely as I could. My back and neck were getting sore from bending over, and my fingers were aching from the repetition.

The loudspeaker coughed itself on then and the bugle rang out, calling the end of the period. For the first time in my life, that bugle sounded as sweet as the ice cream truck jingle that played its way up my street back home. I stood up all the way and stretched backward, pushing out my chest to undo the bent position I had held for too long.

I emptied my pail into one of the green containers on the tray and rubbed my hands together to get some blood flow back into them. I saw that there was a tint of blue stained onto me like a new skin.

"All right," I said with great relief. "It was a real pleasure, Earl. I'm off." I headed toward the path that would lead me around the cabin and away from the farm.

"It's Wednesday," Earl called after me.

"I know it's Wednesday," I answered right away.

"It's double elective on Wednesday." He said this without looking up, the rhythm of his hand swinging from bush to basket and back again like a dance he could do in his sleep. "Always has been."

An urge to yell rose in my throat so suddenly that I almost choked on it. I pictured Jordana sitting in the back of the speedboat, feet up, wind in her hair, soaking up the sun. I pictured Carly on the volleyball court, laughing at how many hits in a row she could miss, trying to convince the counselor that they should play a game where you hit the ball *under* the net instead of over. And I pictured my mom at her computer, writing betrayal after betrayal and hitting send, loving the freedom of an empty house while her kids were shipped away and her husband was at work.

And then I saw me. Standing here with achy muscles and dirty hands, surrounded by plants and bugs and soil and buckets and an oldish guy and a fashion-obsessed Aster. Earl seemed to read the misery my face couldn't hide and gave me some space, moving farther down the row of blueberry bushes.

"Why do they even use the bugle if the period's not over?" I asked. "It's actually rude."

"Rude, Vic?" Earl shook his head. "Maybe a little misleading. And for you and Bella today, perhaps a bit disappointing. But the bugle recording is preset. Maybe try not to take it so personally."

I headed back to my spot, grabbed the pail, and continued picking and dropping, trying to calm my mind and stomach.

About ten minutes later, I heard Bella shout, "Thank God!" She was sitting under the same bush, the berries in her pail now way past the painted line inside, holding a big cup of water against her cheek.

"You can just call me Earl," Earl responded with a chuckle, then added, "You're welcome." He walked over to me next with a cup of ice water in each hand.

"Here you go," he said, and thrust one at me.

I took it and chugged the whole thing in one go. The cold perked me up immediately and I thought of Brenda again, telling Chieko at our first breakfast how hydration was the very best stimulant. She definitely knew what she was talking about.

"Thanks," I said, handing the cup back to Earl. All three cups had the New Hampshire state seal printed on them. I looked at the big boat in the middle of the design with its red flags flapping in the wind and wished I were on it so I could sail away from my mom, her email, and all these backbreaking blueberry bushes.

But I couldn't sail anywhere, so I went back to picking.

Day 5—Wednesday evening

⇒⇒⇒·⇐⇐⇐

Meadow Wood didn't have signs or fences to show where their property ended and the neighbors' began. The woods were the property line. Woods so thick you couldn't see through them.

Brenda claimed the woods provided "the most natural and beautiful property line possible."

And we were not permitted to step one foot over the line.

Aside from the parade of deer ticks the nurses promised would latch onto us if we stepped into the thick of trees, we would also get attacked by poison ivy, poison oak, poison sumac, or if we were really lucky, a combination of all three.

Plus, there were wild animals.

And maybe even Bigfoot.

Seriously, they warned us about Bigfoot so we wouldn't stray off the property.

It didn't work on me, though. Not even when I was nine. I strayed.

I had been straying every summer, always to the exact same spot. As a moody Violet who had learned to avoid her camp sister after the tooth incident, I found myself sneaking into the woods at the edge of junior camp one night after dinner to stew in my sadness. After a minute of weaving between tree trunks and stepping over fallen limbs, I reached a boulder the size of a small car. It stuck out of the ground all bulky and gray with a gritty texture that reminded me of elephant skin. It practically begged me to climb it. So I did. And sitting there, alone on my rock, I felt better.

I kept going back whenever I could sneak away. I never showed anyone my discovery, not even Carly, and I never told anyone about it, either, not even Jamie back home. That secret place was mine alone, and I needed it this summer more than ever.

The sky was just beginning to dim and the air was cool enough to raise bumps on my bare arms. I sat on the hard rock and felt a surge of anger flare up in me again at the big fat lie that poured out of my mom's mouth—that sending me to camp would save me from the bad influence of Jamie.

Jamie never would have broken the rules and left camp property. That was all me.

One hundred percent Vic.

I could hear campers through the curtain of trees, yelling and waving the papers they were recording on. Evening activity was the same treasure hunt they made us do the first week of every summer. We had to run all over the grounds to find answers to questions like *How many chairs are in the dining hall?* and *What color are the canoes docked on the beachfront?* and *What does the sign beside the clinic door say?* As seniors, we were allowed to go without counselors, which made it easy for me to slip away to my rock.

It was my very first chance to be alone, and I needed to be alone.

I needed to think about what I saw.

I'll tell him, I promise, once the kids are gone.

Those words played through my mind like a stuck song lyric. They showed up every time I closed my eyes against the rising sun at flag and every time I closed my eyes to fall asleep on my creaky cot at night.

We'll be together, just wait.

At first I thought it was some romantic gesture between

my mom and dad, which would have shocked me and also seriously grossed me out.

But it wasn't.

I knew because my eyes moved up to the top of the screen and I saw that the email was addressed to Darrin. Which was a monumental problem, since my dad's name was Ross.

That was why.

Darrin was why.

He was why my mom sent me away. And why she sent Freddy away, too, on a different bus, the one headed to Lake Forest. Freddy was only eight, but she pushed him onto that bus with a kiss so quick it half broke my heart to see it happen.

Because she'd rather be with Darrin.

When she put me on the bus that morning, she thought I didn't know, but I did.

I just didn't know what I was going to do about it.

The taps bugle for lights-out was about to sound, so we gathered in the counselor room for another round of "forced bunk bonding."

"My rose"—Jordana went first, still twisting her hair into the style she always wore to sleep—"was kicking butt in the treasure hunt tonight. Simone and Bella and I came in first place."

"Who are Simone and Bella?" Chieko asked. "Sounds like the name of a bad wedding band."

"They're both in Aster," Jaida C said.

"They're lifers, in the oldest bunk." Jordana was in complete brag mode. "And my thorn was that we didn't get a trophy for winning."

"They never give trophies!" Carly sputtered at her.

"Well, they should," Jordana countered.

"They should *not*. It's just an evening activity," Carly answered.

"You're just jealous," Jordana said.

"You're just a butt-butt!" Carly said.

"Butt-butt?" Chieko repeated. "Well said."

"Can someone sane go?" Jaida A asked. "Vic?"

"Sure. My thorn is getting stuck with *farm* for elective this week. Obviously," I said.

"Obviously," Carly echoed in support.

"And my rose is"—I had to think for a second—"my rose is having canteen tomorrow. I'm dying for a Kit Kat."

And then everyone was talking at once about the junk food they couldn't wait to get.

Once Chieko got us all quiet again, Carly spoke up.

"My rose was getting to canter on Rowdy today," she said, gushing.

Not everyone at Meadow Wood did horseback riding. It was an activity you had to pay extra for, and then the riders all got their own separate schedules each week of when they could go to the stables for their lessons. Carly got to skip our bunk activity several times every week to practice riding instead.

"I was talking to Eliza," Jaida C piped up. "She's also in Aster and she's a really good rider, and she said you did great today. And she said that horse really likes you."

"Yes, it would be a *horse* that really likes Carly," Jordana ribbed.

"Jordana, stop," Jaida A and Jaida C said at the same time, then looked at each other and said, "Jinx."

"I'm just kidding, gosh." Jordana leaned back a bit out of the circle.

"My thorn is I don't get to ride again until Friday," Carly finished, then turned to Jaida A and said, "You're up."

"My rose is that I put six letters in the mail today to SeaWorld," Jaida A reported, "and my thorn is that right now there are still people buying stupid tickets to go to stupid SeaWorld."

Jaida C's rose was getting a letter from her favorite cousin, and her thorn was swallowing a mouthful of lake water at swim when someone cannonballed right next to her.

"Your turn," Carly said, nudging Chieko. "You never go."

Chieko closed her eyes and said, with the seriousness of a heart surgeon, "My rose is that Eleanor Roosevelt recorded her wisdom in books so I can feed off her brilliance when there is nothing else to sustain me."

"Who's Eleanor Roosevelt again?" Jordana asked.

"Seriously?" Carly called out.

"Shut up, smarty-pants," Jordana snapped. Then she put on her Annie face and recited, "I grew up a poor orphan, forced to skip school and clean all day."

She sat up on her knees, straightened her posture, and started to belt out the song "Tomorrow," adding hand gestures that had us all laughing by the third verse.

When she finished her performance and the room got quiet again, Chieko continued. "My thorn today is twofold. My thorn is one"—and she held up her pointer finger—"the individual who invented the bugle, and two"—she raised another finger—"the sinister individual who installed the god-awful loudspeaker system at this camp."

Jordana sat up on her knees again and tried to imitate

the screechy sound the loudspeaker made every time it was switched on.

"You sound like a dying dinosaur trying to sing opera," Jaida A said.

And then we all cracked up again.

Every single one of us.

Day 6—Thursday

❯❯❯·❮❮❮

When I reached the field behind Brenda and Earl's cabin the next afternoon, Earl was already squatted over a row of greens, his back hunched, his arms shifting in a pull-and-drop motion. I could hear Brenda inside the cabin, the murmur of her voice on the phone, then the sound of the front door closing as she left to make her rounds.

The sun was hot and bright, and I cursed myself for not bringing a baseball cap to shield my eyes from the glare. My hands were still tinted blue from the day before, and the knot in my neck started to vibrate the moment I looked at the blueberry bushes at the back of the field.

Earl stood up slowly, a crack sounding from his knees like a small balloon popping. He had a faded blue bandanna tied around his forehead, which I had never seen on him before.

I headed back to begin my forty minutes of blueberry pain when Earl called out, "Not back there. Different job this time."

I stopped and turned to face him. "Great. What fun do I get to have today?"

He pointed at the ground. "That fun. Weeding."

I looked more closely at the rows of green sprouting out of the ground. I saw big leaves of dark green and small leaves of dark green. I saw some leaves that were a slightly lighter green.

I looked up at Earl and realized he was watching me try to figure out what was what in all that green. And I think he was trying not to laugh in my face. But if anyone should have been laughing, it was me—I was the one who had to look at him in that ridiculous bandanna.

He cleared his throat, squatted back down, and pulled gently on a large leaf that curled and twisted in on itself like a seashell. "This is curly-leaf kale. This is the plant I'm growing in these two long rows. Steven likes to cook it into omelets and pasta dishes, and even roast it into chips."

He dropped that big leaf and pinched a smaller leaf, thin and flat and narrow. "This is a weed." And he moved his fingers closer to the root and ripped the whole thing out of the ground in one motion. He dropped it in a burlap bag tied to his belt.

"That's it. That's weeding. And we need to do both these rows."

"And by 'we' you mean 'me,' right?"

"You and Bella, when she gets here. And me, of course."

"Well, I hope you gave her advance notice that she'd be weeding today so she could plan her outfit for it." I couldn't help saying it.

Earl bit his lip to stop a smile from sprouting and said, "How 'bout you and me just get started? I'll be pulling the lettuce weeds right here next to you. I've got gloves if you prefer to wear gloves. And it's hot today, so if you need a break, take a break. Here's a bag to put your weeds in."

I took the bag from him and watched him move to his row. He crouched down and started to pull. "Oh, and you can snack as much as you want. Food doesn't come any fresher than this." To make his point, Earl ripped off a piece of lettuce and shoved it in his mouth. "Clean energy, from the sun right to your gut."

I knew Jordana didn't have snacks at water-ski and Carly wouldn't get any food at volleyball, but chomping on free fresh vegetables could not make up for missing out on more relaxing activities with my friends.

After this week, I was done. I would not miss elective sign-up again. I would not get stuck with farm again. Not for the rest of the summer. I was so sure of it I said it out loud.

"You do know I'm done with farmwork after this week, right?"

"So. Am. I!" Bella stomped up behind us. She was wearing the same denim shorts overalls as yesterday, but with both suspenders snapped in place this time, over a red-checked blouse that reminded me of the tablecloths at the Italian restaurant I had gone to with Jamie and her mom and aunt last year.

"I got a farmer's tan in just one day! Look!" Bella pulled up the bottom of her overall shorts to show us the difference in color between her exposed and hidden skin.

"That's a sign of good hard work," Earl said. "Congratulations."

"Congratulations?" Bella repeated, scowling.

She sounded so upset I actually felt bad for her. "You can even that out by the lakefront easily," I told her. "Two days in a bathing suit and it'll be gone."

Bella looked back at her leg and poked the darker skin tone, then rubbed it as if she could just slide the tan onto the whiter part of her leg.

"You think?" she asked.

There was a pretty big difference in color, but I told her, "Sure. Probably."

Bella addressed Earl. "I need an activity not in the sun." Then added, "Please."

"No problem." Earl set her up in a thin strip of shade next to the cabin, rinsing out seed containers and stacking them in groups of ten. Watching her work with the hose water away from the sun's heat made me feel like I had been outsmarted by Bella, which did not help my mood.

Earl was busy with his own work, pulling and dropping weeds, his bag puffing out at his hip as he inched down his row like an overgrown snail. I was starting to get a headache from the sun and not enough water at lunch earlier.

"You can buy all this stuff, you know," I reminded him. "At the supermarket."

"Where do you think the supermarket gets it?"

"They get it from professional farmers," I answered quickly. "With gigantic farms and lots of workers."

"Soon as you sell it, you're professional." Earl kept his head down as he spoke, focused on the work in front of him.

"So you're saying you're a professional farmer now, too, and not just a camp owner?"

"Appears so." He let out one quick laugh and added, "Since I sell what you're helping to pick, you're kind of like a professional farmer, too."

There were a lot of things I didn't know—what was happening with my parents, how good a camp sister I was going to be, how Jamie was managing at home without me—but one thing I knew for sure was that I was *not* a farmer, professional or otherwise.

I was a thirteen-year-old girl going into eighth grade who was supposed to be enjoying the summer with friends on the beautiful lakefront campus of Meadow Wood. But instead, I was covered in sweat, fighting a headache while yanking weeds behind a cabin with Bella, the tanning queen of Aster bunk.

"It's easy to shop at stores," Earl started, "but it's just as easy to grow it in your own backyard."

"It's not *just* as easy," I shot back at him, more aggressively than I meant to. The heat was really getting to me.

"Okay, true," he relented, backing off a bit, "but it's better."

"Please explain to me how this is better than walking into an air-conditioned store and picking out clean vegetables organized on shelves without having to bend over?"

Earl stopped weeding and let his knees drop to the ground. He stared at the lettuce plant before him, then reached down and raked his hand through the loose dark dirt resting on top of the row. "There's a calm here," he said, still looking down. "A quiet. Plants take their time, each small moment, better than anything else I know." He rubbed his hands together, dirt falling like pixie dust, catching the light so it shimmered as it fell. "There's a certain peace in that."

The air got really still and the afternoon heat settled itself right across my shoulders.

There was no way I could know what a certain peace felt like to a sixty-something-year-old man like Earl, but I definitely knew what a certain peace was to a thirteen-year-old girl on summer break.

Peace was sleeping in until chirping birds and revving lawn mowers woke you, and then staying in bed for *another hour anyway* just because you could.

Peace was spooning peanut butter out of the jar with Jamie while binge-watching old TV shows, which is what I would be doing if my mom hadn't sent me to camp.

Peace was floating on rafts at the pool and checking out the lifeguards.

Peace was lounging on the back porch in the dark, shining flashlight beams into the night sky as Jamie and I whispered our deepest wishes and fears to each other.

Peace was definitely not weeding.

When I looked over at Earl, my mouth open, ready to explain all this to him, I saw him curved back over his row, looking, touching, picking and pulling, lost in his work. It was like he forgot Bella and I were even there. And he did look relaxed, extremely relaxed, like some meditative trance had taken over.

So I crouched down and got to it. I tried to copy him and find the peace he was talking about.

I really did.

But twenty minutes later, after my thighs had slow-burned past pain to complete numbness, and my fingers had lost their ability to grasp, and sweat had coated my arms to a glossy sheen, I knew that Earl was seriously disturbed if this brought him any kind of peace.

And I had a tremendous urge to pull that faded blue bandanna off his peaceful forehead and pound it into the ground like a weed that needed to be taught a lesson.

But thinking that and doing it were two very different things.

Day 6—Thursday

→→→·←←←

After a dinner of spaghetti, garlic bread, and salad, we raced to canteen and elbowed our place in line. Canteen was a small wooden building strategically surrounded by the soccer field, the waterfront, and trampled lawn. It had a large piece of wood in front that flipped open from the inside to make a window for ordering. It also had an oversize padlock on the rickety door in back that only Brenda and Earl had the key to.

The crowning achievement for all Meadow Wood campers was to sneak out in the middle of the night and break into canteen to pillage the soda, ice cream pops, and candy bars that filled the fridge and freezer inside. It was usually senior campers who tried. And so far, no one had ever succeeded. We all knew the warped plywood door wasn't that hard to budge, but the creaks and squeaks that rang out at the slightest touch were so loud it always made the invaders scurry away like terrified mice.

I had tried once, back in Clover, to break into canteen with Jordana and Carly, but we didn't even make it to the building. We were halfway across the lawn when we heard Earl's golf cart revving nearby. The three of us beelined for the rocks at the waterfront and dove behind them to hide. I accidentally slammed my knee into a smaller rock when I landed and had a bruise bigger than my fist for three weeks afterward. My bruise looked like a side view of a man's head, so Carly and I named it Bruno Bruiser and took a picture of it with the disposable camera she always brought to camp. I still had the photo. I showed it to Jamie once, but she didn't get it. Maybe some things were only funny at camp.

We *lived* for our weekly canteen visits. Junior campers had canteen on Tuesdays, intermediate campers went on Wednesdays, and us seniors had it every Thursday night. Canteen offered more than just snacks—you could restock on soap, shampoo, hair bands, stamps, envelopes, and other supplies you might run out of before the end of camp. But the real attraction was the junk food. The meals in the dining hall were good, but summer just wasn't summer without Popsicles that turned your tongue blue and bright orange soda that was so sugary it made your teeth hurt.

It was all Asters at the front of the line, of course, and the few who strolled over late just butted in to join their friends. Those girls were fifteen years old, already in high school, but some of them still acted like the cliquey girls I couldn't stand at my middle school back home.

"They just cut," I told Carly, nodding at two Asters who'd just arrived.

Carly shrugged. "I'd let you in line if you were late. That's what friends do."

"Oh." I realized she was right. "I'd let you cut, too."

Carly grabbed my hand and started swinging it while she lifted herself on her tippy-toes. "What's taking so long? All I want in life right now is *sugar*!"

"I see Brenda coming," I reassured her. "It'll open in a sec."

Jordana was in line in front of us, waving like crazy to get Simone's and Bella's attention. They eventually turned and waved at her, but then turned back to their Aster bunkmates and pretended not to hear Jordana's request for "frontsies."

And then the cheering began.

Marigolds started the "Go Bananas" cheer, clapping as they called out the letters *B-A-N-A-N-A-S* over and over. All the Aster girls joined in, adding foot stomping to the clapping. The cheer got louder with each round while Brenda fumbled with the padlock and ushered two counselors in with her to help her flip open the window and distribute the food and supplies.

Chieko appeared beside me, one hand holding her Eleanor Roosevelt book, the other palming her forehead like she was auditioning for a headache commercial.

"This was not in the brochure. I swear to God." Chieko shook her head at me. "There was no mention at all of this coordinated screeching."

"You mean cheering," I corrected her.

"How about we cheer for some peace and quiet?" she called out into the storm of noise around her.

The crowd behind us increased their volume even more to spell out, "*B-A-N-A-N-A-S*! GO, GO BANANAS!"

"You'd think our lives were at stake here and not just some Snickers and root beer." She tucked her book into her back pocket.

"I told you," I said. "Camp is pretty much just two straight months of people cheering and clapping at each other."

"Who even made these cheers up?" Chieko asked. "'Go Bananas'? Where do we want them to go? And why are we picking on bananas? We need the potassium."

"Chieko, I think you made a serious mistake by signing up as a camp counselor," I told her.

"I know. I'm in my own personal hell. But that's kind of why I did it."

"You *wanted* to spend your summer in hell?" I was confused.

Chieko shook her head, pulled out her book again, and whipped it open to a page she had dog-eared. "See? Right here. This is what I'm spending my summer doing."

She shoved the book in front of my face, and I read the underlined sentence out loud. "'You must do the thing you think you cannot do.'"

"Yup." Chieko nodded once in agreement.

"Says who?" I asked.

"Says Eleanor Roosevelt." She flipped the book closed to show me the cover.

"Did Eleanor Roosevelt know you'd be surrounded by constant screaming for weeks on end?"

The volume had reached a level that was even beginning to hurt *my* ears. "*G-O-B-A-N, B-A-N-A-N-A-S*, GO BANANAS, GO, GO BANANAS!"

"Good God." Chieko squinted her eyes closed and pushed her hands even tighter over her ears. "I should have packed more Tylenol."

"Get some from clinic," I told her.

"I can't go there. They even cheer at clinic. It's insane. And inane. It's *insane* and *inane*."

"What's 'inane' mean?" I asked.

"It means this." And she motioned at all the screaming,

clapping, stomping girls around her. "It means foolish, stu-pid, vapid, idiotic, absurd, and any other synonym you can think of."

"I bet you aced your verbal SAT." I patted her on the shoulder.

"And I will pass my vocabulary skills on to you, young one. That's why they pay me the big bucks." Then Chieko clutched her stomach and fell over herself laughing while repeating "big bucks," which made it pretty clear that the counselors at Meadow Wood got paid next to nothing.

The line moved quickly once it started, and in less than two minutes it was my turn to order.

"A root beer and a Kit Kat Big Kat bar, please." The root beer was for Carly, since she won the Jordana bet, but she already told me we could split it.

As the counselor turned to grab my items, Brenda stepped into her place and said, "Hi, Vic. Can we talk?"

I stalled a moment, hoping my snack would arrive so I could rip into it while Brenda talked to me, but the counselor was slow and Brenda was quick.

"Come to the back." And she turned toward the door, a look on her face I hadn't seen before. I had no choice but to walk around and meet her, my stomach grumbling for candy.

She stepped out of the canteen, looked down at me from

her lofty height, and said, "I'm very sorry to tell you this, but there's no money in your canteen account."

My mouth opened but no sound came out.

"There *was* money, when camp started, but your mom called today and pulled it out. She said you didn't need it."

I felt my lips come together to form the beginning of *What?* but then they just froze again.

"I'm sorry, Vic. You can get canteen today, on me, but after that you'll have to sit it out unless your parents send in the money."

I felt my head nod in understanding, even though I didn't understand it at all.

The sound of wrappers being ripped and Popsicles being sucked filled the air. Soda can tabs popped open, followed by the sounds of greedy gulping, loud burping, and laughter. I wasn't a part of any of it.

My mind whirled.

I'll tell him, I promise, once the kids are gone.

We'd been gone for six days.

Did that mean she told him? Did my dad know about Darrin? Did my dad leave? Did he storm off in anger, taking credit cards and closing accounts to punish my mom? Was my mom on her own? Was that what she wanted—to be on her own, with Darrin?

The grass under my feet rolled and spun, and I had to lean against the canteen wall to steady myself. My heart started pounding so hard and heavy in my chest I thought Brenda would hear it. Sweat started to bead up over every inch of my body, even though I felt nothing but a cold, clammy dampness drenching me.

Brenda took my hand and gave it a squeeze, then slid something into it as she said more words I didn't hear. I shoved whatever it was into my back pocket as she turned and went back into canteen, leaving me dazed and alone.

I stayed there a minute, breathing in and out, waiting for my heart to stop beating in my ears. Once I had my balance back, I walked away. I left the canteen and my friends and Chieko and walked, quickly, to the main office, which was just one small room off Brenda and Earl's cabin. I heard Carly's voice shout, "Vic?" but I didn't answer and she didn't come after me.

The door was unlocked and the office was empty, so I marched right in like I owned the place. I picked up the phone and dialed home with a rock in my throat so big I almost couldn't breathe.

She answered on the first ring.

The disappointment in her voice when she heard me say hello got tacked onto the list in my head of all the reasons I was furious with my mom.

"I can't get canteen," I said, as slow and steady as I could manage.

"Yes, I know," she said, after a pause. "I'm sorry. We're having some unexpected financial issues."

"Who is?"

"Us. We are," she answered.

"Did Dad lose his job?" I asked, knowing the answer.

"No, of course not. He's just—"

"He's just gone, right?"

She gasped. "Why would you say that?"

"*You're* the only one having financial issues. Because he's gone and he's in charge of the money and he was so mad he left you with nothing, right?" I wasn't going to make this easy for her. I could taste my anger, bitter and salty on my tongue.

"Have you talked to him?" my mom asked immediately. "Where is he?" Even the four hundred miles between us couldn't keep the desperation in her voice from reaching me. And I almost felt bad for her.

Almost.

Because those words still pressed on my brain.

We'll be together, just wait.

So I mustered the courage I didn't know I had and heard myself say, "If you need money so badly, why don't you ask Darrin?"

My stomach clenched and I felt dizzy the moment the words were out. I had crossed a line and could never go back. No more pretending I didn't know.

There was a silence so thick and heavy it could have suffocated us both.

"Vic, I don't know what you know," she started, a quiver in her voice that was either very angry or very sad, and possibly a mixture of both, "or what you *think* you know, but please understand that I'm trying to sort it out."

"Did you take Freddy's canteen money, too?"

"Freddy is fine," she said, but the fact that her voice jumped an octave made it clear to me that she had pulled all the money from his account, too.

"How could you do that?" I spit at her.

"He has everything he needs. I packed it all myself. Extra money for candy is not a requirement. I'm sure there are other kids who never get canteen food."

"No, Mom, there aren't. *Everyone* gets canteen. It's part of camp."

"Well, that's ridiculous. Even your father said the extra money for canteen was a scam. We already pay a small fortune for you to go to camp, you know. It's a luxury, how you get to spend your summer up there."

"I didn't want to go to camp!" I screamed at the top of my

lungs. "And neither did Freddy. I didn't want this 'luxury'! *You* wanted the luxury of not having me and Freddy around so you could be with *Darrin*!" I spit his name out of my mouth like a piece of gristle. "If I was Dad, I would have left, too."

I didn't hear what she said next because I slammed the phone down with such force I worried for a second I might have broken it.

The air around me hummed with emptiness while I caught my breath.

I had never hung up on my mom before.

I had never hung up on anyone before.

I left the office, shutting the door carefully behind me. I could hear the seniors talking and laughing and cheering down at canteen.

So I went the other way, past the flag and through junior camp and into the woods. I climbed on top of my rock to sort out the spinning in my brain, and that's when I realized, as I sat down and went to hug my knees into my chest, that there was a Kit Kat Big Kat bar in my pocket. It was the free canteen snack Brenda had gifted me. I remembered she had squeezed my hand and slipped something into it but was too distracted at the time to realize what it was. Now the chocolate was melting and I could feel the squish and goo of it through the wrapper.

I peeled half the plastic back and dropped the whole mushy thing to the ground. Then I waited. While the sky grew dark and the sound of slamming cabin doors echoed behind me, I watched the chocolate bar disappear under a mob of swarming ants.

Day 7—Friday

>>>·<<<

"Do you want help at the farmers' market tomorrow?" I asked.

Earl was poking around one of the raised plant beds, his white-T-shirted back to me, when I arrived at the garden. It was Friday afternoon, my last farm elective day, and I had remembered to grab a baseball hat when I left Yarrow. I arrived early on purpose so I could talk to Earl before Bella showed up.

He turned around slowly and looked me dead in the eye. "Good afternoon to you, too," he answered.

I sighed heavily and tried again. "Good afternoon. Do you want help at the farmers' market tomorrow?"

"I do," he said. "Are you offering?"

"Yes. I'll help," I said, but added, "If you'll pay me."

He cocked his head to the side slightly as he continued to stare at me.

I rushed to make my case. "You said there's a lot of work to do and you need another pair of hands and it's really early in the morning and it's not actually *camp*, so if I'm going to do all that work, I think I should get paid."

He scratched at his chin and said, "I see."

I watched him put it together then—my empty canteen account and my offer—and waited for his answer.

"Paid in blueberries?" he asked.

"Paid in *money*," I answered impatiently.

His eyes crinkled up and I realized he was teasing me, which made me feel kind of stupid for falling for it.

"Okay," he said, and he pulled the blue bandanna out of his back pocket and tied it around his forehead again. "That's fair."

"Yes!" I couldn't help cheering for myself. Cheering at camp was contagious.

"I've already got a permission slip for off-site travel and field trips," Earl shared his thinking, "but I should call home to make sure the ride to town and back in the truck is okay."

"It'll be okay," I assured him. My mom didn't seem to care what I did this summer as long as I wasn't in her way.

"I still have to call. But if she agrees, you're good to go. Follow me." Earl walked toward the blueberry bushes. They were shrouded in their white nets and bulged like heavy clouds.

He pointed out the tray of small cardboard containers. "We're gonna pick and fill these baskets today."

"But we already did that, on Wednesday."

"I sold those, to Bear Café. Sold those Wednesday evening."

"What?" I couldn't believe he was going to make me do all that backbreaking picking *again*. "Why would you do that? Those were for the market."

"You can't pick Wednesday to sell on Saturday. That's too long. Some of what you pick now will get used in the dining hall tomorrow morning, and the rest we'll sell at market, so they're less than twenty-four hours old. That's fresh. The kale and lettuce won't get picked till the morning of."

It made sense, but it didn't make me happy.

"Fine," I huffed. "How do you get these net thingies off?" I started to tug, but Earl stepped in and showed me how to release the cinch and ease them off gently.

It turned out I didn't mind the work that day, the picking and pinching and bending and crouching and hot sun on my back. I was actually excited to sell the berries tomorrow so I could put money back in my canteen account, and also in Freddy's. I would take care of my brother and myself, even if my mom wouldn't.

Bella showed up late, wearing a turquoise bikini top and

shorts rolled up so high she might as well have just gone ahead and worn the bikini bottom instead. She went to her end of the blueberry bushes and started picking, but lifted her right leg out to the side each time she reached in to pull a berry. Then she switched arms and swung the other leg out to the side as she picked.

I watched this routine for a few rounds, then rubbed my eyes and looked again, unsure of exactly what I was seeing.

Bella caught me staring and explained, without stopping her leg lifts. "Simone got aerobics for elective all week and I'm missing it. So I'm doing exercises here. There's no reason this can't be a toning activity."

"Right." I nodded, wishing Carly or Jamie were there to witness this with me.

"It's working," she assured me. "I can already feel it in my glutes."

"Glutes, yeah," I urged her on. "Tone away." She looked ridiculous, but I kind of admired her anyway. She knew her problem—missing out on exercise because of farm—and fixed it, and didn't care how it looked to anyone else.

I tried to suck in my gut and squeeze my stomach muscles as I hunched forward into the bush as my own exercise. Within a minute I had a weird ache in my belly and new pain in my back, so I dropped that idea and just focused on the work. Bella continued with the leg lifts for a while, then changed to squats each time she dropped a berry into the container.

The forty-minute period passed quickly, and I still had energy left when the bugle sounded.

I finished filling the last container and slid it onto the tray with the others.

"Where do you want this?" I asked Earl, who had been patiently lifting bugs off his lettuce leaves, one by one.

"Just leave it there. I'll take care of it."

Bella placed her container of berries on the tray next to mine, then stopped to watch Earl pinch a few bugs off a leaf of romaine.

"You know, I have an Ultimate Power hair dryer that could blow those suckers off in two seconds flat. You want to borrow it?"

Earl chuckled. "That is a generous offer, Bella, but I think I'll stick to my method here."

"Suit yourself." Bella shrugged. She adjusted her bikini top as she walked away, calling, "See ya, wouldn't want to be ya" as she went.

Once she was gone, I said, "So we have a deal. I'll see you tomorrow."

Earl nodded.

Right before I turned the corner and disappeared around

his cabin, he called, "See you at five."

I froze in my tracks.

"Five?" My mouth dropped open. "You said the market was at eight."

"I did. It is. We have to be all picked and packed and set up by eight o'clock. And it's a half-hour drive away."

"Five o'clock in the morning! That's insane," I flailed. Then I thought of Chieko. "And inane! That's insane and inane."

"Nice vocabulary," Earl said.

"There is nothing *nice* about this," I huffed back.

"See you at five," he repeated, and waved me off.

"You're really gonna wish you didn't," I muttered as I trudged myself back to Yarrow.

Day 7—Friday evening

-»»·«««-

Evening activity was Game Hopping, where you could "hop" to any other cabin in your section of camp to play cards or board games. Carly and the Jaidas had just started a game of Pictionary with two Marigolds who had come over. Chieko was "supervising" from her bed in the counselor room, which just meant she was curled up reading a book. I was about to leave to check on Vera since I wasn't in the mood for games, but Carly convinced me to stay for one round.

Jaida A started to draw a long, clean line on the board with her black marker. Before she finished the last piece of a rectangle, the guessing began.

"It's a ruler!" Jaida C yelled.

"It's a plank of wood!" Jodi, one of the Marigold girls, called out.

Jaida A shook her head at the guesses and kept drawing. She put little wavy lines inside the big rectangle.

"It's a diving board," Carly tried.

"It *has* to be a diving board," Sasha, the other Marigold girl, agreed.

Jaida A put a circle around the rectangle, and then traced over the rectangle again.

"It's a piece of paper with a list. On a table. It's a grocery list!" Jaida C called.

"It's a book list!" Carly screamed. "It's a list of books to read!" Her whole face beamed at the thought of a long list of book titles.

Jaida A lowered her marker to tease Carly. "You are *such* a book nerd."

"And proud of it!" Chieko's voice thundered from the front room.

"Any other guesses?" Jaida A asked.

"It's a bookmark?" Jodi tried.

"Time's up," Jaida C announced. "What is it?"

Jaida A put the cap back on the marker, dropped it on her bed, and answered, "A three-course meal."

"What?" Jodi asked.

"That's a rectangle inside a circle," Sasha added. "How is that a three-course meal?"

"Oh my God," I said, shaking my head as I figured it out.

"I know, I know!" Carly jumped up. "It's Jordana's stick of gum!"

Jaida A broke into a gigantic grin while Jaida C and Carly fell over laughing.

"A stick of gum is a three-course meal?" Jodi asked.

"It is if you're Jordana," I answered.

"You Yarrows are seriously weird," Sasha said. She picked up the marker, uncapped it, and called, "My turn."

Of course Jordana wasn't there for any of this. She'd run to Aster the second the bugle blared the beginning of the period and was probably knee-deep in a round of Truth or Dare.

When I got to Chicory, I found Vera sitting in the middle of her neatly made bed with a stack of playing cards in her hands. She was playing solitaire.

So were six other girls in the room.

"So, the idea of game hopping night is to play *with* people," I said as my greeting.

Vera looked up from the spread of cards laid out in front of her and flashed me a big smile, then looked back down and placed a five of clubs under a six of diamonds.

"How are you, Vera?"

"Great! I taught everyone solitaire because we didn't like

any of the other game choices and they didn't know how to play."

A few girls nodded to agree, but none of them lifted their heads. They were too busy flipping cards over, studying the spreads before them, and adding on to the columns of numbers stretching across their cots. It looked fun, and I began to think a round of solitaire might be exactly what I needed to distract me from the things I didn't want to think about—my mom, my missing dad, my empty canteen account, Darrin.

"Well, I don't want to interrupt. I just wanted to check on you—"

"No, it's okay. I play this all the time."

I looked down at her ankles. "Your legs look better. The rash is practically gone."

"You were right about clinic. The cream they gave me worked right away. It had calendula in it and some essential oils. Calendula is in the same plant family as marigolds, and you'll be in Marigold next summer, right, Vic?"

I didn't know where I'd be at the end of August, let alone next summer, but I nodded anyway. "Do you want to go outside for a minute, by the rocks, and talk?"

"Sure," Vera answered. "I'll be back in a few," she told her fellow solitaire players, sounding more like a counselor than a junior camper.

Vera slipped her bare feet into her sneakers, and we walked outside into the dimming light. We found two flat rocks by the lake and sat with our backs to Chicory.

"So, have you been canoeing yet?"

"No, but it's on the schedule for tomorrow. And I already asked Jordyn about it. She said she'd go in a boat with me."

"That's great. And how about feeling homesick?"

"I'd say I'm only ten percent homesick now. Maybe eight. It's decreasing as I adapt to the environment."

"Have you been writing to your mom? Sometimes that helps."

"I write a diary entry for her every day. The plan is to mail them all on Fridays so she'll get a week's worth at a time. She gave me seven prepaid envelopes, Priority Mail. I just put my letters in and seal the flap."

"Wow, you two really planned ahead." My mom had sent me with only six stamps. She said I could buy more at canteen as I needed them, but that was before she stripped my account, before she knew she was going to need to.

"My mom is very organized. It's the only way she knows how to be," Vera said. "I appreciate the example she set, because now I'm very organized, too."

"My friend Jamie is like that," I shared. "Even inside her backpack, she keeps her folders and notebooks sequenced in the exact order of her classes every day."

"I do that, too," Vera said approvingly.

"I don't."

"Is your mom organized? She could teach you."

"Yeah, she is. Or . . . was."

"She was but isn't anymore?" Vera shuddered at the thought. "What happened?"

"You know what? I shouldn't have taken you out of your cabin when you were in the middle of an activity with so many friends. You should go back in."

"Okay," Vera agreed without a pause. "They might have questions about how to end the game, when you run out of options. I'm their only resource for solitaire."

"And people need resources." I smiled at her. "You better move it."

Vera gave me a quick hug and ran back inside Chicory, her pigtails swinging above her shoulders with each step.

Instead of walking straight back to Yarrow, I shuffled slowly along a different route, my mind tripping over thoughts of home, of the change in my mom from organizational queen to someone I didn't even recognize.

I remembered being little, younger even than Vera, and playing for hours at a time in my mom's closet. Her clothing had hung in neatly color-coordinated sections like a fabric rainbow, and her shoes were all stored in clear plastic boxes with typed labels taped to the end.

I remembered planting flowers with her by the walkway to our front door each spring, where she made me carefully follow her red, pink, white, purple color pattern. When Freddy was four and put a white next to a red one, she sent him inside for a drink so he wouldn't see and then quickly changed it out to the correct color.

I even remembered the day she brought home a shiny white filing cabinet and a box of hanging folders, so excited you would have thought she had just bought a dream car instead of boring office supplies. She spent hours labeling and ordering her files, filling the folders with papers that had been living inside old cardboard boxes under her desk. She placed one small plant on top of the cabinet and dusted the surface regularly to keep it shiny clean.

But the night before I left for camp, when she thought she hadn't sent in a permission form, she didn't head calmly to her filing cabinet to solve the problem. She frantically rooted through a giant stack of junk on her bedside table, and then through a pile of mail on the kitchen counter, and then through a tower of newspapers and magazines on the laundry room floor.

I went straight to her cabinet in the kitchen to look in

the file labeled *CAMP*, but ended up never even opening the drawer. My breath caught in my throat when I saw what a mess her precious cabinet had become. It was hidden under a pile of papers, catalogs, coupons, empty glasses, and one bowl of partially eaten pretzel rods. The plant was pushed to the back and its leaves wore a thick layer of dust. There were fingerprints, gray and filmy, on the handles and sides of the cabinet.

I went back upstairs to her bedroom and saw that the order in her closet had also disappeared. Half the shoe boxes were empty. Stray shoes lay all over the floor like giant pieces of fallen fruit. Some hangers had shirts hanging off by one shoulder while others were completely bare. Skirts and tops were crumpled in balls on the carpet. The fabric rainbow was completely gone.

When had it happened, this change in my mom, and how had I missed it? What else had I missed?

She ended up printing out a new permission form that night for me to hand in Saturday morning before I boarded the bus. And when I did hand it in, the counselor told me that it was already on file. My mom had sent it in weeks ago but had completely forgotten about it. Apparently, it was all too much to keep track of—camp forms for your two kids and a secret boyfriend.

When I finally got back to Yarrow, I could hear Pictionary

shouting from outside the cabin.

"It's a pile of pennies!" Jaida C guessed.

"Nope," Jodi answered.

"They're marbles," Sasha tried.

"Nope," Jodi said again, and then I heard the squeak of the marker against the board as she drew more.

"How about those bouncy balls we use for playing jacks? They're balls!" Sasha guessed, and everyone laughed.

"Nope."

"Over the course of this evening," Chieko's voice called out, and I could tell that she was still on her bed in the counselor room, "your skills at this game have not improved one iota."

"It's harder than it looks, Chieko," Jaida C defended herself.

"Time's running out . . . ," Jodi reminded everyone.

"It's a bunch of grapes," Carly guessed.

"Nope," Jodi said. "Not grapes."

When I heard that, I walked over to the side of the cabin where the window was. I looked through the screen at the drawing on the board, shook my head, and then said, "They're blueberries."

They all screamed in surprise at my sudden appearance. Their screams morphed into laughter, but Jodi still managed to say, "You're right! Blueberries is right!"

"We get Vic!" Carly called once she caught her breath.

"Our team gets Vic."

"No way! We get her," Jodi argued.

It felt good, being wanted, even if it was just for a silly game.

I walked around to the front door of the cabin and let myself in.

"Greetings, stealth Pictionary master," Chieko said, lowering her book onto her chest.

"Greetings. Wanna play a round?" I asked her.

She surprised me when she closed her book without even marking the page and slid off her bed. "Why not?"

And we walked back to the camper room together.

Day 8—Saturday

>>>·<<<

When Earl and I pulled into the market lot at seven fifteen the following morning, there were already two long rows of tents set up, facing each other like partners in a line dance. Each tent had a truck parked behind it, trunks opened, baskets and crates of brightly colored foods bursting out of them.

I noticed all this through half-closed eyes, of course. Chieko had to set her watch alarm for me and rip me out of bed to get me to Earl on time. Being in a truck with him now was way worse than a school morning, when I never had to set my alarm earlier than seven a.m. Luckily, I was a roll-out-of-bed-and-go girl. I went to bed in the sweatshirt and shorts I was wearing now so I wouldn't have to bother getting dressed, and my hair was in the lopsided ponytail I'd slept on all night.

All I did when I got up was brush my teeth and zombie-walk to Earl's cabin. It was painful, but I kept reminding myself that I was going to get paid.

"We're space sixteen," Earl told me. "Down by that end."

He maneuvered the truck carefully down the middle aisle, which would soon be full of shoppers, and then turned behind the row. He stopped when we reached a rock on the ground with *16* chalked onto it.

"Very high-tech," I commented.

"Help me get the tent up and then we'll unload."

I pretty much just stood there, holding one leg of the tent steady while he fiddled with the other three. I helped him carry the two folding tables into the tent and open them. I wiped them clean so he could lay a waxy tablecloth on top. The cloth was pale yellow with different kinds of flowers printed all over it.

"Earl," I said, eyeing the fabric suspiciously, "please don't tell me those are all the flowers the Meadow Wood bunks are named after."

"Because you said please"—he looked straight at me—"I will definitely not tell you that."

"But they are, aren't they?"

"I plead the Fifth," Earl said, then turned to pull more boxes out of his truck.

I lined up the baskets of blueberries on one table while Earl set out his kale and lettuce bunches on the other.

"Dang it," he cursed.

Dang it was a curse for Earl.

"I knew I'd forget something." He shook his head and pursed his lips.

"What'd you forget?"

"Signs," he answered. "Forgot my price signs."

"So we'll just tell them what they cost."

"No, people don't like to ask," he told me. "People like to see it themselves."

"Oh."

"We just need some paper. Or cardboard. I got a marker in the truck. Go to a stand and ask if we can have a piece of paper."

"Me?" I didn't want to talk to anyone. I still wasn't even 100 percent awake. Vera probably would have gauged me at about 68 percent.

"Yes, you. Go on." He shooed me away.

"But I don't want to," I resisted.

"It's part of the job." He stared me down to show he wasn't joking.

I turned and stalked off.

People were bustling around me, lifting and lugging and

setting up displays. Some were talking in clusters of two and three, thermoses in their hands, shouting greetings across the lot. No one looked like they knew how early it was.

And no one was dressed in shorts. Every person I saw wore long pants, mostly faded and worn, but still pants that went all the way down to their ankles. I felt a cold breeze rush across my thighs and suddenly felt self-conscious, just like I did the day I showed up for the sixth-grade town hall field trip in jeans while all the other girls were in dresses and skirts.

I pulled my thick hoodie over my head and hid inside it. The sun was up but was acting as groggy as I felt, so there was still a chill in the air. I wandered past two stands of strawberries, a stand of mixed greens, one of gourmet mushrooms, and another of blueberries that looked identical to ours.

I stopped in front of a stand that looked like someone had picked every single flower in five acres of meadow and arranged them all together in one small space. Buckets covered the tabletop and the ground around it, each stuffed full of flowers bunched in pouffy bouquets. There were hundreds of flowers. The sight of so much color boosted me to a full 89 percent awake.

"We're not open yet, but you can still shop if you want."

I looked up to see a guy about my age with a *Ramos Family Flowers* apron standing before me, his hands wrapped around a paper coffee cup. His hair was dark and cut close to his head, and he was looking at me with eyes green as the kale I had pulled that morning with Earl.

"Are you wearing contacts?" I asked before I could stop myself.

"Excuse me?"

"Colored contacts, on your eyes?" I clarified.

He made a face. "No."

"Oh," I said, and continued to stare at his eyes.

They were crazy green.

Captivating green.

Mind-controlling green.

His dark olive skin made them stand out even more.

He kind of laughed then, maybe at me.

"Did you want to buy something?"

"What? Um, no." I broke my stare and scanned the table of flowers in front of him. "But do you have a piece of paper, or cardboard, that you don't need? That I could have?"

"Probably." He bent down and searched behind his table. I saw that he was wearing jeans, too, except his weren't ripped or stained anywhere. They were a deep blue and looked as though they had been ironed.

When he couldn't find any paper behind his table, he walked over to the Ramos Family Flowers truck and pulled a piece of torn cardboard out of the back. There was no way he was old enough to drive that truck. He couldn't have been more than a year older than me. Then I noticed someone stretched out in the passenger seat, leaning back with their eyes closed and their feet on the dashboard. He had the same dark hair.

"Will this work?" He held it out before me and flipped it to show me both sides.

"That's perfect. Thanks a lot."

"You're welcome," he said, but then he didn't let go when I tried to take the cardboard.

"Are you waiting for a secret password or something?" I asked, squinting at him.

"Kind of, yeah," he answered, then said again, "You're welcome . . ." He was staring at me, his mouth open, like he wasn't quite done with his sentence.

And then I got it.

"Vic," I said. "My name is Vic."

"You're welcome, Vic," he said, emphasizing my name in a way that made me blush.

I turned quickly to hide my face and leave.

"And I'm Angel. Since you asked."

I heard him laugh as I hurried back to Earl.

Three hours later our two tables were completely bare and we started to break down our area, a whole hour before the market ended. The smell of kettle popcorn filled the air, even though that stand was at the complete other end of the lot. The salty-sweet aroma had been making my stomach growl all morning. Earl had packed two peanut butter sandwiches for us since we left camp before breakfast was served, but we'd eaten those hours ago and my stomach seemed to have no memory of mine.

"Very successful day," Earl announced.

"Great," I managed to get out before a yawn stretched my face into a wildly unattractive state.

Earl laughed at me. "You'll be tired all day now. Which reminds me." He rooted around in his pocket and pulled out a wad of five- and ten-dollar bills. He counted through them, then handed some to me. "Here's your cut."

It was more than I expected. And something about that, about Earl handing me money I had worked for all on my own, lifted me up. I suddenly felt taller, and older. I felt the tiniest bit in charge of my life for the moment, and it warmed me from the inside out.

"And here." Earl handed me a white paper bag.

When I opened it, a waft of warm cinnamon sugar hit me. Two cider doughnuts nestled beside each other in the bottom of the bag, heating my hands through the paper.

"They're from Hoefel's Donuts. Best you'll ever eat."

"Wow." I had to close my mouth to stop drool from sliding out. "Thank you. So much."

"You're welcome. So much." Earl imitated me perfectly. I realized then that just because I couldn't relate to his joy of weeding didn't mean I couldn't relate to him.

I offered the bag to him. "Want one?"

"Nah, gotta watch what I eat, on account of my ticker." And he pointed at his chest, the left side, where his heart was. "You enjoy them."

And I did. I tried to take small bites and I chewed as slowly as I could, but I still finished them both before we even found our way out of the lot and onto the main road back to Meadow Wood.

Day 9—Sunday

➤➤➤·◀◀◀

I spotted Freddy the moment I stepped out of the van, his skinny arms and legs pumping like machinery as he sprinted toward me.

"Vic!" he shouted. "Hey, Vic!"

He was a whole shade darker from the sun, and the buzz cut he'd gotten before camp was already growing out. It was the first brother-sister visitation of the summer. Every Sunday a few vans would load up girls at Meadow Wood and drive them over to Forest Lake so siblings could spend some time together.

"Freddy Spaghetti!" He launched himself into my arms with such force I almost fell over. His hug felt bony and soft at the same time. "I really missed you," I told him, finally peeling him off me and running my hand over his stubbly hair.

"It's only been a week," he said, trying to balance out the enthusiastic greeting he'd just given me. "You usually go four weeks without seeing me, until I come up on Visiting Day with Mom and Dad."

"Yeah, I know," I admitted. "It just feels different this year." Because it was different this year.

"So how's camp? Do you like it? Do you like your counselors? What's your favorite activity?" I had so many questions I was worried we wouldn't have time to cover even half of them during our visit.

"They have the best rolls in the world in the mess hall, and we can eat as many as we want!" Freddy's eyes lit up, and he licked his lips as he thought about them.

"Rolls, huh?" That was the answer I got to all my questions. They must be pretty amazing rolls.

"We have a chart in our bunk, and we're keeping track of who eats the most by the end of the summer."

"You're charting your bread consumption?" That was definitely a summer-camp first.

"My counselor Michael is going to be a teacher, so he has us do a lot of charts and graphs and stuff. He's practicing on us, but it's fun. We're gonna start a bar graph tonight after canteen, but it's gonna be a *candy bar* graph. Get it? Candy *bar. Bar* graph."

I laughed and slipped Freddy's hand into mine. "I get it. Very clever."

We walked down to the waterfront and sat where the grass met the sand. The sun was soft and the sky was dotted with cotton-candy clouds. A whisper of a breeze came off the water. The lake was flat and still, disturbed only by a family of ducks that landed on the surface, one after another in a triangle shape, then paddled off together toward one of the floating docks.

"See that brown building over there?" I pointed across the lake at Meadow Wood. "The second one from the end?"

"Uh-huh." Freddy held his hand over his eyes like a visor and followed my arm.

"That's my cabin. My bed is in the back half of that building, on the left side."

"Cool. So I can see you."

"And at night you'll know exactly where I am, sleeping right across the lake from you."

"Can you send smoke signals, like one puff of smoke to say hi and two puffs to say good night?"

"There's no chimney in the cabin, Freddy. And playing with fire is generally frowned upon at Meadow Wood. Just like it is here."

"Only counselors are allowed to light the bonfires," he admitted. "Your camp looks pretty."

I watched Freddy scan the shoreline across the lake. Every shade of green sparkled back at us in the gleaming sun. If you were a beach-ocean-coast kind of person, the scenery in New Hampshire might not do much for you, but if you were a lake-trees-mountains person, there was no place more breathtaking than the land Forest Lake and Meadow Wood stood on.

"Does my camp look like that," Freddy wanted to know, "when you look over here from your side?"

"Yeah, it does," I answered. "Both our camps are insanely beautiful." I hated to admit my mom might have been right when she used the word *luxury* to describe this place. It really was a blue-and-green kind of paradise.

Freddy and I braided stalks of grass still attached to the ground while we caught up. He told me about his bunkmates and about his counselor Michael, who taught him how to throw a Frisbee and lent him comic books at rest hour. He told me about the beginning of Color War and his swimming group and how cool it was to have a top bunk.

I asked enough questions to realize that Freddy had no idea what was going on at home. His first canteen was later that day, so he hadn't learned yet that his account was empty.

After the thirty-minute visitation was up and counselors started to gather the girls back to the vans, I asked Freddy to introduce me to Michael.

Michael took the money I handed him and agreed not to tell Freddy about it. I could tell that my brother was in good hands. It actually brought tears to my eyes to know my kid brother was okay. Getting up before dawn on a Saturday had been more than worth it.

Day 10—Monday

→→→·←←←

The archery range was tucked back in one corner of Meadow Wood, the tire-size targets set in front of a wall of trees. Chieko was the instructor, which was kind of hard to imagine at first. But once we had a session with her and saw her in action, it made sense.

At the beginning of the period she reviewed the names of all the equipment with us and made a big deal about safety practices. She actually sounded like a mom when she went through the list of dos and don'ts, and she called on us one at a time to repeat them.

Then we watched her shoot.

Five arrows.

Five bull's-eyes.

She practically split an arrow with another arrow, like they do in cartoons.

Chieko was *that* good.

The Chieko with a bow and arrow in her hands at the range was nothing like the cranky, sarcastic Chieko we lived with in the cabin. She seemed like a different person when she was shooting, as if the archery range were the only place she could let her guard down and really be herself.

We lined up across from our targets and began to shoot our ten arrows each. When Chieko got to me, she lifted my right arm and pulled my elbow out to the side, then helped me reposition my feet. I aimed and let go. The *thwack* sound the arrow made as it pierced the straw tire was strong and satisfying. Suddenly, all I cared about was hearing that *thwack*.

I shot again and missed.

"Slow your breathing. Don't rush," Chieko told me.

I took a deep breath and tried to slow myself down. I felt my chest rise and fall. I heard a breeze whisper through the leaves in the treetops. I focused on the ring inside the ring inside the ring on the target. I made myself as still as I could.

I took aim and held it, then let go.

Thwack.

My new favorite sound in the world.

I did it again, but only got a half *thwack*. The arrow was hanging off the edge of the target like a downed power line.

The next one missed completely.

Instead of loading up my next arrow, I turned and asked Chieko, "How are you so good at archery?"

She shrugged. "I don't know. I just am."

"That's helpful," I replied. "Thanks so much, counselor."

"I have a steady arm," Chieko explained. "And good aim. And I know how to be still. And think still. Plus I practice a lot, or I used to. I competed my freshman and sophomore year on the team."

"At college?"

She nodded yes.

"But not anymore?"

"Nah. I'm not going back on the team this fall." She took my bow from me then, set an arrow, got in her stance, pulled back her right arm, and released.

Thwack, right in the center circle.

"Why not?"

She dropped her stance and handed the bow back to me. "Because of Randy."

"Oh." I had no idea what that meant. "Who's Randy?"

Chieko took a deep breath and let it out hard and fast, then quickly said, "Randy was my girlfriend. Randy was the love of my life, who stomped on my heart like bubble wrap until it was deader than dead."

"Oh," I said again.

"Whatever."

"Sorry I asked," I said. "Really."

She shrugged. "That's why I'm here. I needed to get away, go somewhere new and do something different."

"And you chose camp? 'Cause, no offense, but you really don't seem like a camp person."

"No kidding. That's why. Remember what Eleanor said? 'You must do the thing you think you cannot do.'"

"Oh. Right." I threaded an arrow, aimed, shot, and missed. "But couldn't you have just gone home for the summer? To be with your high school friends and your family, instead of coming here?"

"Living at home is not an enticing option," Chieko answered without a pause.

"How come?"

"Because my mom . . ." She paused a moment before continuing, "My mom is not particularly pleased with who I am. And I don't enjoy being reminded of that on a daily basis."

"Has your mom seen you shoot? Who wouldn't be pleased with that?"

132

Chieko let out a quick huff. "Let's just say I'm not the kind of daughter she dreamed she would have and leave it at that."

She called over to Jaida C to point her front foot more to the right, then turned back to me to add, "That's one of the ways I'm like Eleanor. She got flak from her mom, too. Eleanor and me—we're soul sisters."

"Oh," I said, suddenly wishing I had a soul sister of my own, even though I wasn't sure what a soul sister was. Or how you got one. Jamie and I were really close and liked to pretend we were sisters. Was that the same thing?

I loaded an arrow and shot before I was ready, my mind too busy with this new information. My arrow disappeared into the grass with a quiet hush a few feet in front of the target.

I dropped my bow and asked, "But wait. Won't Randy be at school when you go back in the fall?"

"Uh-huh."

"Will you be okay by then?"

She shrugged and took my bow again. She loaded another arrow, pulled back, held her position gracefully like a dancer en pointe, then released.

Thwack.

Bull's-eye.

"You have to stay on the archery team, Chieko. You're too good to quit."

"Can't. Don't want to see Randy."

"'You must do the thing you think you cannot do.'" I threw her quote right back at her.

Chieko glared at me.

Then she shouted to the group, "Equipment down." She eyeballed each shooting station, then looked dead at me when she ordered, "Go fetch, little doggies."

She walked over to a shady area under the trees and took a long drink from her water bottle while we shuffled around the range, collecting our old cruddy arrows and comparing the holes we'd made in the targets.

As I pulled my two best hits out of the target, I thought about Chieko and how she suddenly seemed a lot like an archery arrow—tough as the steel point on one end and fragile as the crimped feathers on the other.

Once we were all back in the safe zone, Chieko put her water down and went to help Carly, who was proving to be hopeless with archery so far. She hadn't hit the target once.

"You are going to be my success story this summer, Carly," Chieko told her as she stepped beside her and nudged her front foot into a better shooting position. "Just you wait."

Day 12—Wednesday

→≫·≪←

At the beginning of rest hour I told Chieko my stomach hurt and asked if I could go to clinic.

"Your stomach is rock solid and you're totally fine, but please, go wherever it is you are really sneaking off to." Chieko said all this without pulling her eyes away from her book. Maybe she was still a little mad at me from archery.

"You don't know if my stomach hurts or not." I was offended that she assumed I was lying.

Even though I was totally lying.

She lowered her book, which was another one about Eleanor Roosevelt, and stared straight at me. "You are holding stationery and a pen and a clipboard. A stomach-sick person would be holding tissues or a bucket, and their hair would already be back in a knot to keep it clear of any impending streams of barf."

"Jeez, detective, you really figured me out."

"It wasn't hard."

"I'm not going to barf. I just feel queasy." I was sticking with my story. "Clinic has medicine for that. I've had it before."

"Does clinic have medicine for bad lying?"

"If you let me go, I can find out," I answered.

"Whatever. Go to 'clinic.'" Chieko gave me an exaggerated wink. "I will not stand in your way, for, as my soul sister Eleanor Roosevelt once said"—and she read directly from her book—"'Life was meant to be lived and curiosity must be kept alive. One must never, for whatever reason, turn his back on life.' So go. Be free. Escape rest hour. Face your life and keep your curiosity alive."

"You're a little nuts, you know that, Chieko?" I said, realizing how happy I was that she was my counselor.

"Nuts are good for you. High in protein. And fats—the good kind." Then she sighed loudly and announced, "Great—now I'm craving nuts. Thank you oh so very much."

"They have almonds sometimes at canteen," I told her.

Chieko clutched her stomach with one hand and draped the other across her brow. "Why must Thursday fall but once a week?"

She wasn't mad at me anymore.

"I'll be back soon," I said with a smile, and slipped out the screen door.

I crossed the fields, walked past clinic and past the flagpole, pausing a moment to notice the four flags hanging, one above the other, like limp dish towels on a loose clothesline. It was probably the most pathetic flagpole display in the entire state.

I moved swiftly through junior camp, past Violet, Daisy, and Chicory, and was relieved to see the grounds around them deserted. I looked over my shoulder and then slunk into the woods, stepping carefully over roots and twigs until I reached my rock. I climbed on top, my back to camp, and looked at the tiny bits of lake I could see to the left through the tree trunks and branches around me.

I had stationery because I planned to write a letter.

To my mom.

I needed to tell her that she was the worst mom on the face of the planet.

That she'd ruined our family.

That I would never forgive her.

I needed to write out everything I was feeling so it would stop weighing me down like a bag of wet sand strapped to my back.

But I couldn't even write *Dear Mom*.

Instead, my grip loosened and I watched the pen fall to the rock, then roll, slowly, off the side to the dirt below.

And that's when I felt it seize my heart and squeeze: fear.

More than angry or betrayed or surprised beyond belief, I was scared. At the end of August, camp would be over and I would be going home.

But what was home now?

Before the email I was never supposed to see, home meant my mom and dad and Freddy and me in a yellow house on a dead-end street in central Pennsylvania.

Home meant the uneven stone path to our front door that we had to line with orange cones every year at Halloween so trick-or-treaters wouldn't trip.

Home meant endless bags of pretzels in the kitchen snack drawer, and the fuzzy green carpet in the den that was thick enough to hide your toes in.

Home meant pancakes on weekends, and a street party every Labor Day, and raking leaves for our neighbor who was too old to do it herself.

But then my brain switched tracks, and other thoughts flooded in.

Home also meant dinners in front of the television, just the three of us, because Dad was working late again.

Home meant last-minute phone calls from my dad at some hotel, explaining he'd have to stay another day. Or two.

Home meant Mom watching soap operas like they were breaking news reports, and Mom shopping for things that she never even bothered to unpack out of the bags, and Mom staring out the window at nothing.

The more I thought about home, the more memories came flooding back to me, like scenes in a movie.

Scene: Mom's and Dad's muffled voices behind the bedroom door, growing louder and angrier until they sounded like two claps of thunder crashing into each other.

Scene: Freddy and me gnawing frozen waffles on the bus ride to school because Mom was stuck in bed with another migraine.

Scene: Mom and Dad showing up separately, and sitting separately, at the seventh-grade Welcome Back to School night.

It was suddenly so clear: They were in lousy shape. They had been in lousy shape for a long time, with or without Darrin.

And I had never noticed, not really, until the email.

We'll be together, just wait.

Was Mom planning to leave but Dad beat her to it?

Would Dad come back?

Would we have to move?

Who would I live with?

In August, camp would end and Freddy and I would travel hours by bus to get back home, but what were we going back to?

For the first time, I felt thankful that I was at Meadow Wood and that Freddy was safe and happy at Forest Lake. I didn't want to be anywhere near my mom or my dad.

I grabbed my clipboard, scrabbled off the rock, and picked up my pen from the weeds on the ground. I eased my way through the dim, shadowed woods and stepped into the bright junior camp area.

I had to make it back to Yarrow in time to sign up for canoe elective with Carly this week, and I had to pretend my stomach was better from my pretend visit to clinic. Ironically, my stomach actually hurt now. A lot. Like I was having one of my mom's migraines but in my gut.

It was the pain of knowing there was no way I could undo what had already happened at home.

And I knew clinic didn't have medicine for that kind of hurt.

Day 13—Thursday evening

→→→·←←←

"I'll start," Carly offered, "and then as soon as we're done, I'm getting in the shower."

The horse smell on her was pretty strong. No one was going to stop her from showering.

"My rose is that I did my first jump on Rowdy today," Carly announced. "I was terrified but I did it." She seemed to have a new obsession. She talked about riding now more than she talked about reading. She had even started referring to Rowdy as "her" horse.

"My rose is about the horses, too," Jaida A jumped in. "I talked to Brenda, and from now on they're going to pull all the fruit scraps from the kitchen so I can take them to the stables every day. For the horses."

"I didn't know you were doing that!" Carly was so happy

she looked like she had just walked into her own surprise party.

"They weren't even composting the scraps. They were just trashing them!" Jaida A said, completely exasperated. "And my thorn is that by the time I got my turn at canteen today, there were no Kit Kat bars left. And I had been *dreaming* of a Kit Kat for a whole entire week!"

I immediately felt guilty for the Kit Kat Brenda had slipped me last week, the one I had dropped to the ground in the woods. I could still picture the ants attacking it and wondered if the wrapper was still there, buried under dirt and leaves, or if they would have devoured that, too. All I knew for sure was that I wouldn't be able to eat a Kit Kat again for a very long time.

"You never said your thorn, Carly," Jaida C pointed out.

"My thorn is that my mom's letter said Lola, at home, got a new babysitter and it might be hard for me to get my job back in the fall."

"Ouch. You've been replaced," Chieko said.

Carly scrunched her eyebrows at that. "I might be able to get it back."

"No, you're out. Trust me," Chieko said. "Once someone new comes along, forget it. It's done."

Carly looked like she'd been punched in the gut. I couldn't help but wonder if that was what happened with Randy—if

Chieko had been replaced by someone else. But there was no way on earth I was going to ask her.

And then I thought of my dad, of him being replaced by Darrin. Did my dad have someone hidden away, too, that I didn't know about because he was more careful with his emails? And did Darrin and my dad's maybe-lady have kids of their own? Would they replace Freddy and me? My stomach started to feel wobbly and I hugged myself around the middle, as if I could squeeze all the bad thoughts out of me.

"Why don't you go, Chieko?" Jaida C said, steering us to a new topic. "Tell us your rose."

"My rose is nuts. I craved nuts. I pined for nuts. And at canteen, I got nuts. California almonds. My nut quest has been fulfilled."

"All hail the almond," Jordana called out, and performed a seated bow.

"My *thorn*"—Chieko really emphasized the word—"is that we are all required to refer to the *bad* event of the day as a *thorn*. I find this ill-conceived. Thorns are honest. Thorns don't deceive. If you touch a thorn, it's going to hurt. If you squeeze it, you're going to bleed. A thorn doesn't lie. A thorn is true. So a thorn is not a *bad* thing."

Everyone was quiet after her speech. Even Jordana, who had been braiding and unbraiding her hair the whole time, dropped her hands to her lap and considered Chieko's words, her hair unfurling.

"I never thought about it like that," Jaida A admitted. "That's a really good point."

"But thorns make you bleed. You said it yourself," Carly argued. "And most people would consider that a bad thing. So it makes sense that we use thorns for the negative part of our day."

A debate followed, but I didn't join it. What Chieko said made perfect sense to me. The moment you saw a thorn, you knew exactly what you were in for. You knew it could hurt you, so there was no terrible surprise when it did. Getting hurt by something unexpected—like a lying mom or a disappearing dad or, for Chieko, maybe, a cheating girlfriend—was a whole lot harder to deal with.

Jaida C called us all back to order by yelling, "People, we have to finish. Carly needs a shower, for Jake's sake."

"Oh, my hot Jakey!" Jordana folded her hands over her heart and swooned.

"Vic, you go," Jaida C ordered, and gave my knee a squeeze. It reminded me of the way my mom used to hold my hand when I was little and squeeze it three times to say *I love you*. I would squeeze three times back and smile up at her, thinking we had a special secret code, just the two of us. Later I learned Jamie did the same exact thing with her mom and also with her aunt Julie. And so did Carly with her parents. It turned out there was nothing special about it at all.

"My rose is canteen, definitely. I got a root beer and an ice cream sandwich, and I surprised Vera with M&M's, so now she thinks I'm the best camp sister in the whole entire world," I bragged.

"Better than Jennifer Maskers?" Jordana asked, tapping her front top tooth.

"Oh my God, *everyone* is better than Jennifer Maskers," Carly answered.

"Don't remind me," I said, my tongue moving immediately to the tooth that broke on that ridiculous lollipop. "And my thorn that shouldn't be called a thorn because I totally agree with Chieko"—I looked at her and she gave a firm nod—"is that tomorrow I'm going to smell like horse because I'm allowed to skip tennis so I can watch Carly ride third period."

Carly shouted, "You'll be equestrian-smelly like me! We can be the stink sisters!"

I wanted a soul sister, like Chieko had with Eleanor Roosevelt, but maybe I would have to settle for a stink sister instead. "My dream come true."

"The more stink, the merrier," Carly said, and hugged me tight with both arms.

"The more stink, the stinkier," Jordana corrected.

"How intensely lovely for the rest of us," Chieko noted. "At next canteen maybe someone should purchase more soap."

Day 14—Friday

>>>·<<<

The path to the stables wasn't far from our cabin. It took just a few minutes to walk the narrow trail that cut through some woods until it opened up to a large round fenced area with an old tack and stable house on the side. The trail was shady and dark and the mosquitoes were out of control. Carly didn't seem to notice, probably because she was dressed from head to toe in riding gear: denim jeans tucked into leather boots, long-sleeved shirt buttoned up to her chin, riding gloves, and a black helmet. Aside from her face, there was nowhere to bite.

I was another story, however. I was in my usual T-shirt, shorts, and sneakers outfit, with my hair stuffed into a high ponytail so even the back of my neck was on the menu for the blood-hungry insects. I slapped and swatted at them the entire walk. When I looked at Carly to complain, I saw that she was drenched in a slick layer of sweat. It was hot and humid, and she was dressed for a fall harvest hayride. For a moment I couldn't decide which was worse, the sweat or the bites.

Carly smacked me on the elbow, hard.

"Oww! What was that for?"

"Mosquito," she answered. "You're welcome."

The bites were worse.

The horse smell became noticeably stronger as we reached the end of the trail. Carly's pace picked up and her lips spread into a smile, but mine went the opposite direction. I wasn't used to the smell of so much horse, or manure.

"There's Holly," Carly gushed. "She's my favorite instructor. And look, there's Eliza! She's riding Festival."

A girl trotted around the ring on a white horse with a tan mane and tail. She was also completely covered in clothing with a dark helmet on her head. It was pretty impressive that Carly could identify anyone in all those clothes.

"I think Brenda's been scheduling Eliza and me together, even though she's way better than me," Carly explained.

I leaned on the fence while Carly went into the stable to get Rowdy. Holly gave me a welcome wave from the other side of the ring, where she was boosting a junior camper into a saddle.

Carly came out of the stable sitting straight and tall on

Rowdy, one hand holding the reins while the other stroked his mane. I watched as she walked Rowdy around the ring a few times, then gave a little kick and took him up to a trot. She popped up and down in the saddle like a jack-in-the-box that couldn't decide if it wanted to spring up or stay down. Her face became more serious as she took him up a notch again and began to canter.

Every time a hoof hit the ground, a puff of dirt rose up like magic dust. Holly called out an instruction, and I saw Carly change her position slightly in response. My eyes started to glaze over as the steady drumbeat rhythm of the canter lulled me into a trance.

But then my trance was broken by the sound of Earl's golf cart chugging up the narrow trail behind me.

"Fancy meeting you here," he said as he pulled up beside me, his walkie-talkie spitting static from his hip.

"I'm watching Carly ride. She's getting good."

He followed Carly for one full pass around the ring. "She must be," he said, "'cause Rowdy is not the most cooperative horse."

"He cooperates for Carly," I said. "She loves him."

Earl turned off the cart, left the keys in the ignition, and walked around the ring to a damaged area of fencing. He inspected the failing wood, tapping and prodding in different spots, and then took a bunch of measurements. The bottom of his jeans collected more brown dust every time a rider trotted by, but he didn't seem to care.

Tomorrow was Saturday, and he would be up before the sun, picking greens from his garden and driving them over to the market way before the bugle rang. As far as I knew, he would be going alone. I knew how much work it was, so I couldn't help feeling a tiny bit guilty about it.

But then I talked myself out of that. It wasn't my fault Meadow Wood grew more food than it could use in the dining hall. I had made enough money in one Saturday to fill both my and Freddy's accounts for the next few weeks, and who in their right mind would wake up that early on a Saturday if they didn't have to?

Earl said he liked all that farming work, anyway, that it gave him peace. I was going to find my own peace by staying in bed until the last possible second before dragging myself to flag.

And that would definitely be *after* the sun came up.

Day 16—Sunday

→›»·‹«←

Jordana was the first one out of bed when the bugle blared, which was a sure sign that something was up. She also skipped her usual stream of early-morning cursing. Instead, she bounced around the cabin while getting dressed and was the first one out the door for flag, which was as unbelievable as anything you might read in the *Guinness World Records*.

Once the whole camp was assembled, Brenda said her good mornings and was reminding us of the July Fourth firework plans when she was interrupted by the sound of Earl's cart churning toward the flagpole. The Marigold girls stepped aside to let him through, and he drove into the middle of the circle to park beside Brenda. As soon as I spotted the bouquet of flowers on the passenger seat in place of his overflowing tool kit, I knew what was going on.

It happened every July.

A chorus of "Awww" filled the air, and Brenda started shaking her head at her husband, even though she was grinning with every inch of her face at the same time.

Earl climbed out of the cart and nodded at one of the drama counselors, who took the cue and started a round of "Happy Birthday." The whole camp joined in, singing with an energy not usually available at this hour. Earl hoisted the bouquet out of the cart and presented it to his wife. I wondered if he'd bought it yesterday at the farmers' market.

Jordana sang along—she couldn't resist an opportunity to sing, ever—but she looked like she was bursting out of her skin with impatience while she was doing it.

"What's your deal, Jordana?" I asked her. "You in some kind of race to get to your bagel and cream cheese?"

She shook her head at me and didn't answer.

When the "Happy Birthday" song was done, a bunch of junior campers broke into, "Are you one? Are you two? Are you three? Are you four? Are you—"

Earl waved his hands to stop them while Brenda laughed and shook her head some more.

"Your breakfast'll be stone cold if you count to the right number," Earl ribbed.

"It's true," Brenda agreed. "I'm blessed and grateful to turn sixty-four today." Then she turned to Earl and said, "I'm catching up to you, mister. In just three years I'll be all caught up!"

Brenda made this joke every summer.

Earl hopped into his cart and drove away while Brenda got us back on track, calling two girls from Goldenrod to assist with the flag raising. One girl held the stack of folded-up flags while the other attached them to the rope in the usual order. Then they hoisted them up to the top of the pole, tied off the rope, and returned to their bunkmates.

And that's when we saw it.

As if on cue, a gust of wind whipped through the sky and the flags flapped out to their full rectangular shapes.

The last flag, the *Nature Nurtures Life* flag, had been swapped out. In its place was another burlap flag with the words *CANTEEN Nurtures Life* printed on it, surrounded by drawings of candy bar wrappers and soda cans.

Laughter broke out like the July Fourth fireworks Brenda had tried to tell us about. I'm pretty sure I even saw her crack a smile before she righted herself and forced a stern director-like look onto her face.

Jordana was laughing more enthusiastically than everyone else. She was also staring straight at a group of Aster girls. I followed her gaze and saw Bella, Simone, and a few others from that cabin high-fiving. Bella looked over at Jordana, gave her a thumbs-up, and mouthed, "Awesome!"

Jordana beamed from ear to ear and returned the thumbs-up sign. I guessed Bella and her friends had included Jordana in their prank.

Brenda started to lower the flags, then changed her mind and retied the rope back in place. She probably decided it would be better to remove the *CANTEEN* flag later in the day without a crowd watching.

"You did *not*." Carly smacked Jordana on the arm in admiration.

Jordana pursed her lips together and didn't say a word. Which was really impressive for Jordana.

"You know what? Canteen really *does* nurture life," Jaida C said. "At least at Meadow Wood."

"I wish today was Thursday," Jaida A said, staring at the flag, the Twix and Sprite pictures flapping firmly against the soft blue sky.

"Canteen," Carly agreed, her voice going soft and dreamy. "Every day should be canteen day."

Day 16—Sunday

→→→·←←←

Freddy and I sat by the water and threw pebbles into the lake while we talked. It was sibling visitation at his camp again, and we had fifteen minutes left together. Freddy's only problem that week had been running out of soap. Except he didn't exactly run out of it—he lost it.

At Forest Lake, the boys bathed *in* the lake. They stripped down to nothing and jumped in with special environmentally safe bars of soap and bottles of shampoo and scrubbed themselves right there in the water, dunking under to rinse off. Freddy had been having trouble holding on to his slippery bar of soap while also cleaning himself. Every attempt to grab it from where it was floating in the water made it slink even farther away. He had lost three bars of soap in the last week.

"Can't you buy more at canteen?" I asked him.

"I don't like their soap. It smells weird," Freddy complained.

"All right, I'll get you soap from my canteen and bring it to you next Sunday, okay?"

"Okay."

"Will someone share with you till then?"

"Yeah. But not many of us have any soap left. We all keep losing it. It's harder than it looks, you know, to hold it in the lake."

"It must be," I said, and ran my hand through his uncombed hair. He had lots of new highlights from the sun that never showed up in my dark hair no matter how much time I spent outside.

"Are you homesick at all?" I wanted to know.

Freddy was quiet for a minute, rolling a stone back and forth across his palm. Then he said, "I miss the big pillows on the floor by the TV, and I miss TV. And I miss my video games. But that's it."

"That's it?"

"I thought I would miss the pool at home, but the lake is better."

"The lake is colder," I pointed out.

"I like it. Camp is fun. I thought it would just be okay here, but it's better than okay." He flopped onto his back and gazed up at the blue sky.

I stared at the speckles of sunlight glittering across the lake and repeated Freddy's answer in my head: better than okay. It seemed like a goal, like something to shoot for. Earl was better than okay when he was working in his garden. Chieko was better than okay when she was shooting at the archery range. Carly was better than okay when she was riding Rowdy. Freddy was better than okay at Forest Lake.

But Freddy didn't know what I knew. Freddy didn't know that his dad was gone and his mom was with some guy named Darrin.

And I did.

How was I supposed to be okay with that?

Day 17—Monday night

→»·«←

"This camp has reached an all-time low," Jordana complained.

"You guys cheer about *bananas*. I think you hit your *low* a long time ago," Chieko countered.

Tonight's Evening activity was s'mores over a bonfire and the July Fourth fireworks over the lake.

Except it was July 10.

Apparently, professionally run July Fourth firecracker shows were available well after July Fourth.

We didn't know if Brenda had waited too long to schedule it, or if it was the Lake Forest director's job to schedule and he forgot, or if the firecracker company was short on staff and couldn't fit us in until now. We all just knew it was tough to argue that Meadow Wood *hadn't* reached an all-time low if the best we could do was have Independence Day fireworks a week *after* Independence Day.

We all changed into long pants and drenched ourselves in bug spray. It was late, already eight thirty, and dark enough for us to head to the waterfront and start on the snacks.

The night air was cool and crisp and the campfire was roaring, kicking up smoke and that incredible wood-burning smell. If you ever wanted to bottle the smell of summer camp, that would be it.

Carly linked arms with me and announced, "Happy birthday, America!"

"You mean happy *belated* birthday, America," I corrected her.

"Belated is better than not at all," Jordana chimed in. "I remember the year my mom forgot *my* birthday. It was awful."

"Your mom forgot?" Carly asked, her voice rising in shock.

Jordana's face crumpled into the beginning of a cry, and Carly reached out to rub her shoulder. Then Jordana perked back up with a huge grin. "Nah, I just made that up. But if you ever are starving for attention, tell people that. They'll feel so bad, they'll slobber sympathy all over you."

Carly smacked Jordana on the back. "You are such a butt-butt! I believed you."

"That's because I'm such a talented actress." Jordana held her head high and posed like a diva.

"Then you should have no problem acting like it's really the Fourth of July," Chieko said, nudging her toward the s'mores station. "Move it or there'll be no marshmallows left."

After I made two s'mores for Vera and left her happy with her bunkmates, I found Chieko sitting on the rock wall that separated the beach from the grass. She was staring up at the sky impatiently.

"This isn't an exercise in imagination, is it?" Chieko asked. "I mean, there really will be actual fireworks in the actual sky?"

"That's how it usually works," I answered.

"Well, what in God's good name are they waiting for? We've been down here for hours."

"I think it's been like twenty minutes."

"Whatever."

"What's wrong?" I asked.

She answered with a shrug.

"What can I do to help you feel the spirit of this historic day?"

"Nothing historic went down on July tenth," she snapped back.

"But we're pretending it's July Fourth, remember?"

"Jordana's pretending. I can't pretend. See?" And she looked me square in the eye then, her complete lack of enthusiasm smeared over her face.

"Okay. You're miserable. I give up." I decided to stop talking.

Chieko sighed heavily, then pulled up one of her pant legs to reveal a swollen pink bump on her ankle.

"A stupid flesh-crazed mosquito bit me on the ankle right in the middle of my stupid tattoo. It's itching so badly I'm ready to eat my own leg to make it stop."

Her tattoo was a capital *R* painted in a fancy calligraphy style. And there was a swollen, ugly bug bite smack in the middle of it.

"First of all," I said with a cringe, "eating your own leg is extremely gross. And second, clinic has stuff that could fix that in half of half of a second."

"So, a quarter of a second?" Chieko simplified.

"It's summer. No math, please," I said.

"You started it."

"Whatever," I replied.

"Don't take my word. Whatever is *my* word. You have to get your own word."

"I like whatever. I've been using it," I confessed. "And I used inane."

"Then I have had great impact on you, young one," Chieko said, nodding slowly.

I pointed at her leg. "Is the *R* for Randy?"

Chieko looked back at her ankle. "Yeah. Pretty symbolic, don't you think? A mosquito bit me right on the Randy? Like a message from a higher power."

"No. Mosquitoes just go for the ankle a lot. Easy access."

"Uh-uh. It's symbolic," Chieko insisted. "My advice to you—don't get a tattoo for another person. Don't be an idiot, like me."

"You're not an idiot."

"Promise me," she demanded.

"Okay, I promise." Then I asked, "Did she get one for you, too?"

Chieko looked at me, her face a blank sheet.

And then an explosive *BOOM* rang out so loud that even the sand on the beach seemed to jump in surprise. A field of color burst over our heads and the air filled with sudden squeals and shouts. Next came the noise of bodies scrambling to get to their place for the show, and then came quiet, like a blanket of hush draped across the entire waterfront.

Brenda was seated a few rocks down with a junior camper on either side. I spotted Earl resting in his golf cart at the other end of the beach. Vera was sitting next to a bunkmate who already had her hands over her ears and wore a look of terror on her face. Vera would explain the science of chemical reactions to talk her down, I was sure.

Chieko and I both leaned back on our rocks and let the night sky take over. The steady rhythm of pops and cracks and the flashes of light were hypnotic. Blue, red, purple, and white lights climbed and twisted together as they shot up, then exploded, sparkling and glowing on the way down. The surface of the lake reflected the shimmering light like a mirror. I loved knowing that Freddy was watching the same show from his side of the lake.

My eyes started to tear from so much staring and not enough blinking. Clouds of smoke began to collect in the sky, changing the black backdrop to a hazy gray.

"See that one?" Chieko whispered, pointing at a single streak of light zooming straight up into the sky. "That was me and Randy."

The streak of light reached its full height, hung in the air silently for a split second, and then exploded, light shooting off in every direction with a fierceness that made me squint.

"And that's me and Randy now," Chieko continued in a whisper. "Broken into a gazillion tiny pieces of fire and ash."

Her gaze was glued to the spectacle in the sky, connecting everything she saw with everything she felt.

I could do that, too.

I locked onto one streak of light and followed its climb, tracking it as it soared like a wish. And then I watched it pop and shatter, like a family breaking apart. It split into separate trails of fading light, each one glittering and twisting in its own lonely downward spiral. That one, on the left, was Freddy falling to Forest Lake, and that one next to it was me, spinning down to Meadow Wood. There was my dad, on the right, escaping away, and there was my mom, hissing toward some other place, probably toward Darrin. The light withered and fizzled out until there was nothing left but wispy smoke and air.

How was that for symbolic?

Day 19—Wednesday

➤➤➤·◄◄◄

When Chieko found me sprawled on my bed trying to balance a pen on my knee at rest hour, she threw an Eleanor Roosevelt book at me.

"You are the epitome of bored. Feed your mind," she ordered.

"I am," I said, ignoring the book, which landed next to my shoulder. "This is very Zen, what I'm doing."

"Really? What do you know about Zen Buddhism? Where did it originate?"

"Asia," I answered quickly.

"Asia is huge. Where in Asia?"

"Somewhere . . . very chill," I said.

Chieko laughed. "Nice try. If you read more, you would know the answer. Read a lot, know a lot."

"You sound like a public service announcement," I said. "And what's with your Eleanor obsession, by the way?"

"I'm not obsessed with her. I'm inspired by her. There's a difference. And trust me, you could do with some Eleanor inspiration."

"What's that supposed to mean?" I eyed her suspiciously.

A loud thump followed by an "Owww!" came from the bathroom area.

"Jeez, Jordana! Shut your dumb cubby door," Jaida A yelled, rubbing her leg where it had just collided with the hard wood.

Jordana's cubby door swung in front of the bathroom entrance if she didn't latch it closed completely, which she never did. Twenty-four hours didn't pass without at least one of us banging into it.

"Sorry," Jordana called, but she didn't move from the magazine fest she was having on her bed to fix it.

Jaida A threw her a death stare but then flopped onto Jordana's bed right next to her and started reading over her shoulder.

"Anyway." Chieko turned her attention back to me. "I haven't known you long, but I can tell something's off with you. As my shrink loves to say, 'You're carrying a weight.'"

I suddenly felt naked, like Chieko could see right through

me to the secret I hadn't shared with anyone.

"You go to a shrink?" I steered the subject away.

"Who doesn't?"

"Uh . . . me."

"You're young. Give it time. When you're older, and smarter, you'll find yourself a shrink. A good one can work wonders. Until then, you have Eleanor."

"Well, I doubt Eleanor can help me," I argued. "Wasn't she born, like, a hundred years ago?"

"More—she was born in 1884. And she died in 1962. And in between she led an amazing life. She was the First Lady for longer than any other First Lady in the history of our country. She did all these great things despite life blowing up in her face every time she turned around."

"Something blew up in her face?"

"No, nothing *literally* blew up, you ding-a-ling." Chieko shook her head at me, but she looked amused, not annoyed. "I'm saying she had a lot of bad breaks, but she didn't let them stop her. She kept going. And learning. And helping people. She totally rocked."

"What were her bad breaks?"

"Read the book and find out. I'm not giving an oral report here."

"Could've fooled me," I muttered.

"Okay, forget it then." Chieko leaned over me to take her book back.

"No, okay, okay." I rolled onto the book quickly so it was trapped under me. "I want it. I'll read it."

Chieko smiled like a proud mom. "Good decision. See? You're getting smarter already."

"Gee, thanks," I said back. I propped up my pillow a bit, opened the book to page one, and started to read about Chieko's soul sister.

Day 20—Thursday

->>>·<<<-

The moment the loudspeaker clicked on during rest hour and echoed its shrill screech across camp, Carly looked at me and said, "Two root beers say you're going to Chicory."

Brenda's voice rang through the quiet. "Vic Brown, please report to Chicory. Vic to Chicory."

"Called it," Carly said. She was flipping through a book Holly had lent her on jumping techniques and the scoring systems used at horse shows.

I hadn't really spent any time with Vera since the fireworks, so I fast-jogged to her cabin.

And I don't like to jog.

Ever.

When I reached Chicory, Vera was already outside on the

bottom step, waiting for me. She didn't look upset, though. Instead, her eyes were wide and bright and there was an excited energy bouncing off her, as if her insides were made up of those rubber bouncy balls you got from the twenty-five-cent vending machines.

She sprang up from her step when she saw me and grabbed my arm, tugging me behind her cabin. "I've been waiting *forever*," she huffed as she pulled me with a strength that was downright alarming, given her size.

"Vera, I got here in about one minute flat. I *ran*, for Jake's sake!"

"Who's Jake?"

"It's an expression."

"I think you mean 'for goodness' sake.'"

"No, I mean Jake's." I was not feeling the camp-sister love at the moment. "Why did you have them call me? I thought something was wrong."

"It isn't, but it will be if we don't do something fast."

"That's not dramatic or anything." I rolled my eyes at her.

Vera stopped behind her cabin, crouched down, and stuck her arm through a bunch of tall, grassy weeds. She groped around for a second and then slid her arm back out, pulling a red metal basket with it.

"Do I even want to know?" It could have been anything

from a potato-powered flashlight to a handwritten encyclopedia of insect species.

"Ta-da!" she said, and slid back the book that was resting on top so I could peer into the basket. The basket was her shower caddy, currently emptied of all shower supplies.

"He's my new pet." Vera beamed.

The frog trapped in the container let out a quack-like noise that sounded to me like a cry for help.

"Isn't he sweet?" Vera cooed.

I studied the frog and found absolutely nothing that would make me describe it as "sweet."

"Sure," I answered. "Where did you get him?"

"There." She pointed toward the lake in front of her cabin. "Where the woods meet the rocks in front of the lake. Which is exactly where one would find a wood frog. They like wooded areas and need access to water."

"So it's a he, and he's a wood frog?" I reviewed the facts.

"Yes, *Lithobates sylvaticus*. And the tympanums are larger than the eyes, so male, of course."

"Of course."

"I found him right before lunch."

"And I'm guessing you named him already?"

"His name is Jolly. It's a synonym for Happy, who we lost on the bus ride, as you know."

Of course she named him Jolly.

I had been hearing so much animal welfare talk from Jaida A that I must have absorbed it like water through amphibian skin, because I heard myself say, "And you are honoring Happy's memory by keeping him trapped in a box instead of letting him live his normal, natural, outdoors life?"

Vera's whole body slumped. The words were out of my mouth before I realized how they might sound to a slightly homesick frog-loving seven-year-old girl.

"But he came to me," Vera said, her eyes fixed on the frog staring up at her from the caddy. "Frogs don't do that. They don't come to people. But he came to me."

I thought about the kind of camp sister I always said I wanted to be. "He does seem to like you. He keeps looking at you. Tell me how it happened."

Vera explained that she was sitting by the rocks in front of her cabin when she heard a quacking sound but couldn't find a duck or waterbird anywhere. The sound got closer and louder until finally she looked down and saw a frog leaping toward her. It landed with a final plop right on her sneaker and then didn't move a muscle. So she picked him up, snuck him into Chicory to make him a temporary home, and then put him back outside under the cabin so she wouldn't get in trouble.

"Okay, he definitely *did* come to you. I'm sold on that. What's the plan now?"

Vera smiled wide, like a frog, and explained what insects she needed to collect to keep Jolly fed. She also needed a small container, like a jar lid, to use as a water source so he wouldn't dry out. I told her I'd check out the recycle bins behind the dining hall and snag whatever might work as a shallow pool.

As for the insects, we started to hunt them right then. We flipped a rock that was sitting half under the cabin and pulled out two worms and some other critter I couldn't identify. Vera dropped them in and Jolly ate all three of them while we watched. It was pretty gross but also kind of cool.

While we searched for more, I asked Vera how things were going with her bunkmates.

"Pretty good. I did the canoe thing. Twice."

"And?" I really hoped my idea hadn't been a disaster.

"I canoed with Jordyn. She's from Long Island, New York, and has three pug dogs and lives only with her mom, like me. She likes math and music but doesn't like to read, and she was scared the whole time we were in the canoe because of sharks."

"There aren't any sharks in the lake."

"I know, and I told her that, but she watched the movie

Jaws by accident right before camp and it made her terrified beyond reason."

"How do you watch a movie by accident?"

"I don't know, but now she can't get it out of her head. She has anxiety about all water activities. She even made her mom call Brenda to excuse her from water-skiing. Look!" Vera held up her hand, another slimy worm dangling from her fingers. "Dessert for Jolly!"

"So you made a friend?" I asked. "A good friend?"

"I did. Jordyn said every time we have canoe she wants to go with me because I told her facts about marine life that helped calm her down."

"That's great, Vera." I sighed in relief. "I'm really happy for you."

"And I'm really happy for Jolly, because that's a slug!" She pointed at the cabin wall near me. "Grab it."

"No thanks." I scooted away so she could peel it off the wall herself and feed her new pet. It left a glossy stain of goop on the wall in the shape of a lima bean.

"So I can keep him?" Vera asked me then.

"How about you keep him for a few days and then give him the chance to return to his other life, if he wants to?"

Vera reached into her caddy and stroked Jolly's brown head.

"I think . . ." And she paused for just a second before saying,

"I think that's the ethically right thing to do." She petted Jolly one last time, slid the book in place like a roof on his little house, and pushed the basket back into the shade under the cabin.

I hugged Vera goodbye and promised I would hunt for more bugs after dinner.

As she squeezed the middle of me with her strong skinny arms, she said right into my belly, "You're the best camp sister ever."

I let those jolly words play over and over in my head as I walked back to Yarrow.

Day 21–Friday

→≫·≪←

It was second period and I had volunteered to untangle a mess of life vests by the kayak hut when I saw Earl zip by in his golf cart at a speed I didn't know it was capable of. He didn't even bother to steer around the soccer field. He just hit his horn twice as a warning to the Goldenrod girls scrimmaging there and plowed through. Even the swim counselors on the dock stopped what they were doing, hands lifted to shade their eyes, and watched Earl zoom by.

Jaida A and Jaida C said, "Something's wrong," at the same time, but neither of them added *jinx* or laughed.

Jordana was already far out on the water in her kayak, drifting in a small patch of sun, her eyes closed, her paddle resting across her lap.

"What could be wrong?" I asked, hustling over to the Jaidas, who were ankle deep in the lake.

We all watched Earl and his cart get smaller as he whizzed off the field toward senior camp and then entered the narrow trail through the woods that led to one place only: the riding ring.

My stomach folded over itself as I watched the wheels kick up dirt and disappear into the thicket of leafy woods. Carly had horseback riding second period today. The humid air suddenly shrink-wrapped itself around me and I couldn't breathe. The Jaidas felt it, too, because without any of us saying a word, we dropped everything and ran.

I reached the trail first and flew down it so fast the mosquitoes had no chance of getting a piece of me. I burst out of the woods to find the cart parked outside the fence and Earl and Holly inside it, bent over someone on the ground.

I saw Eliza with a huddle of young girls at the other end of the ring. The girls were whispering and watching while Eliza held tightly to the reins of a brown horse. The horse couldn't have looked more bored if it tried.

The only sound was Earl's walkie-talkie spitting static, and then Brenda's voice: "Did you arrive? Over. Do you need backup? Over."

I knew from the process of elimination.

From the buckle and twist in my gut.

From the dry swell of my tongue that wouldn't let me swallow.

I knew the way you just know.

It was Carly.

When Earl and Holly eased her up to a sitting position, a yelp of pain soared through the quiet like an archer's arrow. It pierced me in the chest and made me want to run toward my friend and away from her at the same time.

From everything Chieko had told me about Eleanor Roosevelt, I was sure that Eleanor would choose toward.

It occurred to me right then that Vera would, too.

I hopped the fence and ran to Carly. I reached her just as she was finding her way to her feet, Earl under her left shoulder and Holly lifting her by the waist.

"It's her shoulder," Holly rushed to say before I touched Carly. "Something's wrong with her right shoulder."

Carly's face looked like all the color had been drained out of it, and a line of sweat painted her upper lip. Her helmet was still on but was twisted, squishing loose hairs onto her damp forehead and cheek in that way I knew she hated.

"Take my radio," Earl instructed me, "and tell Brenda to

meet me at the lot. Tell her she's taking Carly to the hospital."

I fumbled to get the walkie-talkie off his belt, and I fumbled to press and release the right buttons to get my message through.

Holly settled Carly into the golf cart and supported her against the jolt of Earl starting the engine. Carly's eyes were closed, her left arm clutching her right tightly against her stomach. Streaks of tears lined her cheeks. Earl drove slowly at first, gliding carefully over the roots and bumps on the wood trail, and then floored it once he hit open flat field. I chased after the cart but couldn't keep up and lost sight of them as they veered around cabins through the camp entranceway to the parking lot.

The Jaidas caught up with me after another minute, and Jaida C put her arm around me as we walked back to the beachfront. "She'll be okay."

"What happened?" I still didn't know.

"Eliza said she was jumping and fell off the horse," Jaida A answered.

"Or she was thrown," Jaida C added. "Eliza wasn't sure because she didn't see it happen. She just heard her hit the ground."

I shuddered as I pictured it. "Was she riding Rowdy?"

"Yeah," Jaida A said. "Her favorite."

"Not anymore, I bet," Jaida C said.

From a distance, we saw Earl return from the parking lot. He parked his cart in its usual spot in front of the main office and went inside. We waited, staring hopefully at the building as if it would answer our questions and calm our fears. And because we were all lost in our own thoughts about what had just happened, we jumped completely out of our skin when the bugle suddenly rang out, screeching its end-of-activity song to let us know it was time to return to our cabins and get ready for third period.

"Are they ever going to fix that junky thing?" Jaida A grumbled, grabbing two paddles from the sandy beach and walking them over to the storage rack.

"In your dreams," Jaida C answered, lifting the pile of still-tangled life vests.

Jordana pulled her kayak out of the water and flipped it over to drain. "How come you guys never came out? The water was so flat and perfect just now."

Jaida C helped Jordana carry her kayak to the hut and started to catch her up.

I picked up a small canoe paddle half-buried in the sand and slammed the end into the ground. I wedged it to the side and flicked a softball-sized chunk of damp sand toward the lake. The sand chunk hit the water with a hollow *plunk* and left a big divot on the beach, deep enough to twist an ankle.

I started to trudge back to Yarrow but then turned around, grabbed a handful of sand, and tapped it back into the hole, smoothing it out with my foot. I didn't want anyone else to get hurt.

Day 21—Friday

➤➤➤·◄◄◄

"Mail delivery," Chieko called out as the screen door slammed behind her. It was rest hour and we still hadn't heard anything about Carly.

"A letter for Jaida A, two for Vic, and a flatty for Jordana. Do tell what's inside that baby." Chieko tossed each item on the correct bed and then sat next to Jordana to see what she'd gotten.

We weren't allowed to receive packages at Meadow Wood. The camp would only accept "flat" mail, which meant paper in envelopes. The envelopes could be large, like Jordana's was today, but they still had to be flat. That way, no one could send food or toys or any equipment we weren't allowed to have.

Jordana ripped open her manila envelope and pulled out

color pages of Broadway stars that had been cut out of a celebrity magazine. She also got magazine pages of other pop stars and actors.

"Yes! My mom's the best!" Jordana squealed and hugged her treasure to herself. "These are going up now." She hopped up from her bed and started clawing through her cubby in search of her duct tape, which was supersize and neon pink so shouldn't have been that hard to find.

Chieko left Jordana's cot, clearly disappointed with the loot, and asked me who my letters were from.

"Don't know yet," I answered. I tried to sound calm and cool and not the way I actually felt, which was like a tornado was ripping through my insides. One of the letters addressed to me was in my mom's perfect cursive writing. The other envelope had lettering that looked like chicken scratch, which I recognized immediately as my dad's.

I had to take deep breaths and swallow slowly a few times to make sure I wouldn't hurl up the tuna salad sandwich I'd had for lunch. As if Carly being rushed to the hospital wasn't traumatic enough for one day, now I had both of my parents in my hands, with no idea at all what was waiting for me inside their envelopes.

I had never been afraid of a letter before in my life.

I decided to read my dad's first. There was no return address on the envelope, and it was written on hotel stationery, the hotel chain he always stayed in for work.

> Dear Vic,
>
> How are you? How's camp? I hope you're having fun with Carly and the crew and you're having nice weather. I wanted to let you know that I'm not staying at home right now. Your mom and I are having some problems, so I moved out. You know my cell number—I'm sure Brenda will let you call if you need me. Give Freddy a hug for me. I know you're taking good care of him when you see him on Sundays.
>
> Love,
>
> Dad
>
> P.S. I won't make it to Visiting Day this year. I have a business meeting in California that same weekend. Your mom will be up to see you, though.

I read it three times in a row, searching for any hint of emotion about what was happening. I couldn't find a shred. The letter was so short and simple that I knew my seventh grade language arts teacher would write in the margin, in her favorite purple ink, *Expand on your theme. Give supporting evidence.*

And she would definitely have a comment on his lack of transitions. He went right from the weather to moving out like that was a completely normal sequence of topics.

I read the letter a fourth time. If my dad wasn't coming to Meadow Wood for Visiting Day, that meant he wasn't going to Forest Lake, either. Freddy would be devastated. What kind of parent tossed that piece of information in a P.S.? A P.S. was for comments like, *Saw the funniest commercial and thought of you*, or *Been reading the dictionary so I can destroy you in Scrabble!* My dad's P.S. would make the *Guinness World Records* for the worst P.S. in recorded history.

But at least he wrote.

I knew how much my dad hated writing letters. I usually got only two letters from him each summer—one before Visiting Day and one after. I wondered if I'd get a third one this year in place of the visit on Visiting Day.

Probably not.

I couldn't figure out if I should cry or punch something. Part of me wanted to feel bad for him, because of what my mom did, but the other part of me was furious that he'd let it happen, that he didn't sound upset about leaving us, that, in a way, he had already been gone for a very long time.

My eyes drifted over to my mom's letter, which was staring at me with its fancy handwriting on its fancy ivory stationery.

The stamp was a pink heart with the word *FOREVER* printed underneath.

Which made me think of marriage vows.

Which made me think of irony.

Which made me think of Vera, since she was the youngest person I had ever heard in my life use the word *irony* in conversation.

And thinking of Vera reminded me that I couldn't fix a problem without first naming it. I still wasn't ready to talk about it with anyone, but I could at least read what my mom had to say about it.

I took a deep breath and let it go, then picked up the letter and slid my finger under the seal. I didn't know if I'd find an apology or an explanation or an excuse inside, but after my dad's letter, I knew not to expect much.

> Dear Vic,
>
> Let me start by saying how sorry I am about our phone conversation. I wasn't expecting your call (excuse) and didn't handle myself well. I understand you were very angry at the time and I'm hoping that you're sorry, too.
>
> I'm also very sorry that you learned about Darrin the way you did (apology). I have to add that

it would not have happened if you weren't reading my email, though. Please know I was going to tell you about him after camp.

Your father and I are currently separated. We need to figure out where we are going from here (explanation). He left and I don't know where he is, so if you hear from him, I would appreciate you letting me know. There are some matters he is not legally allowed to walk away from. I am very sorry if this puts you in an uncomfortable position, but I need this help from you. Because Freddy is only eight, I don't think he needs to know about this. I realize I can't stop you from telling him, but I hope you will respect my wishes and let him enjoy his summer at Forest Lake.

I spoke with Brenda and she has agreed to let you call me from the office if you have any news of your father.

I am sorry for all of this, Vic. I really am.
I love you.
Love,
Mom

As mad as I was, I couldn't stop my eyes from welling up as I read the words *I love you*.

But then I kept reading.

My mom had also included a P.S.

P.S. Please understand that I won't be able to come up for Visiting Day for you or Freddy. I don't have the finances in place to support the travel and hotel stay.

A surge of anger churned through my insides, like fire was pumping through my veins instead of blood. She wasn't coming to see us on Visiting Day? And she decided to include that important information in a P.S., just like Dad? Maybe they were meant for each other, after all. I could already imagine the letters they would send each other through their lawyers. My mom's would say, *P.S. If you're late with child support, I'll have you arrested*, and his would say, *P.S. I'm keeping the house. You'll have to vacate by Wednesday.*

Now I *knew* I wanted to punch something, but before I could, the screen door closed gently and Holly appeared in the doorway.

We all stopped what we were doing.

Chieko followed Holly to our room.

No one said a word, not even Jordana.

"Carly broke her collarbone. Straight through. I saw the X-ray."

Jaida A and Jaida C gasped at the same time.

I took a deep breath and held it for a few seconds as I listened.

"Her parents are on their way. They want to take her home to see a specialist. The doctor here says she'll need four weeks to heal, maybe more."

My tuna salad started to swim around my gut again and I closed my eyes, pushing my hand against my stomach to stop all the motion. There was more talking, but I didn't hear it. I was busy trying to erase the image of a straight white bone snapped in two. That had to hurt like crazy.

I interrupted someone to ask, "How is she doing?"

"Better now." Holly's face relaxed a bit as she said this. "They gave her medicine for the pain and put her in a brace. She'll be okay."

"Let's make her something," Jaida C called out.

"Let's make a gigantic get well card," Jaida A suggested.

"Arts and crafts has poster board. I'll snag some," Chieko said, and left immediately.

"And we can use some of these." Jordana held up the magazine pages she had just received in her package. "We can collage some on."

The Jaidas plopped onto Jordana's bed and started choosing which hot guys they wanted to cut out and what to write in speech bubbles above their heads.

"Thanks for taking care of her, Holly," I said as she turned to leave.

"Of course," Holly answered me. "I hate that she's leaving. Her riding was really coming along. I'm gonna miss her."

"Yeah," I said. "Me too."

I collapsed back on my bed and threw my arms over my face. Five more weeks of camp without my best friend *and* no family on Visiting Day. I squeezed my eyes shut and pushed my hands into them until I saw specks of color bloom and explode in the darkness, like July 10 fireworks. I tuned out the chatter of my bunkmates and sank into the realization that my summer couldn't possibly get any worse.

Day 21—Friday evening

>>>·<<<

After dinner I begged Chieko to let me skip evening activity, which happened to be our first social with Forest Lake. The dance was from eight to ten in our rec hall and I wanted to spend my night watching Jordana flirt about as much as I wanted to revisit the dentist who fixed my broken tooth four years ago. The fact that Chieko agreed showed just how bad she felt for me about losing Carly.

Once everyone in Yarrow was primped and gone—Jaida C had gone to Marigold to do hair after she did Jaida A's and Jordana's—I stretched out on my cot and tried to dive back into Chieko's Eleanor Roosevelt book. It was hard to concentrate, though. The music in the rec hall was pumping so loud I could hear it through the walls of the cabin. It was mostly just bass and beat, like listening to someone's heart through a stethoscope. It also wasn't helping that Carly's bed above me was stripped bare. There would be no more bed tents. Her parents had been only two hours away, vacationing in Vermont, when they got the call from Brenda. They drove straight here, packed up all of Carly's stuff, and whisked her out of the hospital in a blink.

I didn't get to say goodbye.

None of us did.

After reading the same sentence four times in a row and absorbing none of it, I realized reading wasn't going to work right now. I got up, tucked the paperback in my back pocket like Chieko did, grabbed a flashlight, and walked out of Yarrow. The mosquitoes swarmed around me as if they were having their own social, dancing around me in twos and threes. I slapped at them as I walked.

I remembered the small bugs I saw Earl picking off his lettuce leaves and wondered if frogs ate those. I'd have to ask Vera. For now, I headed to the trash area behind the dining hall and started searching for insects for Jolly. I quickly found two grubs in the dirt but realized I had nothing to put them in, and there was no way I was going to palm those suckers all the way to Chicory. Grubs were called grubs for a reason—they were 110 percent grubby gross.

I walked over to the recycling dumpster and found an

empty plastic tub that would work as a bug carrier. I killed a mosquito on my arm and dropped it into the tub, not sure if it was a food option for Jolly or not. I returned to my twin grubs on the ground and wondered how I was going to get them into the tub without touching them.

I picked up two short twigs and tried using them as chopsticks. I was pretty good at them, but I still couldn't get them to work on the bugs. Next I tried one stick in each hand so I could use them like salad tongs, but the grub kept falling before I could get it into the container. After too many minutes of this, I got so frustrated that I flicked the stick under the grub to get some lift, but the stick snapped and the disgusting grub and tons of dirt flew into my face instead.

I gasped as gobs of damp earth hit my eyes. I blinked furiously while I clawed dirt off my cheeks and out of my hair and spat grit out of my mouth. Then I slumped down on my butt, kicked the stupid tub away with a grunt, and bawled my eyes out.

This wasn't what summer vacation was supposed to be. My list of horribleness was just way too long:

My mom was cheating on my dad.
My dad had taken off and disappeared.
My brother and I had been shipped away for two months.
My mom apparently had no money.

My parents were not coming on Visiting Day.

My best camp friend had left for the summer.

My evening activity was scavenging for bugs so I could feed my gifted camp sister's secret pet.

If there was a rock bottom, I was several grimy, grungy, rotten feet beneath it.

So I cried.

I cried until my face was soaked and my eyes were puffy and I thought I didn't have a single tear left in me.

And then I cried some more.

When I finally ran out of tears, I wiped my face on my T-shirt and exhaled long and loud and hard.

The grubs were gone and I wasn't going to look for them.

"Stupid frog food," I muttered.

Which made me think of Jolly.

Which made me think of Vera.

Which made me think again about what her mom said: to fix a problem you had to name it.

"Okay, Miss Smarty-Pants," I said to no one, "we'll do it your way."

So I named it.

"My summer totally sucks," I said out loud to the empty space around me.

I ran through my long list of horribleness again, but this time I said it all out loud instead of inside my head. I belted out my problems in a voice that was angry and sad and scared all at the same time, and when I was finished, I had to admit that I felt a lot better than I did before my bug-flinging breakdown.

My problems were *out there* now, floating around in the clean New Hampshire air. Maybe now I would finally be able to get a good look at them and tackle them from the other side.

I suddenly wanted to know more about Eleanor and this magical inspiration Chieko said she would give me. I was *ready* to know more. The book was still in my back pocket, so I wiped my face again on my T-shirt, retrieved the empty tub to drop back in the dumpster, and headed across camp to my rock.

Day 21—Friday evening

>>>·<<<

The sky was lit up with stars, but they weren't strong enough to break through the ceiling of leaves that hung over my rock. I switched on my flashlight and shined it over the tree trunks that circled me. The grooves in the bark stood out more in the dark, the browns richer and the shadows deeper. Limbs looked like arms reaching out to their neighbors, and leaves looked like hands holding on to a friend. I realized that the trees weren't all that different from the plants Earl kept in neat rows behind his cabin. Trees took their time also, each small moment growing on the next.

I had about an hour before I'd have to return to Yarrow and listen to Jordana complain about her brother blocking all her fun at the social. I opened my book and started to read. It took only a few pages of reading to learn that Eleanor was an orphan by the time she was ten years old. First her mom died—the mom that Chieko said wasn't so great to Eleanor—and then a couple of years later her dad died, too.

Both parents gone. Just like that.

I couldn't relate. I had one great brother and two less-than-perfect parents who I knew loved me. Compared to what Eleanor had to deal with, my family situation didn't seem so bad at all. Maybe Chieko felt the same way, because she had underlined a lot on this page of the book.

I finished that chapter and read the next one, too, which described the school in England Eleanor was sent to and the amazing student she became there. Then I put the book on my lap and rubbed my eyes. The sky was almost completely black now.

I flashed my light around me again and saw details I'd never noticed before. I saw how a broken limb from a tree had patched itself and how a new limb was growing somewhere else. I saw how a plant curved and reached itself around a stump to find its way to better light. I saw life surviving and thriving all around me.

Maybe it was just because I had let myself bawl my brains out, or because I had finally named my problems out loud, or because I was light-headed from excessive blood loss to mosquitoes, but I definitely felt a certain peace at that moment. I felt like all that was wrong in my world could be made right somehow, if I just gave it a chance.

My book slipped off my lap then and landed on something that crinkled like plastic. I didn't need my flashlight to know it was my Kit Kat wrapper. It had been picked clean and torn in two but was still bright red and easy to identify. I hopped off my rock, collected the trash, and picked up my Eleanor book, which had landed open, facedown. I smoothed out the pages and brushed off the dirt, but stopped as my eyes caught something written by hand on the last page: *"My experience has been that work is almost the best way to pull oneself out of the depths."*

It was Chieko's handwriting. Under the quote she had written *Eleanor* with a question mark, and then the name of some website where she must have found the quote. It definitely sounded like something Eleanor would say.

And if anyone knew how to pull themselves out of the depths, it would be Eleanor.

I read the sentence again.

I read the sentence out loud.

I let the words soak into my brain.

I repeated them over and over as I clutched the book to my chest.

And I knew what I was going to do.

Day 22—Saturday

→>>·<<←

"I figured you could use some help," I said.

Earl, who was bent over a row of lettuce, cutting and bagging in the dark, jumped and dropped what he was holding.

"I'm sorry," I apologized immediately.

"Dang it, girl!" he said, turning toward me, his hand across his chest like he was about to say the Pledge of Allegiance. "You nearly gave me a heart attack."

"I didn't mean to scare you. I'm sorry."

He lifted his second hand to join his first, like he was manually holding his heart inside his body. "What are you even doin' here? It's five o'clock in the morning. There are roosters still sleeping." His voice was agitated, higher than normal. He stood up and shook out his legs, his knees cracking inside his jeans.

"It's market day. I came to work."

Earl squinted at me. "For money?"

"No." Then I thought better and told him, "I mean, if you want to pay me, yeah. But really I just came to help. Either way."

He paused a minute, dropped his hands from his chest, and pulled a bandanna out of his back pocket. He used it to wipe some sweat from his face, then tied it around his forehead.

"You already have permission to take me," I persuaded. "You told me when you called my mom she didn't even let you finish your sentence about where we were going before she said yes."

He nodded at that. "Okay," he said, his voice back to normal. "I could use a hand."

He gave me a box to fill and jutted his chin where he wanted me to start.

I got to work.

Six hours later we were sitting in rusty beach chairs behind our two tables, our gorgeous display of lettuce, kale, and blueberries nearly all gone. Earl had real price signs propped up this time, all written by Brenda in her neat retired-teacher handwriting, and the cash box was so stuffed with bills and coins that Earl locked the whole thing in his truck and just made change out of what he kept in his pocket.

The market was emptying out as the heat soared. Earl and I had each drunk two bottles of apple juice between sales, and my stomach was grumbling for something more solid to fill it.

"When can we pack up?" I asked Earl, after a particularly loud rumble.

"Let's give it another fifteen minutes or so. Then we'll go."

I wiggled my toes inside my sneakers and told myself fifteen minutes would go by in a flash. And it did when you had a line nine deep and were busily bagging produce and counting out change as fast as humanly possible, but it passed slow as that slug Vera fed Jolly when no one stopped at your stand. I spread my fingers out in my lap and examined them, counting how many cuts, nicks, and scrapes I had from picking plants and berries.

"Hey, Vic. Remember me?"

I had counted six when I looked up to find Angel standing on the other side of our table, grinning down at me. The deep forest green of his eyes hit me again like a magic spell I had to shake my way out of. I closed my hands and stood up so fast my chair tumbled over backward behind me. I righted my chair while Earl watched, his mouth half-open like I was putting on the most mesmerizing performance he'd ever seen.

"So, do you?" he asked.

"Do I what?" I asked back.

"Do you remember me?"

"Uh-huh." I nodded. "You're the flower guy."

"The flower guy? That's it?"

"The flower guy Angel," I expanded.

Angel was not the kind of name you forgot.

"Very good." He nodded approvingly. "You weren't here last week. I didn't know if I'd see you again."

And then my stomach rumbled so loudly it sounded like there was a whole separate creature living inside me.

"Or hear you," Angel added, and laughed hard. Earl joined in, the two of them cracking up.

"Thanks, guys," I told them, folding my arms over my gut, hoping to quiet it down. "Very kind of you. Really."

"Aww, I'm sorry, Vic," Earl said, pulling his bandanna off then to wipe the tears from his eyes. "Take this. Go get yourself some doughnuts."

He handed me a ten-dollar bill. "Take Angel with you so I won't have to worry about you fainting from hunger on the way. It's not far—I can see the stand from here."

"Very funny," I said, but swiped the money out of his hand. "How many do you want?"

"None for me. I'll eat this last tub of blueberries if they don't sell. You go get enough for the two of you. I'll keep an eye on you from here," Earl said, but I wasn't sure if it was directed at Angel or me.

"Okay, I'll be right back," I assured him.

Angel led the way.

I glanced sideways at him as we walked. I had to look up a few inches to get another peek at his eyes. I realized half of what made them look so green were the long dark lashes above and below them. They reminded me of the unit we had in art last year on contrast. I probably would have paid a lot more attention if Angel's eyes had been one of the examples the teacher pulled up in her slideshow.

"They charge more for doughnuts here than they do at their store, but they're so good no one seems to care."

"They have a store?"

"Yeah, in town. It's near our flower shop." He pointed at the Ramos Family Flowers logo on his apron. "So, where's Meadow Wood Farm? I never heard of it before."

"It isn't a farm. It's a camp. Earl just started a garden at camp and sells some of his food here, that's all."

"Riiiight, Meadow Wood *camp*. I've heard of the camp," Angel said. "Wait—so you don't live here?"

"Nope, just here for the summer."

"Oh."

I didn't want to read too much into it, but I thought I heard some disappointment in his voice.

"Then why do you help him sell? Shouldn't you be playing tennis or singing around a fire pit or something?"

Why did I help Earl?

The first time I helped him it was for the money. I wanted my canteen privileges back and I wanted to make sure Freddy never knew his were gone.

But now it was different.

I was helping Earl because Carly was gone.

I was helping Earl because my parents were a mess.

I was helping Earl because Eleanor Roosevelt said work would pull me out of my *depths*. So far, she was right. At that moment, I felt a lot more like someone beaming on top of a mountain than someone drowning in the depths.

"If I was at camp right now, I wouldn't be about to inhale a bag of Hoefel's doughnuts," was the answer I gave him.

Angel smiled wide at me. He had a dimple on his right cheek I hadn't noticed before. It was like a second smile right next to his bigger one.

We reached the stand and took our place in the back of the line. The smell of cinnamon sugar was intoxicating. My stomach grumbled again.

"No doughnuts at camp?" Angel asked. "That's just cruel."

"We get cookies and brownies. And we have canteen once

a week, which is junk food heaven. We can buy whatever we want there—soda and ice cream and candy bars. But there's nothing like these doughnuts."

"Once a week for canteen isn't enough. No wonder you escape to the outside world on Saturdays."

"Well, really it's because Earl needed help. I'm channeling my inner Eleanor Roosevelt and helping people who need help."

"Oh," Angel said. "That's really nice of you."

"Thanks."

"And a little creepy-sounding—channeling another human being, especially one who's not even alive." He put his hand on my shoulder, steered me forward a few feet, and then let go.

A gentle warmth seeped from my shoulder down through my stomach all the way to my knees. I actually felt wobbly, but that could have just been because I needed food. I did know there was no way I could look up into those eyes, though, or I would blush a red deep enough to match the roses at his flower stand. It occurred to me that this must be how Jamie felt every time she saw Trey, her longtime crush, at school last year. I wasn't sure if I liked the feeling or not.

"So, Eleanor Roosevelt?" Angel asked. "The longest-reigning First Lady of the United States?"

"How'd you know that?" I almost yelled. I hadn't known

the first thing about her until I started reading Chieko's book.

"We studied the presidents last year in school," Angel admitted. "And don't be too impressed, because that's all I know about her."

"Don't worry. I'm not impressed," I lied.

He smirked at that, then asked, "So why her? Why not Mother Teresa or Gandhi or some other saintly person? What's so great about Eleanor Roosevelt?"

I gasped in pretend outrage and squared off on him, hands on my hips. "What's so great about Eleanor Roosevelt?"

"That's what I'm asking." He copied my hands-on-hips pose and grinned ear to ear.

"I'll tell you what's so great," I said. "She changed what it meant to be First Lady. She was the first one to get involved in politics. She pushed the president to pass laws for people who weren't being treated right. She wrote articles and went on the radio. She inspired women to speak up." I crossed my arms in front of my chest and declared, "She was a complete and total rock star."

The elderly lady in front of us in line turned around when I finished, patted my arm, and said, "You tell him, honey." Then she nodded curtly, turned back around, and moved up a few steps.

Angel smiled and raised his eyebrows at the lady's back,

then said, "Thank you for the history lesson, Vic."

"Anytime," I answered.

"I'm *so* hungry. This is torture," Angel said, putting both hands on my shoulders this time and steering me forward again.

I was hungry, too, but suddenly didn't mind being stuck in line. If Jamie could see me now, she wouldn't even recognize me. Here I was—Vic Brown—at a farmers' market outside camp, shopping for doughnuts with a flower-selling guy who had the world's most gorgeous eyes. I barely even knew him, but I liked him. Which killed my streak. My lifelong never-had-a-crush-on-anyone streak was over.

Gone.

Dead.

Like Vera's first frog.

When we reached the front of the line, we decided to buy a half-dozen bag to split. I reached into my pocket for money, but Angel cut me off. "I've got it," he said, handing over a bill to the cashier.

"But Earl gave me money," I protested.

"It's my treat," he said, giving me the warm bag to hold. "But next Saturday, you have to buy."

"O . . . kay," I said, feeling like I wasn't completely sure what I was agreeing to.

"Great. It's a date," Angel said, then pulled a doughnut out of the bag and bit into it. He closed his eyes as he chewed and I stared at the tiny sugar crystals that glittered around his mouth.

Yep, I had just agreed to my first date.

Earl and I were quiet the whole ride back to Meadow Wood. As we pulled into the long driveway that led to the parking lot, I asked him, "Has anyone signed up for farm elective the last two weeks?"

"Signed up? No." He laughed to himself. "Brenda added slots to other elective choices so it's not possible to get stuck with it, either. Seniors will only be at farm if they want to be. But they'll be eating farm food in the dining hall either way."

"Got it."

"I don't mind gardening alone. Best part of my day is being in that space," Earl added.

"Wow." I folded my arms across my chest in fake anger. "The best part of your life at camp is when you're not with any campers? That's really great, Earl. Thanks a lot."

Earl laughed. "It's not like that," he explained. "Camp is great. But camp is loud. And fast. And frenetic."

"Frenetic?"

"Frenetic," he kept going. "The garden is the other end of the scale, and I like the balance."

"You like to hide," I told him.

"Not hide. I like to . . . be," he decided. "In the garden, I'm with the sky and the dirt and all the green. I can *smell* the green. And the change that happens there, bit by bit—I just love it."

Earl pulled the truck into the spot next to the rusty shed where he stored the folding tables. He turned off the engine, unbuckled his seat belt, and climbed out of the truck. Then he walked over to my side and handed me a thin fold of bills from his pocket. "You take this for your efforts and get on back to your cabin. I can unload myself."

I thanked him for the cash and said, "I can help you."

"I know you can. You did. And I hope you do again, but you've done more than enough for today. Go be a camper."

Before I could say another word, he popped open the flat-bed door and slid out a folding table in one graceful motion.

I started to leave, shoving the money into my pocket so I wouldn't have to explain it to my bunkmates, when Earl called after me, "I hope you're available next Saturday, though. I wouldn't know how to console Angel otherwise."

I narrowed my eyes at him and yelled, "Very funny," then turned on my heel hard so bits of gravel kicked up from the ground.

I could hear Earl laughing behind me while I walked away, but I didn't care. I was busy thinking about Angel and trying to fight back the smile that was spreading across my face. Then I decided to just let the stupid smile do its thing, and I grinned like a goofball the whole long walk back to Yarrow.

Day 23—Sunday

->>>·<<<-

"If this cabin is wiretapped, I'm so fired. We haven't done R and T in days," Chieko announced.

"What's R and T?" Jordana asked.

"Roses and Thorns," Jaida C explained, patting Jordana on the back the same way she did with her camp sister in Daisy.

Jordana scrunched up her brow. "No one calls it that," she muttered to herself. "Like, ever."

"Get your darling selves to my room ASAP," Chieko called. Then she changed her mind and said, "Scratch that. Not ASAP. Right spankin' now."

Once we were settled in a circle on the floor, Chieko asked, "Can we just save some time here and agree that everyone's thorn is losing Carly for the rest of the summer?"

Heads nodded in unison around the circle.

"Okay, so just roses then," Chieko continued. "Mine is finally getting Brenda to order new arrows for the range. That junk they gave me to teach with is beyond funky. They don't even fly right half the time." She rolled her eyes. "I'm done. Who's next?"

Jordana's rose was that her parents were coming up next Sunday for Visiting Day and were taking her out for a fancy lunch and to see a movie in town.

Jaida A's rose was learning she had already saved forty-five pounds of organic trash from the garbage by delivering it to the stables instead.

Jaida C's rose was a mosaic pottery project she had almost finished in the arts-and-crafts shack that came out a lot better than she expected.

And I said my rose was seeing Freddy at Forest Lake earlier that day, that he'd passed a swim test and moved up a level.

But I had a bigger rose. I just didn't want to share it. My bigger rose was Angel.

I couldn't stop thinking about him. Like at breakfast. We always had bagels on Sunday mornings, but today the bagels made me think of doughnuts, which made me think of Angel.

At arts and crafts, the piece of dark green sea glass that Jaida C sank into the concrete slab of her mosaic project made me think of the dark green of Angel's eyes.

At swim, a counselor wearing a bathing suit with daisies all over it made me think of Angel selling daisies at his flower stand.

At lunch, when a kitchen staffer came out to mop up a spill, the sight of him in his long white apron made my mind jump to Angel in his green Ramos Family Flowers one.

Every time Angel popped into my head, a wave of prickly heat washed through my body. I didn't entirely like the feeling, but I didn't entirely *not* like the feeling, either. It was just . . . different. But I was getting used to different. My parents splitting up was different. My best friend leaving camp was different. At least this kind of different didn't make me want to cry.

Anyway, I hoped Carly's rose was that her collarbone was hurting less and that she would still find a way to love riding horses as much as she did before her accident.

And I hoped Saturday would come quickly, because that was when I'd get to see Angel again.

Day 24—Monday

->>>·<<<-

"My pet project is dead since Carly is gone, so I might as well focus my skills on you," Chieko said as she lifted my elbow and repositioned my back foot.

"Gee, thanks. I feel so special," I said, collapsing my stance and dropping the bow and arrow to the ground.

"Don't be a butt-butt." Chieko lifted my arms and pushed me back into position.

"That's Carly's word!"

"Yes, and I'm making sure it lives on at Meadow Wood while she's home recovering in an air-conditioned room with cable TV and a laptop and a cell phone," Chieko claimed.

"Wow, you're not jealous."

"Not jealous enough to break a bone," Chieko countered.

I rolled my shoulders back, checked my feet, then looked at

the target. I pulled my right arm back as far as I could, elbow out, held it a nanosecond, and released.

My arrow soared several feet over the tire and disappeared into the woods beyond.

Arrows flew down the row on either side of me, but none of them reached their target. Instead of the beautiful crisp sound of contact, the air was filled with the *zip-zing* of an arrow releasing, then the quiet *plunk* of it hitting the ground. A collection of grunts and a few curse words followed these attempts.

Chieko stood back watching the archery fiasco, shaking her head in disappointment.

Finally, she threw her hands up in the air and waved them like an overcaffeinated air traffic controller. "Bows down! For the love of God and all things holy, EVERYONE STOP!"

We all stopped.

"You are shaming my skills as an instructor!" Chieko reprimanded us. "Drop your weapons."

We all dropped our gear to the ground.

"Step back and spread out," Chieko ordered.

We did.

"Now stretch your arms up in the air like this." Chieko reached her arms up high, then lifted up onto her tippy-toes to reach even higher.

We all copied.

Next she dropped her torso down and bent at the waist, letting her long, thin arms dangle in front of her calves and her fingers rake through the mixture of grass and weeds at her feet.

We copied.

Then she raised herself back up and stood still as a tree, her eyes closed, her hands held in prayer right in front of her chest.

We stared at her, and somehow she knew it.

"Copy," she ordered. "Eyes closed."

We all copied her stance and closed our eyes.

"Pay attention to your breath." Her voice got softer, more soothing. "Feel your chest rise and fall. Feel your diaphragm fill and release. Feel each breath. Settle into it."

The range fell into silence as we followed her directions. At first, I felt kind of ridiculous, but then I got lost in the darkness behind my eyelids. I felt the world shrink around me as I paid attention to my breathing. I felt both wobbly and stable at the same time, and everything outside me disappeared. Then, after one minute or five minutes or who-knows-how-many minutes, my world expanded and opened back up.

Everything was calm and even and connected and whole.

"Open your eyes," Chieko said softly, breaking us out.

My eyes didn't want to open. I wanted to stay in that peaceful place.

"Guys!" Chieko ordered. "Snap out of it and open your eyes."

Apparently, I wasn't the only one trying to stay in my quiet place.

"Now pick up your gear and get in stance," was her next order.

Once we were lined up and in position, Chieko continued her directions. "Breathe the same way you just were. Find your target. Don't just look at it—feel it. Feel the space between you and it. Connect with it. Then . . . go."

A series of releases and thwacks followed. Every single shot was a hit. And mine was in the middle circle.

Bull's-eye.

Chieko scanned the targets.

"There's hope for you yet," she told us, then said under her breath, "I definitely don't get paid enough."

I smiled at Chieko. It was obvious she loved teaching us, even though she acted like we frustrated her beyond belief. And I smiled at myself for my perfect shot.

"Continue," she said, sounding somewhat exhausted. "And don't assume you know where the target is just because you see it. You have to connect with it. Don't rush."

And then she looked straight at me as she walked off to grab her water bottle and said, "You have to be patient and do the work, or you'll never hit true."

Day 25—Tuesday

->>> · <<<-

When we got back to Yarrow after Taco Night in the dining hall, which included fresh lettuce and the first tomatoes from Earl's garden, I found an envelope facedown on my bed. Mail had been late that day, so there hadn't been any to pass out at rest hour. I saw that Jordana had one letter on her bed, and Jaida C had three.

I was used to not getting mail. My parents had only written once each in the last three weeks, which was typical of them even without all the family drama going on this summer. You'd think they'd make more effort to send reassuring I'm-always-here-for-you letters, considering what was going on at home, *and* considering neither of them were coming up on Visiting Day, but no. I guessed they were both too wrapped up in their own junk.

Which I sort of understood. Because I still hadn't written to Jamie.

I didn't want to tell Jamie about my parents in a letter, but I also felt funny writing a letter that made it sound like everything was fine when it wasn't. So I didn't write at all. And I guessed she was doing the same thing with me, because I hadn't received a letter from her yet, either. Jamie loved to write and usually sent me at least one letter a week when I was at camp. But I knew enough to know she was busy dealing with her community service at the library. I also knew she missed me the same way I missed her.

I flipped the envelope over to read the return address but found there wasn't one. It was addressed to Camp Meadow Wood with the correct mailing information beneath, but it was the very first line that made my mouth drop open and my fingertips tingle. It said: *Farmers' Market Vic.*

As Jordana ripped into her envelope and Jaida C carefully split open the first in her pile, I felt my knees turn to jelly and I lowered myself onto my bed.

Had Angel written to me?

It looked like boy handwriting.

It looked like fourteen-year-old, flower-selling, green-eyed-boy handwriting.

I took a deep breath and opened the envelope.

The paper was small and plain, pale blue with no lines. His writing was in pencil, his letters small, and the lines slanted down to the right. It was dated Sunday, July 16.

Dear Vic,

Bet you weren't expecting a letter from me, but I wasn't expecting to meet a Meadow Wood camper/farmer at the market, so I say we're even. I don't even know if this will reach you, but I'm trying anyway, 'cause you never know unless you try.

I went to Hoefel's store this morning and got the same cinnamon sugar doughnuts. I ate three in a row, but they didn't taste as good as the last time I had them. Wonder why.

See you Saturday (I hope),

Angel

P.S. I did some research on Eleanor Roosevelt. Did you know she volunteered at a canteen? Her canteen gave out coffee and sandwiches to soldiers headed off to war, not Snickers and Sprite to campers, but still. It looks like you really do have something in common with that rock star First Lady.

The second I finished reading the letter, my eyes flew back to the top and I read it again, more slowly this time so I could savor each word.

He wrote to me.

He addressed the letter to *Farmers' Market Vic* and it got to me. Earl and Brenda sorted the mail, so it made sense. *Farmers' Market Vic* could only be me.

This letter made up for all the ones my parents didn't write. It made up for no money in my canteen account and for the lousy P.S.'s my parents had sent me. Angel knew how to use a P.S.—he researched Eleanor Roosevelt for me! That had to mean something. Who randomly researched historical figures just for the heck of it? Who, outside of Vera, I mean?

I scrunched down lower onto my bed and held the paper in front of my face as I read it again. I didn't want anyone in my cabin to see the flush in my cheeks or the beaming smile on my face.

I really wished Jamie were here. She would understand the crazy feelings ballooning inside of me that I didn't know how to explain. I just knew I felt good. I felt happy—a different kind of happy than I had ever felt before in my life.

And I also felt like Saturday would take forever to get here.

Day 26—Wednesday

->>> · <<<-

It was rest hour and I had been called to Chicory. Again.

Vera had noticed Jolly was looking a little less peppy each day, so she'd decided to release him back into the wild. She didn't want to do it alone, though.

"You did get a whole week with him, Vera," I pointed out. "That's something."

"I guess so," she agreed, her voice quiet as a hum. "I'm really going to miss him."

"Of course you are." I put my arm around her as we crouched behind her cabin, looking down at the dejected frog squatting in the corner of the shower caddy. "But maybe you'll see him again. If you sit by the rocks where you found him, maybe he'll come hopping by every once in a while to check in." That kind of thing happened in G-rated movies all the time.

Vera looked up at me with doubt in her big brown eyes. She wasn't buying it.

"He came to you once, didn't he?" I tried. "So it's *possible* he'll come to you again."

"Possible, yes"—Vera folded her arms in front of her chest like a statistics professor—"but not probable."

I sighed my frustration a little too loudly, then said, "All right, well, let's take him over." I picked up the caddy and handed it to her.

"I want to hold him." Vera lifted Jolly out of the container. She cradled him against her chest and gazed down at him lovingly.

"He really does make you happy," I observed out loud.

"He does. Happy and calm. Studies say having a pet with fur lowers blood pressure and reduces the risk of heart attack and stroke. It's called fur therapy, but that's not fair to furless animals. Amphibians can have that effect, too." Vera finished her oral report, then looked at me and said, "I know for a fact that my heartbeat is slower now than it was ten minutes ago. While it's entirely *possible* I could still have a cardiac episode at this precise moment, it is not at all *probable*."

I honestly never knew what was going to come out of her mouth.

Vera continued to stroke Jolly's back. The two of them

together, framed in that moment, were the picture of peace.

I led Vera around the cabin to the rocks by the water, carrying her filthy shower caddy, which was now in serious need of its own shower.

It was so sunny that we had to squint. We climbed over the first row of rocks and then settled on the one where Vera had first met Jolly.

"Okay, my sweet *Lithobates sylvatica*," Vera cooed at him. "Off you go. Return to your natural habitat." She bent down and placed Jolly on her sneaker.

"Vera—" I started, but she cut me off to say, "That's exactly where he was when I found him."

We would do it her way.

"Okay."

We both stared at Jolly, clumped like a sad wad of clay on top of Vera's dingy sneaker. He didn't move a muscle. I glanced at Vera, who was staring intently at her pet, her eyes filled with tears. I reminded myself to be the kind of camp sister I would have wanted to have if I were a seven-year-old Chicory kid saying a tough goodbye.

"Vera, can you keep a secret?" I asked her.

She turned to me, wiping away the one tear that had escaped down her cheek. "Of course I can," she said sadly. "But studies show that keeping secrets is associated with anxiety, depression, and poor health."

"Are you serious?"

"I'm always serious," she answered immediately. "But I think it might depend on the kind of secret."

"Well, I don't think my secret is one of those kinds," I said, hoping I was right. Good camp sisters weren't supposed to give their little camp sisters anxiety, depression, or poor health.

I leaned down to her shoe and gave Jolly a slight nudge, just to slip him off Vera and onto a bit of shaded rock beside her foot. Then I held out my hand. "Come with me."

Vera took a long last look at Jolly, then put her hand in mine and followed me off the rocks, across the lawn, and into the woods. I was preparing an argument to convince her to break the rules and leave camp property with me, but it turned out I didn't need one. She followed me, step for step, without a sound.

"It's like paradise," Vera said in a whisper, taking in the lush green scenery around her. "It's like a green sea forest."

"And this rock is like my ship," I added, running my hand over the boulder we were sitting on, tracing the familiar dents and bumps along its surface.

"How did you find this?" Vera was in a state of true wonder.

"I don't know," I told her, shaking my head. "I just did. Four years ago. I've been coming to this spot since I was nine."

"Wow." Vera breathed it all in and held it inside her like a wish.

"Maybe you could say I found it because I needed to."

Vera nodded at me. "That sounds right."

We sat for a few minutes in the quiet, enjoying the dusky shade of the woods, which felt like a whole other world after the bright light by the waterfront.

"And I can come here whenever I want?" Vera asked all of a sudden.

"Actually, no. You're not allowed to come here at all."

"Why not?" Vera huffed at me.

"Because you're just not," I said.

Vera slumped and stuck her bottom lip out so far a bird could have landed on it as a perch.

I changed my approach. "You could get in a lot of trouble if you got caught sneaking into the woods."

"It's barely in the woods. We couldn't be more than eight meters in. I can practically see Chicory from here!" Vera contested.

"You use meters?"

"It makes more sense. It's a base-ten system," she answered matter-of-factly.

Vera could sulk like a toddler and then whip out an accurate metric estimation in the same minute.

She really killed me.

"Look, I can bring you here whenever you want. You just can't come here alone, okay?" I offered, then added, "I'm kind of a master at getting here and back without anyone noticing."

"Like a ninja?" Vera asked hopefully.

"Sure. Like a ninja. I'm Ninja Vic."

"And I'll be Ninja Vera. The Ninja *V*s!" Vera hopped off the rock and started to twist and kick and crouch like a ninja in training. It was a side of her I hadn't seen before, and unsurprisingly, she wasn't much of a natural in the grace and physical coordination department. But I joined her anyway, copying her moves until I was sure the sadness of losing Jolly had been high-kicked away.

On our way back to the cabin, we stopped at the rocks to look for Jolly. The shaded nook where I had placed him was empty. There was no sign of him anywhere.

Vera let out a loud sigh, then put her hands on her hips the way Brenda always did when a pitcher broke in the dining hall or lightning cracked through the sky during a water activity.

"That's nature for you," Vera said. "He's either hopping back to his froggy friends at this very moment, or he's decomposing in an acid bath inside the belly of a predator."

My eyes popped out of my head. "Vera, I don't think—"

"It's okay, Vic." Vera put her arm around me. "It's the cycle of life." She gave me a quick squeeze and then disappeared back inside Chicory.

I hurried back to Yarrow, making it just in time to sign myself up for farm elective for the rest of the week.

Day 27–Thursday

>>>·<<<

"I cannot *believe* this is happening to me," Jordana huffed, twisting her hair into a tight bun on top of her head. "I'm supposed to be water-skiing!"

We were on our way to farm. There was a last-minute change in the schedule because of an equipment crisis on the waterfront, so Brenda asked Jordana to leave water-ski and go to farm instead.

Jordana wasn't taking it well.

"Are there bugs?"

"We're at camp, Jordana. There're bugs *everywhere*," I told her, as if she didn't already know. "You'll survive this. Trust me."

"Thank God you'll be there with me." She sounded a lot like Bella the way she said *thank God*, but I threw my arm around her shoulders anyway and we walked like that to the garden.

Earl showed us a magazine article about the nutrients in leafy green vegetables and then sent us both to work around rows of lettuce and spinach and kale. Instead of working on opposite ends and meeting in the middle, Jordana insisted on working right next to me. Earl was three rows away, trimming leaves and tying tomato plants to stakes.

The sun beat down on us, but Jordana didn't complain. Instead, she sang Broadway show tunes as she worked, stopping only to push back bits of hair that fell out of her bun. Soon she was a couple of feet ahead of me, busily ripping handfuls of green out of the ground like a robot set on hyper-speed.

A shadow fell over me and I looked up to find Earl there, peering curiously at Jordana. "What can we do to get you to slow down?"

"Huh?" Jordana stopped mid-lyric. "I need to work fast 'cause you've got, like, eight million weeds back here."

I looked around and realized she was right. It was starting to look like there were more weeds than plants.

"You should sell the weeds!" Jordana said. "You have so much you'd make a *ton* of money."

"There aren't many buyers for weeds." Earl glanced at me and I quickly looked away, hiding the grin on my face. "Anyway, what you're doing is not productive. If you don't get the root, they just grow back. Watch me."

Earl squatted down between us and grabbed a weed around its middle. He ripped it out of the ground the way Jordana had been doing and held it out for us to see. Then he grabbed the next weed all the way down at its base, right where it entered the soil, and pulled slowly, straight up. When he held that one before us, we could see the knot of roots that had been feeding the weed beneath the ground. "This here is what we're going for. See the difference?"

Jordana sighed. "Yeah, I see it."

"So the key is to work slow and careful. Don't be in such a rush."

"But it's not fun," Jordana whined.

"It's not?" Earl asked.

"No!" Jordana shouted. "*Canoeing* is fun. *Dance*, which I have next period, is fun. And *canteen*, later tonight, is *amazingly* fun. But weeding is not even in the same neighborhood as fun!" She looked at me for help, like she couldn't believe she had to explain this.

"Earl doesn't get it because he honest-to-God enjoys this," I informed her.

"That's not right. I'm worried. I think you should go to clinic."

Earl chuckled once, then pretended to take his pulse by pressing two fingers against a spot under his neck. "I believe I'm okay for the moment, but thank you for your concern."

Jordana crouched back down to the ground, grabbed a weed at the base, and pulled. She held it above her head, the tangled roots hanging off it like bunched thread. "See? Happy?"

"Thrilled," Earl answered. "Can't fix it without getting to the root of it. How's that for a life lesson?"

"This elective is the *longest lesson* of my life," Jordana groaned. "How many more minutes? I can't wait for dance."

Earl scratched the top of his head and looked off into the distance, his eyes slits against the sun. "You're here now, Jordana. See if you can find a way to enjoy what you're doing while you're doing it."

She stopped weeding and looked at him as if he had just spoken in a different language. She watched him take off his bandanna, unroll it, reroll it the opposite way, and then tie it back around his head. I could tell she was dying to say something about his head accessory, but she held it in.

"Besides," Earl said, looking happy as could be even though his neck was slick with sweat and his arms were covered in patches of dirt all the way up to the elbows, "when you're busy rushing to the next thing, it's easier to make mistakes. Sometimes when you rush, you don't move forward at all.

Sometimes you set yourself back."

He turned quickly then and went into his cabin without waiting for a response.

"What is he, some plant-man prophet or something?" Jordana asked, rolling her eyes.

"Kinda." I shrugged. "Maybe."

A breeze moved through the air, bringing with it the smell of garlic, onion, and tomato stewing in the kitchen. We always had spaghetti on Thursday nights. It was two hours away, but I was already hungry for it.

After a few minutes, Jordana said, "My back is killing me." Then she broke into "It's a Hard Knock Life" from *Annie*.

And even though I couldn't sing to save my life, and even though I didn't have it half as bad as Orphan Annie or orphan Eleanor Roosevelt, I joined in. Singing made the rest of the period fly by. Jordana would deny it if anyone asked her, but I knew from the way she sang and from the way she proudly handed her overflowing bag of weeds to Earl that she had had some fun, too.

Day 28—Friday

->>>·<<<-

"It's getting too hot for my kale," Earl said, pulling off a wilted leaf, the ruffles around the edges hanging limp and lifeless as a popped balloon. "We'll see what we can salvage for tomorrow's market."

It was midafternoon and Earl told me he'd already been in the garden for an hour, weeding and watering and worrying. His cheeks were sunburned pink and his blue bandanna looked soaked with sweat.

"Should I work on the kale?" I asked. I had a baseball hat on to shield my eyes from the glare, but it was so hot I felt like the top of my head was cooking inside it.

"No, I'll handle that. How about you tackle this here?" He walked me over to a row of raised beds I had never bothered looking closely at before. From where I stood, it was just a massive collection of green leaves splaying in all directions. The leaves were as big as my face, and as I scanned all four identical beds, I realized I didn't see anything that resembled food.

I caught Earl looking at me, holding back a grin. "Have some faith, Vic. The goods are in there."

Earl crouched down and leaned into the bed, spreading the leaves and stalks like he was parting a curtain. "Down here," he directed. "Summer squash, in all its glory."

I knelt beside him, peered in, and saw dozens of long cylindrical vegetables, all colored a rich shiny green, speckled with tiny dashes of pale yellow so delicate they looked like they could have been painted on by hand.

"Commonly referred to as zucchini," Earl added.

I sighed. "I know what zucchini is."

He reached in and cut one off, leaving a stumpy stem on the thinner end of the vegetable. "Doesn't get more gorgeous than that," he said, holding it up to the sun and turning it this way and that.

"You're weirdly proud of your vegetables, Earl," I teased him.

"They're my babies," he replied, then handed the green squash to me. "I'm gonna need you to harvest all the zucchini that looks like this. They'll sell beautifully tomorrow."

"Aside from your zucchini babies, do you and Brenda have any kids?"

He let go of the huge leaves and they closed like a tent over the vegetables beneath.

"You know, like human kids?" I asked, trying to make the question breezy.

"Nope," he answered, looking up at me. "And yes."

"No, you *don't* have kids and yes, you *do* have kids—that's your answer?" I asked.

"Brenda and I don't have kids of our own, not the way you mean," he explained. "But we've had hundreds of kids over our summers, and if you do the math, that more than balances out our empty nest the rest of the year, don't you think?"

"I'm not doing math."

Earl smiled. "Just trust me then. All you campers, you're our kids. We plan for you all year and then spend twenty-four/seven enjoying your company all summer."

I smiled back. "I guess it does balance out."

"Although it's a bit shorter this year. Camp ends on a Tuesday, so it's more like seven and a half weeks, not eight."

"Yeah, I've noticed things are a little . . . different this year."

"Fewer campers this year, but it's just in senior camp that numbers are down. Junior camp is big and intermediate is holding steady," Earl explained. "*And* this year we have a productive garden."

"The garden is cool," I admitted. "And Yarrow is very spacious with only five campers living inside. I kind of prefer it that way." Then I remembered that Carly was gone. "I mean, four campers now."

Earl just nodded. "Meadow Wood will always be here." He turned his attention back to the raised beds overflowing with ripe squash.

"So, I should get started on those zucchini, I guess."

"I guess," he repeated, then reached into his pocket and pulled his knife out again, the one he'd just used to separate a zucchini from its stem. "You comfortable using a knife?" Earl asked.

"I've been cutting my pancakes since I was about five years old, so yeah, I think I can handle it," I told him.

"This is no pancake knife. Let me get you the special scissors. You can't hurt yourself with those."

"Have some faith, Earl," I threw his words back at him. "I'm *thirteen*."

He put the knife back in his pocket and showed me how to use the special scissors.

I lifted my baseball cap up a bit off my head to get some air between my scalp and the thick fabric, but I couldn't take it off completely because the sun was too strong and I needed the brim to shade my eyes. Next time I'd have to remember to wear sunglasses and skip the hat altogether.

I developed a system where I cut three zucchini in a row and then moved them to the cardboard box together. I laid them carefully, side by side, as if I were tucking them into bed for the night. Then I went back in for the next three. The more I worked, the more I cared about how good a job I did, how clean my cuts were, and how I packed them so they would stay smooth and perfect for tomorrow morning. I wanted them to sit so beautifully on our market table it would be impossible for a shopper to walk by without buying a few.

The minutes raced by despite the heat, and I ended up staying after the bugle, finishing the zucchini harvest and then helping to collect the last of the ripe blueberries. Blueberry season was pretty much over, but we were still able to fill six containers with the plump dark fruit. I was sure we would sell out in the first hour.

"You better get back to Yarrow and clean yourself up before dinner," Earl called out to me. He was fussing with the coils of hose by the back of his cabin where he stored it.

"I know—I'm completely gross. But that was actually fun," I said, pulling my baseball cap off and using it to fan my face.

Eleanor Roosevelt was right. The work had made me feel happy, grateful even, to be in that yard gardening with Earl. Even without Jordana's singing.

A loud *swoosh* from the cabin sounded and we turned to find Brenda sticking her head out of the window where she'd just slid up the screen. "Earl, you need to get inside and cool off."

"We've been working hard out here." Earl flexed his bicep muscle to prove it. His arm shape didn't change much between the flexed version and the regular version, though, from what I could see.

"I don't like you so overheated. You need to hose off, the both of you."

Earl pointed the hose toward the sky above his head and closed his eyes as the water fell down on him like sweet rain.

"That does feel a whole lot better," he said, then turned off the water and coiled up the hose.

"I'm coming in," he called through the window to Brenda. "See ya later, Vic."

Once he was gone, I uncoiled the hose, turned it back on, and pointed it over my head the way Earl had. I was drenched in seconds. Cold water trickled down my back and legs and dripped from my hair, collecting in pools on the ground before soaking into the thirsty soil. The scorching heat on the top of my head disappeared and goose bumps popped up on my forearms from the sudden chill. It made me want to lie down and sink into the cool, wet ground for a moment or two and just be.

Like a plant.

Day 29—Saturday

→→→·←←←

"How honored I am to be your personal alarm clock." Chieko was shaking me awake with the finesse of a grumpy gorilla.

"I'm up. Stop. I'm up." My vision came into focus and I took in Chieko's puffy, tired face. She had sleep lines across one cheek from lying against a creased sheet. It looked like a scar.

"Jeez, do I look as bad as you this early?" I whispered.

"If you mean do you look like total butt-butt, the answer is yes," she answered without a pause.

"I miss Carly."

"She's fast asleep right now on a thick, comfy mattress and will probably wake up to breakfast in bed, so I doubt the feeling is mutual."

"Thanks, Chieko. You might want to work on your

nurturing skills before you have kids," I advised, rubbing my eyes and propping myself up on my elbows.

"Why would I have kids?" she shot back.

I let out a giant yawn and sat up the rest of the way. "Can we talk about that some other time, please?"

"Whatever." Chieko shrugged.

At least she had stopped shaking me.

"Sorry you had to wake me again," I added.

"Next Friday night you can wear my watch to sleep and wake your own self up at five in the morning, thank you very much," Chieko said.

"Fine with me," I agreed.

"No, won't work," she said. "I never take this baby off. Ever." She stroked her wristwatch affectionately, then started poking me in the shoulder.

"I'm *up*. Stop!" I begged her.

She stopped.

I pulled my knees into my chest and stretched my neck up and down. I always woke stiff and sore after an afternoon in the garden.

"So you're going back to bed, right?" I asked, trying to converse myself into wakefulness.

"Hmm, let's see. I could take advantage of these early hours to wash and blow-dry my hair, paint my face, shave my legs, and give myself a mani-pedi. Or I could drool into my pillow for another glorious hundred and fifty minutes." She looked me dead in the eyes. "What do you think?"

I knew the answer. Since she'd mentioned shaving her legs, my eyes moved to the black *R* tattoo gleaming up at me from her ankle.

Chieko, tired and grumpy as she was, noticed my gaze and covered the *R* with her hand. "I hate that stupid thing. I wish it would evaporate."

"People get tattoos removed," I mentioned.

"Yeah, but it doesn't always work. And it's crazy painful—worse than *getting* the tattoo." She shuddered. "Plus, it's prohibitively expensive."

"Prohi-huh?" I furrowed my half-awake brow.

Chieko stated each word clearly for effect. "It is trust-fund, rich-kid, Daddy-Warbucks-from-*Annie* kind of expensive."

"Oh."

"Not to mention," she added, "that it's the ultimate sign of defeat."

It had never occurred to me to think of it like that.

"No, it isn't."

"Of course it is," Chieko countered. "It's defeat with a capital calligraphy *D*. Come to think of it, maybe that should be my next tattoo."

I lightly smacked her, and she lightly smacked me back, twice. One smack as she said "de" and the other as she said "feat."

"*Or* it's a new beginning, which is more like a victory when you think about it." I immediately thought of my parents and the life waiting for Freddy and me when camp ended, realizing those words applied to me, too. I had a new beginning waiting for me, and approaching it as something positive seemed a better way to go.

Chieko shook her head at me. "Another discussion for another time, young one. You need to move it. Those vegetables ain't gonna pick themselves." When she stood up, the cot creaked angrily at the shift in weight.

"And these campers ain't going to *sleep* themselves if you guys don't shut your traps," Jordana grumbled from under her covers.

Chieko picked up a pair of balled-up socks from the floor and chucked them at the motionless heap that was Jordana's body.

"Camper abuse," Jordana mumble-yelled, and knocked the sock roll off.

"Go back to sleep, knucklehead," Chieko called back.

"I'm *trying* to," Jordana called out, then rolled over to face the wall.

I dragged myself to a standing position, threw on the clothes I had set out the night before, and headed to the bathroom, where even my toothbrush looked annoyed at the early hour. Or maybe the toothbrush was just a toothbrush and I was hallucinating because of severe exhaustion. It was too early to tell.

Angel came to our stand at eleven with the same apron, the same friendly greeting, and the same ridiculous green eyes. He talked to Earl for a minute and then asked if it was an okay time for me to take a break.

"I'm almost sold out, so go right ahead." Earl waved us off. "Just stay between here and Hoefel's, where I can see you."

Angel grabbed my hand and walked in front of me, leading me through the crowd. He looked back over his shoulder twice to make fun of my grumbling stomach, which was embarrassingly loud again.

The line at Hoefel's Donuts was ten long. We stood side by side, our clasped hands hanging between us like it was the most natural thing in the world. His hand was bigger than mine and his skin was calloused and cool against my palm. My hand was growing clammier by the second. I wanted to let go, rub the sweat off on my shirt, and then retake his hand, but I didn't know how to do it without him noticing. How did his stay so dry? Jordana would probably know a trick. But if I asked her, I would have to fess up about Angel, and there was no way I was going to do that.

I bet Vera could research an answer for me. But she wouldn't be able to do it until camp was over and she was back in Pennsylvania, with access to her computer or her library or her other resources.

So I was stuck with clammy palms.

Maybe he wouldn't notice.

Once we got our doughnuts, we sat on a bench in the shade and ate, white sugar crystals falling to the ground like snow each time we took a bite.

"Your stand's almost empty again," Angel said, looking in Earl's direction.

"We didn't bring as much as usual, but yeah, we did well. Did you?" I asked.

"Not our best day. Guess people wanted food today more than flowers."

"Sorry," I said.

"It's fine. We do most of our business at the store. Bouquet deliveries, weddings, that kind of stuff. This is just extra," he explained, and gestured at the tents. "It's fun to be a part of the scene."

"Fun?" I asked.

"Yeah, fun. What? You don't like it?" His gaze was intense.

"Um . . . I like working in the garden with Earl," I started to explain, thinking it through as I went. "I didn't in the beginning, but I do now. A lot, actually. And I like working at the stand okay. But I don't like getting up early. Waking up that early, when it's still completely dark out, is a complete nightmare for me."

Angel laughed and nodded. "You get used to it. And then, after a while, you start to like it. Being up before everyone else, before the sun even—it's pretty Zen."

"Zen?" I repeated, raising my eyebrows at him.

He nodded again. "Spiritual. Meditative. All that." Then he added, "Plus, my mom and dad both say it keeps me out of trouble."

I smiled at that because it was such a parent thing to say.

"It's one of the few things they agree on," Angel added.

"What do you mean? They don't get along?" I asked, feeling ashamed that I was hoping his parents had problems like mine.

"No, they get along fine. *Now.* They're divorced." His voice was breezy as he said it. "Very divorced."

"Oh," I said. "Sorry."

"No, it's good. I mean, not at first, right when they split— that was a mess." He shook his head, remembering. "But now it's good. I live with my mom during the school year and see my dad on the weekends. I live with my dad during the summer and see my mom on Sundays. I work the shop and market all summer and my dad pays me. I like it."

"And the work keeps you out of trouble," I repeated.

"Exactly. You can't be out all night with friends when you have to get up at the butt-crack of dawn to work."

"Guess not," I agreed. I took my last bite of doughnut and rubbed my fingers together, sprinkling the extra sugar onto the pavement below. Some colony of ants was going to have a serious party when it found the spread of sugar we were leaving behind.

"What are your parents like?" Angel asked.

I paused.

I could answer any way I wanted to.

I could make something up.

I could flat-out lie.

He lived in New Hampshire and I lived in Pennsylvania and it would be easy for him to never know the truth. And it was for just that reason, I think, that I told him everything. I didn't even know I was going to do it. I just heard myself talking and I heard what I was saying and it was all about the smoking oven and the burning cookies and the email on the laptop and the canteen money disappearing and the phone call in Brenda's office and even the letters I'd received with the terrible P.S.'s. And he listened to every word, holding my hand again.

And even though I had eaten my weight in doughnuts and should have felt as heavy as a beached whale, I felt the exact opposite. I felt light and airy and free.

I felt relief.

I was a doughnut-stuffed feather of relief.

Angel looked toward his dad at the flower stand and watched him make a sale. He cleared his throat and said, "Well, for my family, starting over was a whole lot better than fighting through the mess of trying to keep things the same."

His words made perfect sense to me.

"Say that again."

Angel paused long enough to tilt his head and take me in from a different angle. Then he said, more slowly this time, "Starting over was a whole lot better than fighting through the mess of trying to keep things the same."

I closed my eyes and breathed in deeply.

"You want me to write it down for you, too?" he joked.

I shook my head and opened my eyes. "And things got better?"

"Things got a lot better," he confirmed.

I nudged him with my shoulder. "All right then. Cool. Thanks, Angel."

"You're welcome, Vic. And speaking of writing"—a sly smile crept across his face—"get any other mail lately? Anything with, I don't know, a decent P.S.?"

I lifted my hand to my chin. "Hmm, let me think. That letter from my mom, the one from my dad, nothing yet from my best friend, Jamie—oh wait! Yes! There was one short note from some guy with an Eleanor Roosevelt fetish. Apparently, he likes to mail random facts about her to people he hardly knows. Very bizarre."

"He sounds awesome to me," Angel claimed. "Intelligent. And thoughtful. And handsome."

"He *sounds* handsome?"

"Definitely."

I shrugged. "He's all right."

Angel shoved me playfully.

"Okay, fine. He's a little bit cute." I felt heat creep onto my cheeks when I admitted this. Then I got serious and turned toward him, staring him straight in the eyes. "But seriously— what's the deal with your eyes? They have to be color contacts. Nobody has that kind of green."

"I am the chosen one." He made prayer hands in front of me and bowed in his seat.

"So unfair." I crossed my arms and glared at him.

"What about your eyes? They're like steamy hot chocolate when you don't put too much milk in. How cool is that?"

"I'm guessing not *cool* at all, if they're *steamy*."

"You're too smart for your own good, you know that? Why don't you put some of that wit down on paper and write me a letter back?"

"I don't have your address."

"Not a problem." He pulled an index card out of his apron pocket with his name and address already printed on it. "One letter before next Saturday, okay?"

"We'll see." I pocketed the card.

"Man, you're tough," he said, but he was smiling as he said it.

We walked back to Earl's stand at a much slower pace than we left it. He had already started to pack up, just the tent and tables left to fold and stash away in the back of the truck.

"Want some help?" Angel asked Earl as soon as we arrived.

"No, thank you. I'll just take my assistant back." And he smiled.

"I better go then," Angel said. "I'll see you next Saturday, right?" There was a softness in his gaze.

"Of course," I said, grinning. "This is where the doughnuts are."

"Right," he said back. "It's all about the doughnuts." He took my hand and squeezed it, then flashed a big smile at me and walked away.

His eyes sparkled like wet grass when he smiled.

And apparently, mine were delicious like hot chocolate.

Who knew?

Day 30—Sunday

>>>·<<<

There was very little eating and a whole lot of wiggling, shouting, and chair tipping at breakfast on Visiting Day morning. Campers were bouncing off the walls with excitement about seeing their families, who would be arriving soon. Everyone at camp had a parent or family member of some sort coming to see them.

Everyone except me.

And I was pretty sure Chieko already knew, because she wasn't acting like her usual morning-crabby self. She had gone out of her way to give me the best mini cereal box on the table (Frosted Flakes), she handed me a napkin before I spilled instead of throwing one at me after, and she announced to the rest of Yarrow that "sharing was caring," so whatever junk food they got from their families should be spread all around.

She definitely knew.

At nine fifteen, right as campers were being herded to the parking lot to greet their families, the loudspeaker switched on with a jolting screech and bellowed out my name, calling me to Brenda's office for a telephone call.

I knew it was my mom before the announcement even ended.

"Make yourself comfortable, Vic," Brenda said, her lips pressed together in a sympathetic smile. "Take as long as you need." She left the office quickly, shutting the real door and the screen door behind her.

I stared at the receiver lying on the desk like a stranded turtle on its back with four legs in the air.

Tactic One: I could slam the phone and hang up without even saying hello. (Not very Eleanor.)

Tactic Two: I could pick up the phone and give the most colossal silent treatment of recorded history. (Not very Eleanor.)

Tactic Three: I could pick up the phone and attack, yelling every insult I could imagine at her for ruining our family. (Not very Eleanor.)

Tactic Four: I could pick up the phone and listen. And try. I could start working on a new beginning. I could do the thing I think I cannot do. (Very Eleanor.)

I lowered myself into Brenda's hard metal chair and picked up the phone.

"Hi, Mom," I said.

It wasn't easy, but it wasn't too hard, either.

Meadow Wood cleared out almost entirely at lunch, since parents were allowed to sign out their kids and take them to eat in town. Yarrow's table was completely empty. Even Chieko had been pulled away, helping Brenda with visitors, answering questions and giving tours.

I looked at the salad bar crammed full of special offerings, options we never had on regular Sundays, like chickpea pasta and fresh-tomato-and-mozzarella salad, and even a huge serve-yourself bin of strawberry and cream dessert.

But I didn't have an appetite for any of it.

I spotted Earl sitting at the head table, his spine curved over his plate the same way he curved over a row of greens in his garden. I had never bothered him at a mealtime before, but today I couldn't stop myself.

"Excuse me," I said once I reached his side.

"Good afternoon, Vic." His plate was half-empty. He took a sip of ice water, then asked, in a quieter voice, "How are you holding up today?"

"I'm fine. It's Freddy I'm worried about," I answered.

"Of course," Earl responded, nodding his head slowly. He took another sip of water and pushed his plate away. He wiped his mouth with a napkin he pulled from his lap, then said, even more quietly, "Meet me at the truck in ten minutes."

I was there in two.

I thought Earl would just drop me off at Forest Lake's entrance and then return in an hour to drive me back to Meadow Wood, but he pulled into a shady parking spot instead and climbed out of the truck with me.

"I'm guessing it's rest hour about now," he said.

"I think so. I know where to go." I started walking quickly across the fields to the wooded area where Freddy's cabin stood. But when I noticed the distance growing between Earl and me, I stopped and pretended to tie my shoe to give him a chance to catch up. Once he was beside me, I started to walk again, this time matching my pace to his.

We walked silently, the sun shining down on us so we were stepping on our shadows the moment they formed. I pointed ahead once we entered the shade of the woods. "That's it, right there. That's Freddy's."

"All right then," he said, taking it in. "Haven't been here in a while. Forgot about these bunks. They make our cabins look like the Four Seasons."

I laughed. "I'd definitely rather live at Meadow Wood than in one of these," I admitted.

"Different camping experience," he said. He squinted at the cabin, examining the joints where the taut tent fabric met the wooden flooring.

"Thank you, Earl," I said.

"You're very welcome." He nodded.

When I opened the door and stepped inside, Freddy was on his cot, flipping through a comic book so ragged and crinkled it had probably been read two hundred times already. He looked up at the sound of the door, and the way he leaped up and threw his arms around me was like a scene from a movie. I hugged him tight and lifted him off the ground.

Freddy's counselor, Michael, was smiling ear to ear over our reunion. "See, Freddy? You never know when something amazing is going to happen."

Earl introduced himself to Freddy, shook Michael's hand, and then starting zinging questions at Michael about tent maintenance, insulation, weatherproofing, and a whole bunch of other things I would never in a million years want to know.

"So, Freddy, what do you wanna do?" I asked.

"They're giving away free ice cream at canteen. Michael already got me one, but let's get more!"

Michael was my hero. He was more than a counselor to

Freddy; he was like a dream older brother. I wouldn't have minded having one of those myself. But then I thought of Chieko and realized she was kind of like an older sister to me—a cranky, sarcastic, very glass-half-empty but reliable older sister.

"Then take me to the canteen." I hadn't been able to eat lunch, but my appetite was back full-force now.

"I'll race you there," Freddy challenged me.

"Good luck, squirt," I threw back at him, and we sprinted out of the cabin together.

Day 32—Tuesday

→→→·←←←

It took only one glance at the letter Chieko handed me at rest hour to know that it was from Carly. Her handwriting was round and fat like overlapping bubbles, and she dotted her *i*'s with circles so they looked like the beginning of a stick-figure drawing—a head and body with no limbs. I remembered then that Carly was left-handed, so breaking her right collarbone didn't get in the way of her writing.

I pulled my legs onto my bed in the crisscross applesauce position we always sat in at bunk meetings back in Violet. Carly and I always sat next to each other, and we always made sure my left knee touched her right one.

Her stationery was yellow and had pictures of books stamped around the edges like a frame. Carly had written titles on the books: *How to Break Your Collarbone*, *How to Miss Your*

Camp Friends, How to Fall Off a Horse, How to Not *Fall Off a Horse, How to Milk an Injury, How to Be Bored.* I laughed out loud and started reading.

Dearest Vic!

I miss you so much! That was the worst way to leave camp ever!!! I'm so sorry I didn't get to say goodbye. I have the card you guys made me up on my wall, and I look at it constantly. I miss Yarrow! I miss our awful cots and I miss banging into Jordana's stupid cubby door and I miss canteen. But I don't miss the bugle!!!

The good news is that my collarbone is getting better. It barely even hurts anymore. The bad news is I'm not allowed to do much while it heals—no biking, no swimming, no trampoline, and definitely no horseback riding. I've been reading a book a day, every day, and I've watched every cute animal video on YouTube, and I'm still going insane with boredom!!!

My doctor said I can't ride for at least

THREE MONTHS. Then my parents said not for SIX MONTHS! So I threw a fit and we reached a compromise: I'm grooming horses at a riding school!!! I'm going every other morning to brush the horses (with my left arm only) and feed them. I already have a favorite. She's light brown with a dark mane and her name is Anna and I LOVE her. She nuzzles into me the second I walk up to her. I can't wait to ride her! Oh! And tell Chieko there's a horse here named Franklin Roosevelt. He was married to Eleanor, right? How random is that?

I hope camp is fun. I think of you every time I drink a root beer (which is a lot—my mom feels so bad for me she's been keeping the fridge stocked). Tell the Jaidas that I got my parents to make a donation to PETA. I told them all about the abused orcas and they wrote a check right away. Cool, right?!

This is for Jordana:

There was a stick of gum in its wrapper taped to the paper.

Tell her it's Sunday brunch: pancakes, eggs, toast, mixed fruit, hash browns, orange juice, and a cappuccino. It should keep her full for half a day, at least. Ha!
And this is for you:

There was a wrapped strawberry/apple fruit leather taped to the page.

It's the only flat candy I could find. It's really good, though—I'm addicted to them now.
Write to me soon because I miss you and I am sooooo bored.
Love you so much,
Carly

As much as I loved getting Angel's letter, Carly's was even better. Reading it made me feel like Carly was right there next to me, knee to knee, ready to walk to the dining hall or stand at flag or complain about the cold water at swim.

And Carly wasn't afraid after her fall! Or maybe she was

afraid, but she wasn't letting it stop her. She still loved horses and she still wanted to ride, and she found a way to keep horses in her life until she could again. The next time we did R & T, I would tell everyone that that was Carly's rose.

I wanted to write back, but I didn't have any special Carly stationery to write on. I'd have to get to the arts-and-crafts shack this week and design something really awful for her. And in my letter I'd have to tell her that Eleanor Roosevelt's real name was Anna, just like her new favorite horse, so there were actually horses named after the president *and* the First Lady in her stable. I couldn't wait to tell Chieko.

I couldn't write to Carly yet, but there was another letter I really needed to work on. I flopped onto my stomach, pulled out a page of plain lined paper, and wrote in my neatest handwriting:

Dear Angel,

Day 34—Thursday

→»·«←

"I'm sorry to inform you," Brenda announced at flag in her steady camp-director voice, "that there will be no canteen today."

All of senior camp started gasping and shouting, "What?" and "That's not fair," before Brenda could even finish her explanation.

I was one of the gaspers. After all the sweaty, backbreaking work I'd done to restock my account, how could we not have canteen?

Brenda rested one hand on her walkie-talkie while she waited for the huffs and complaints to end. I was about to say, "Of course this happens on *our* canteen day" when my eyes fell on Jordana.

Jordana was not gasping.

Jordana was not complaining.

Jordana looked nervous. She was squeezing her hands into fists, pumping them open and closed anxiously, and staring frantically at the Asters. For an actress, she was doing a pretty lousy job of looking innocent.

Chieko's gaze landed on Jordana right after mine did, and I watched her read Jordana's face like a page in a book. Chieko lowered her sunglasses—she wore sunglasses to flag whether it was sunny or not—and muttered, "Way to go, Orphan Annie."

Jordana scowled.

Brenda cleared her throat and addressed the crowd. "It *is* unfair, I agree. It's unfair that all of you will do without because a few individuals thought it wise to break into canteen last night." She said this while holding her mouth in a perfect straight line. She sounded like someone who had been a camp director for a gazillion years and had seen everything.

She was a rock.

Or she just did an excellent job of impersonating a rock.

"After these campers broke in and took their fill, they neglected to close the refrigerator and freezer doors. This forced the motors to work much harder to regulate the temperature. The motors burned out and both appliances are dead. I doubt we'll be able to repair them."

The huffs and complaints grew about one hundred decibels

louder. Instead of shushing us, Brenda lifted her hands in a *go ahead* gesture, giving us time to moan and complain.

I turned to Jordana. She looked like a statue of regret.

"You killed canteen," I accused her.

"No, I didn't," she tried.

I stared at her with my best *you have got to be kidding me* face.

She stared back, as if looking at me long and hard enough could undo what she'd done with her hotshot Aster friends last night.

"The doors were left open? That was you," I said.

"How do you know?" she asked, her confidence draining like a defrosting freezer.

"You leave your cubby door open all the time!" Jaida A chimed in. "We're always banging into it to get out of the bathroom. I have actual bruises from walking into that stupid thing."

"Oh. Sorry," she said, sounding especially pathetic as she looked down at Jaida A's thigh for a lingering bruise.

"You're just supposed to break in, take a few snacks, and then run for it. You're not supposed to break equipment," I whisper-yelled at her.

"I didn't mean to. I was just the lookout. It was Bella and someone else," Jordana whisper-pleaded back. "I was just following them."

"Why? Why are you trying so hard to make them like you?"

"I'm not *trying*." She sucked her teeth at me and looked away angrily. "You don't understand. Just forget it."

"Forget what? Forget to close a door?" I knew it wasn't a very Eleanor thing to say, but I couldn't help it.

"It's not *that* bad. We can still get candy bars," she argued.

"No we can't. Canteen isn't air-conditioned—it's a sauna in there." Jaida C joined our hushed conversation. "They have to keep all the chocolate in the fridge or it melts. Which means it's all ruined."

Jordana dropped her eyes to the ground as she let out a quiet, "Oh."

Chieko stepped toward our huddle and said, "Please direct your attention to the Aster bunk. Three of those girls look suspiciously peaked and queasy, wouldn't you agree?"

We all looked over. Bella looked like she had something sour stuck on her tongue, and Simone looked like she was trying not to throw up. The girl next to them, Gabbi, was fidgeting and looked sweaty.

"Agreed," Jaida A and Jaida C both said.

"Alas, the faces of guilt. None of my campers are missing the irony here, I hope," Chieko continued. "Our Canteen Nurtures Life flag team is, in fact, the same team who just decimated canteen."

Jordana turned her back to the flagpole and rubbed at her eyes.

Brenda called her meeting to order, finished her announcements, and then called on the Violets to share a song they'd made up in their cabin during rest hour.

My stomach grumbled for breakfast while the junior campers sang. Jaida C stood next to me, braiding Jaida A's hair. I ached for Carly. Missing canteen would be a lot more tolerable if Carly were still here.

I looked over at Chieko. Her lean body was moving slowly in a forward and backward rocking motion, like she was half-asleep or floating in some deep meditation. I was jealous of her peaceful state and wished I could do what she was doing. I got really close that day at archery, I remembered. Maybe if I practiced—

But my thought was interrupted by an unenthusiastic dismissal shout of, "Meadow Wood!"

Chieko jumped at the noise as if a firecracker had gone off under her feet, and I flinched so hard I had to put my hand over my heart, the way Earl did, to steady myself.

No canteen, no Carly, and a mild heart attack scare all before eight o'clock in the morning. Even mile-high chocolate chip pancakes with whipped cream for breakfast couldn't make up for all that.

Day 35—Friday

->>>·<<<-

E arl was in a mood, same as yesterday. He barely greeted me when I showed up for elective and just pointed, caveman-like, to show me where he wanted me to work. There was no nutrition article to read, no lesson about photosynthesis, no discussion of recipes for the dining hall.

I knew why he was so grouchy. It was canteen. Every year campers tried to break in and every year he stopped them. But this time they'd succeeded, and I bet it stung.

Apparently, it was going to be a zucchini-patch-weeding day for me. I grabbed an empty bag to stash the weeds in and crouched down at the end of one raised bed. I parted the leaves and let them rest against my shoulders, the way Earl showed me, and started to pinch and pull. Each time I leaned in to grasp a weed, my sunglasses slid down my nose. I pushed them back into place, shoved the weed into the bag, leaned back in to grab the next one, and the glasses slid down again. The fact that I was already sweating wasn't helping.

Earl was suffering in his own way, from the looks of things. He was grunting and huffing while trying to set up some kind of drip-hose watering system along his plant rows, and it clearly wasn't going as he'd hoped.

We had been at it for only twenty minutes, but it felt like two hours to me. I caved first.

"Earl, can we take a break?" I waited for an answer, and when I didn't get one, I added, "Please?"

Earl threw down the portion of hose in his hand and looked at it with disgust. Then he said, more to the hose than to me, "Yeah, take a break."

He walked toward me, sweat dripping down his arms and staining his white T-shirt, then past me and into his cabin. I was about to douse myself with the hose when he came back out, a cup of ice water in each hand.

"Hydrate," he said.

I thanked him and drank greedily.

Once both our cups were empty, I asked, "So what's gonna happen with canteen? Will we get it back?"

Earl let out a short huff. "Good question. And I don't know

the answer." He looked down and said to his feet, "Still can't believe it."

"That they got in?"

"That I didn't hear them," Earl said. "I always hear them. That door is louder than thunder. Haven't oiled it in years for just that purpose."

"It was probably the middle of the night. You were fast asleep," I tried to console him.

"No"—Earl wouldn't accept the excuse—"that never mattered before. I'm just old. I can't hear as well as I used to. I can't wake up fast. I just . . . can't."

"You're not old," I said, even though the first word that popped into my head whenever I thought of Earl was *old*. The second word was *garden* and the third was *hardworking*. Earl was one of the hardest-working people I had ever met.

"You'd be surprised, the things that change as you get older. Can't even sleep the same."

"You can't sleep?"

"Twists up my back. Brenda got me a body pillow for it. Most ridiculous thing I ever seen." Earl looked embarrassed for the first time ever.

"Does it work?"

"Like a dream. Best invention in the galaxy." Earl laughed

and pressed the cold cup against his cheek to cool the pink flush that was spreading there.

"Getting old, it happens so fast you don't see it coming." He gestured at the space around him, at his bigger-than-a-garden but smaller-than-a-farm yard overflowing with plants and bushes and neatly tended rows of care. "Everything gets older back here, but the growing is slow. When I'm back here, my growing old feels slower, too."

That's the kind of smart Earl was—he found a way to slow down time. Being in the garden really was a kind of slow-motion experience. Being in the woods, alone on my rock, was kind of like that, too.

Earl put his cup on the ground and tightened the knot on his bandanna. "Back to the garden now."

"Do you have anything I could do that doesn't make me lean over? My glasses keep sliding down my nose, and it's driving me nuts."

"All the work back here has you bent over, you know that. What happened to your hat?"

"My head feels like it's on fire when I wear the hat."

"That's what bandannas are for," he said, as if he were stating the most obvious fact known to man. "No heat trapped on your head, no glasses sliding off your face, no sun in your eyes, and all the sweat gets soaked away. Next to my sleep pillow, it's the best invention in the world."

"No way I'm wearing a bandanna," I told him. "Not happening."

"Suit yourself." He shrugged. "But Steven's counting on us. He wants to make his famous chocolate chip zucchini bread for everyone tomorrow."

I looked at the green zucchini shining in the afternoon sun and felt a whole new motivation. Steven's chocolate chip zucchini bread was insanely amazing.

"You play dirty, Earl." I glowered at him.

"I'm a gardener, Vic." He held his soil-stained hands out in front of him. "How else would I play?"

Day 36—Saturday

→>>·<<<-

Saturday's market was a total wash.

Literally.

As soon as Earl and I started loading up the truck with zucchini and kale, the sky let out a rumble louder than a hundred garage doors closing at the same time, and then spewed rain down on us.

We spread a tarp over the flatbed but only had time to tie it down in three spots before a knife of lightning sliced the sky right above our heads. The rain was pelting us so hard it almost hurt, and we both raced for the safety of the front seat. We hopped in our sides and slammed the doors shut behind us. The furious drumming of rain softened and we sat like that, sealed in our small dry pod, catching our breath while staring out the windshield at the watery world around us.

"So," I wondered, "was that in the forecast?"

Earl thought for a moment, then said, "Well, come to think of it . . ."

"Earl!"

"I was going to the market either way, so what does the forecast matter?" he defended himself.

"Well, that answers my next question." I sighed and squeezed water out of my ponytail onto the truck floor. "Will there be other people there?"

"Most of the vendors will be there, you can count on that," he said. "There just won't be as many shoppers. You can count on that, too."

Fewer shoppers meant less work to do at the stand, which meant more time to spend with Angel.

If he showed up.

It took us forever to get to the market because the rain wouldn't let up and Earl had to drive way below the speed limit. He was hunched forward in his seat, hands gripping the steering wheel like he was hanging from a ledge, squinting through the back-and-forth rush of the windshield wipers to read the blurry road in front of him. By the time we finally pulled into our space, he looked completely fried.

"No rush to set up just yet," he said wearily. "Rain's bound to lighten soon. We'll do it then." Then he closed his eyes, folded his hands in his lap, and leaned back into his headrest like it was his favorite pillow cradling him.

Earl was right. Almost all the regular vendors still showed up, and at least half the shopping population decided to stay dry and cozy at home rather than face the morning storm just to buy a few local vegetables.

Which worked out perfectly for Angel and me.

The hard rain finally calmed itself into a steady drizzle, and Angel made his move then. He showed up with an umbrella and a smile and a bright-green-eyed invitation. Earl told me to take my time. Business was slow.

The air hung thick over us, heavy and soggy. Angel and I huddled under his umbrella on our regular bench eating doughnuts while we argued over which one of us had gotten more drenched that morning.

I'm pretty sure I won.

My toes still squished loud enough to hear inside my water-logged sneakers and my sweatshirt sleeves were water-stained from the elbow all the way down to the cuff. My hair was still damp, even though his was dry as a bone.

"One of the advantages of a crew cut," he bragged.

"Yeah, I'm not so sure that look would work on me," I answered.

"You never know till you try. We have scissors in the truck." And he acted like he was going to run over and fetch them.

"I'll stick with my rainy hair, thank you very much."

"Rainy hair?"

"It's been rained on, so it's rainy."

"You're weird," he said.

"Gee, that's exactly what I've always wanted a guy to say to me."

"No," Angel laughed, "weird in a good way." He stared at me for a beat, then broke the last doughnut in half and gave me a piece. "In a really good way."

I didn't know what to say to that, so I just bit into the doughnut and chewed.

When Angel finished his last bite, he crumpled the paper bag into a ball and stashed it in his apron pocket. Then he slipped his hand over mine and asked, "Any news from your parents?"

"No," I told him, my gaze settling on his tanned skin. "We had Visiting Day last week and neither of them showed up, but I already knew they weren't coming."

He nodded and waited for me to say more.

"I got to visit Freddy, though, at Forest Lake, and I loaded him up with so much ice cream he got sick to his stomach and had to spend the rest of the day in bed reading comic books!"

"You say that like it's a good thing," Angel chided me.

"It is. He was in the infirmary, so he didn't have to watch all the kids hugging their parents goodbye, and he didn't have a chance to get sad about not seeing his own. It was brilliant."

"And this is why you're weird," Angel laughed at me. "Who else would even think of that?"

"Another weird person," I answered.

"The *good* kind of weird person," he clarified.

A silence fell over us as the light drizzle became heavier. Angel huddled closer to me to stay under the umbrella.

"So, can I have your cell number?"

I laughed so hard I almost spit doughnut crumbs at him.

"Gee, that's exactly what I've always wanted a girl to do to me. Laugh in my face when I ask for her phone number." He crossed his arms over his chest and slid away enough that rain was hitting him.

"I'm not laughing at you," I said, trying to pull him back over. "It's just that my cell phone is in my bedroom in Pennsylvania, so I won't get your call for another few weeks."

"Whoa, your camp is harsh. You can't have a phone at all, not even for emergencies?"

"We're not even allowed to use the regular phone without permission. There's no contact at all with the outside world for us Meadow Wooders. Except by flat mail." I rolled my eyes as I said it.

"What's flat mail? Is that something Eleanor Roosevelt invented?"

I laughed, then explained.

"So we'll keep writing letters, then," Angel said. "Fine."

"Unless . . ." An idea started to hatch in my mind. "You know what? Give me *your* cell number. Just in case."

"You're not going to break into the office for the phone, are you? I don't think they could take that after the canteen tragedy."

I had caught Angel up on the latest camp drama. "No, not break in. But maybe . . ." I didn't want to make any promises I couldn't keep, so I didn't finish my sentence. "Just write your number down for me, in case."

He ripped off a piece of the bag in his apron pocket and printed his number on it. "Here. But don't do something dumb and get kicked out of camp," he said.

"Why not?"

"Because then you'd get sent back to Pennsylvania and there would be no more doughnuts, that's why not," he answered.

But I knew it wasn't about the doughnuts.

Day 36—Saturday evening

⇢⟫·⟪⇠

Chieko agreed to let me skip the social before I even started pleading my case. I didn't have to explain how lousy I felt after waking up early, standing in wet clothes for six hours, and packing and unpacking heavy boxes of food with Earl all morning. And I didn't have to confess how pointless the dance was for me, since the only guy in New Hampshire I was interested in was not going to be there.

She had just said, "Whatever," and brushed me off quickly so she could get back to her book.

I crossed the fields, trudged up the hill, and made my way to Chicory. Vera was on her bed when I arrived, even though the rest of her bunkmates were in the counselor room, engaged in a serious jacks tournament.

"Vic!" She looked up the moment I came in and hopped off her bed to hug me.

"Vera, why are you hiding in here?" I asked right away. "Remember what I said? You have to try."

"I did try. I got out on the first round," she explained. "Eye-hand coordination is not a strength of mine."

"Oh." It wasn't hard to believe that. "Don't you want to watch the others?"

"It gives me anxiety. My canoe friend Jordyn is the reigning champ, and it's just too stressful to watch her play. What if she loses her title?"

"I think you can just call her your friend. Drop the 'canoe' part."

Vera tilted her head at me.

"So, you wanna take a walk with me?" I asked. "I bet I can get your counselor to let you go."

"Oh, you don't even have to ask," Vera said, waving the idea away like it was an annoying fly. "She loves it when I'm not here."

We climbed onto the rock and sat side by side, the quiet hum of the woods surrounding us.

We talked about the books she was reading, the letters she

received from her mom and her favorite teacher, and the pinch pot she was making at arts and crafts to use as a water dish for her next amphibious pet.

Then she said, out of the blue, "You should have named this rock. Back when you first discovered it—you should have given it a name."

"I did."

"What is it?" She turned toward me, eager to know.

"Rocky."

She blinked, hard.

"You named this rock *Rocky*?"

"I was *nine*," I reminded her.

"I'm only seven and I can do a lot better than *Rocky*."

I took a deep breath and let it out slowly.

"Rocky is so pedestrian," Vera continued.

I really didn't want to snap at a seven-year-old kid who couldn't play jacks to save her life and used the word *pedestrian* in casual conversation.

"You should have named it something more original," she kept going. "Something poignant."

A seven-year-old kid who used the word *poignant*.

"Something unique," Vera said.

"The first thing I thought of was Rocky, okay?" I wished she would drop it.

"The first thing I thought of was Ferdinand. Like that gentle bull from the book. It's a text-to-life connection that has meanings on many levels, plus layers of symbolism. I would have named it Ferdinand."

"Then go find your own rock and name it, Vera," I snapped.

Her face grew cloudy and it looked, for a quick second, like she might cry. But she gathered herself together and said, "I don't think you're supposed to talk to your camp sister like that."

"Well, I don't think you're supposed to call *your* camp sister *pedestrian*," I said back.

Her whole body deflated.

"I'm sorry," she said, her voice cracking. "I always do that. I get bossy when I'm upset. I know that about myself."

I saw Freddy when I looked at her then, the way his face crumpled before he cried, the way it strained to fight against the tears and the way it broke when he lost the fight.

"It's okay, Vera." I held my arms out to her for a hug. She leaned into them and snuggled like she couldn't get close enough. "Why are you upset? Because of the jacks tournament?"

"No. I'm homesick again."

"You're allowed to be homesick. You've been away for weeks, and sometimes Visiting Day makes it even harder. It's okay," I assured her.

"Are you homesick?" she asked, and I could hear the hope in her voice.

"Yeah," I said. "I am, a little bit." And it was true. My home was a mess, but it was my mess. I missed it even though I didn't know what it would be when I got back.

"I don't know what I would do without you, Vic," she said to my shoulder.

"Well, then, we're a good match, because I don't know what I would do without you, either." And I really meant it.

She snuggled into my lap and squeezed me like a koala clinging to a tree branch. Then she lifted one small fist up to the sky and cheered quietly into my sleeve, "*V* team!"

Day 39—Tuesday

→≫·≪←

I had just finished adding the last bit of brown glitter to my Carly stationery when Ruth, the arts-and-crafts counselor sitting next to me, said, "Oh shoot! I forgot to drop these at Brenda's."

She was holding a small bag of rubber stamps.

"I'll take them for you," I offered quickly, reaching for the bag.

"Tell her they're all good to go except for the return address stamp. That one was so gooped with ink I couldn't save it."

I headed toward the main office, a small bubble growing in my stomach the closer I got. I still wasn't sure if I would be able to go through with it. I couldn't tell if my bubbly stomach was because I was about to maybe tell a small lie, or if it was because I was maybe, possibly, going to be talking to Angel on the phone in a few minutes.

It was probably both.

I caught Brenda just as she was leaving the office.

"Ruth asked me to bring these stamps to you. They're all fixed except for one."

"Excellent, thank you. Can you put them on the desk for me? I have to get to the stables."

"Sure." I could feel myself losing my nerve. I didn't even know how to say it.

Brenda's eyes widened as she noticed the piece of stationery in my hand. "Oh, Vic—did you hear from your dad?"

I followed her gaze to my paper. Only the back side was visible, but lines from my drawing showed through so it looked like a letter.

"Do you need to call your mom? Go right ahead. Nobody's in there. You'll have total privacy." Her walkie-talkie rumbled on her hip and static came through, followed by a voice saying, "You coming? Over."

"I've gotta go. Just make sure you pull the door shut on your way out." And she left.

It was that easy. I didn't even have to say anything. Brenda had said it all for me.

Inside the office, I sat in the chair behind the desk and

looked at the telephone. It was an ancient, clunky-looking thing with a receiver and a twisty cord and a bunch of buttons, but it was about to connect me with Angel. Whoever invented this sucker was my new hero. After I finished learning about Eleanor, maybe I would research the phone guy. But for now, I lifted the receiver to my ear and dialed the number I had memorized. Between each ring, I could hear my heartbeat thumping in my chest. The bubble in my gut seemed to split into many smaller ones that started knocking into each other like the balls on the bocce court.

He answered after the third ring. "Hello?"

"Hi."

There was a short pause. Then he said, "Farmers' Market Vic?"

I could practically *hear* his smile.

"Ramos Family Flowers Angel?" I said back.

"Hi! How are you doing this? How are you calling me?"

"With this odd contraption called a telephone. They're really neat-o."

"Very funny," he laughed. "But seriously? Where are you?"

"I'm at camp. In the main office."

"I told you not to break in," he scolded.

"I didn't. Brenda *told* me to use the phone. To call my mom because of, you know, the whole situation at home."

"So I'm your mom now?" Angel asked.

"Yep," I answered. "I'd like more allowance."

"Did you clean your room?" he said, using his version of a stern mom voice.

"As far as you know," I answered.

"Fine. But I can only pay you in doughnuts."

"We should research that next," I decided at just that moment. "Who invented the doughnut?"

"I have my laptop right here. I can look it up." I heard him tapping on a keyboard.

"Just so you know, I might have to hang up suddenly if someone comes in, and I'll have to call you 'Mom' when I do. So don't think I'm hanging up on you, okay?"

"Maybe we should say our real goodbye now, then, while we have the chance."

"That's . . . a little weird," I said.

"The good kind of weird," he answered.

I smiled at that. I bet we both did.

"So here I go," Angel said. "I'm really glad you called. I'll see you on Saturday, okay?"

"Okay."

"Bye, Vic."

"Bye, Angel."

It was quiet for a second, and then I heard more tapping

sounds through the phone. I looked out the window and saw campers in the distance, running on the soccer field and splashing in the lake, but no Brenda and no Earl headed my way. I relaxed back into my chair.

"Here we go—Hanson Gregory," Angel reported. "An American ship captain. He's credited with inventing the doughnut *shape*."

"When?"

"In 1847. When Hanson Gregory was making these cakes, he kept running into the same problem. The centers of the dough stayed gooey and raw while the outside cooked, so he popped the centers out. With the hole in the middle, they cooked evenly all around. The doughnut was born."

"So he named his problem and fixed it," I realized.

"The gooey center problem? Yeah, I guess so."

"I'll have to tell Vera."

"Who's Vera?"

"My camp sister."

"What's a camp sister? Is it like a flat mail thing? Is she a flat camp sister?"

"No, she's a real 3D camp sister, and she's seven years old, and she's awesome."

"Cool. Tell me about Vera."

So for the next ten minutes I did, until I heard the churning sound of Earl's cart growing closer and louder. I hopped out of the chair like it was on fire, said, "Gotta go, Mom!" and hung up the phone as fast as I could.

But not so fast that I couldn't hear Angel answer me as the receiver moved from my ear back to its base. I had to laugh when I heard him say, "Bye, honey."

Day 41—Thursday

>>>·<<<

The sun's heat pressed down on my back like a hot iron. I was bent over the tomato bed, tying stems to metal poles and poking little holes around the plants to fill with water. My sunglasses kept sliding down my sweaty nose until I was so frustrated I flung them off with the force of a hurricane wind. They cracked when they hit a tomato pole and landed in three pieces, one lens popped free of the frame, reflecting the sun's rays back up to the sky.

"That's why farmers don't wear sunglasses," Earl's voice rang out from behind me.

"Really?" I barked, embarrassed to be caught in my mini tantrum. "I thought it was because farmers work at the butt-crack of dawn," I said, using Angel's word, "so they don't have to deal with the heat and the stupid sun blasting them."

"That they do," he answered. "But I'm a camp employee first, farmer second. And this is when I get to work back here."

I let out a frustrated sigh.

"Unless you want to work at five a.m. with me every morning of the week instead of just on Saturdays?"

"No thanks," I said without needing even half a second to think about it.

"Good. I was hoping you wouldn't take me up on that." He twisted his bandanna around his head so the sweatier part from the front moved to the back. "Time for a breather. I got somethin' for you." And he wandered off toward the back door of his cabin and disappeared inside.

I walked over to the tiny stripe of shade by the hose rack and felt the temperature drop by ten degrees just by stepping out of the sun. I peeled my T-shirt away from my slick back and redid my ponytail, smoothing every loose strand against my head with the glue-like effect of my sweat.

Earl came back with two cups of ice water and a package tucked under his arm. "This came for you." He presented the bulky package, a rectangular manila envelope that was so stuffed it was busting at the seams. My name was scripted beautifully across the front, with Meadow Wood's address in a smaller script underneath.

"That's my mom's writing," I said out loud.

"That's correct."

"But that's not a flat package," I stated the obvious.

"You're two for two," Earl replied.

"But we can only get flat packages at camp."

"You are currently standing on land that belongs to this cabin, which is privately owned by myself, as mentioned before, so you're not technically 'at camp.'"

"All this time I've been working at farm I haven't been at camp?" I asked, soundly confused.

"That land"—he tossed his chin in the garden's direction—"*is* camp. But I think you're missing the point here. Take the package."

He shoved it at me.

I took a gulp of my water, then put the cup on the ground and used both hands to tear the sticky seal open. Inside was a large bag of Swedish Fish, a box of fat pretzel rods, and three Kit Kat Big Kat bars.

And a note.

> Dear Vic—
> I'm sorry about canteen. And I'm sorry I missed Visiting Day. And I'm just sorry.
> I love you,
> Mom

P.S. Remember that spot on your carpet where you and Jamie spilled the chocolate syrup? I finally got the stain out!

"I hope the candy didn't melt," Earl said after a minute. "Your mom called first to make sure we'd let you have it. You'll have to store it here, though, not in Yarrow, and come fetch your snacks when you want them."

I nodded okay and stared at all the goodies in my hands. And the note.

"She's trying, Vic," Earl said quietly.

"Uh-huh," I agreed. "I know."

I pictured my mom standing in the candy aisle in our town grocery store, shopping for the treats in my package. I pictured her writing the note and addressing the envelope, then waiting in line at the post office to have it weighed and mailed to me.

The money I was going to earn on Saturday felt like an opportunity.

"Could you do me a favor?" I asked Earl. "Could you turn my pay from the market this Saturday, however much it is, into a check and mail it to my mom?"

"You don't want to give it to her yourself?"

"No. I want to send her a surprise in the mail. Like she did for me."

"Okay." He nodded once and smiled at me. "She'll be touched, you doing this for her."

"Maybe," I said. "Hopefully."

My mom was trying. That's what Earl said when he gave me her very not-flat package.

I was trying now, too.

Earl downed his entire cup of water, chewed on an ice cube, then said, "Let me stick that inside for you before the chocolate melts. We gotta get back to work. Steven needs greens for tomorrow's dinner. We're growing the healthiest campers in New Hampshire here at Meadow Wood!"

I handed him the package.

"Thanks, Earl," I said, "for everything."

He stopped with the stuffed envelope cradled in his arms and looked at me before saying slowly, "Thank you for everything, too, Vic."

The wood door clapped against the warped frame as it closed behind him, and a gigantic cloud drifted in front of the sun and hung there. It was like being in a room where the light was suddenly switched from full blast to dim. I stepped back to my tomato patch and knelt down, feeling gratitude wash over me like a prayer. I ran my fingers through the loose, dark soil and felt grateful for the water I was about to feed it. I felt grateful for well-placed clouds, and grateful for surprise packages, and grateful for a friend like Earl.

And I felt grateful my mom had finally learned how to use a P.S.

Day 42–Friday

→→→·←←←

Chieko handed me two letters at rest hour. One was in my dad's chicken scratch handwriting, and the other was in Angel's. I was definitely saving the best for last, so I slid Angel's under my pillow and opened the envelope from my dad first.

> Dear Vic,
>
> How's camp? It's hard to believe it's August already. I miss you. Not coming up on Visiting Day was harder than I thought it would be.
>
> I'm still in California. There's enough work to do out here that I volunteered to stay a while. I remember the report you did on earthquakes in third grade. According to the map you made, I'm not near a fault line.

Anyway, it made sense for me to stay here, since work covers my hotel room, and your mom and I still need time to figure things out. I know this must be upsetting and confusing to you. I'm sorry. I don't know what else to say, because it's upsetting and confusing to me, too.

Give Freddy a big hug for me.

Love you,

Dad

Aside from my dad admitting he thought it would be easy to *not* see me for the entire summer, it was an okay letter. At least I knew where he was now, and I could tell my mom if she hadn't already found out. And knowing that he was upset and confused, and that he felt bad enough to apologize for it, automatically made me feel less mad at him.

He included a P.S.

P.S. Here's a take-out menu from a pizza place by my hotel. Thought you might be able to turn it into stationery for a future Carly letter.

I unfolded the long red menu. The front of it said *ARTY PIZZERIA—Make Every Meal a Masterpiece*, but my dad had penned a capital *F* right in front of the *A* in *ARTY*. I couldn't not smile at that. Fart jokes were more Freddy's department than mine, but at least he tried. It let me know that no matter what was going on between my parents, I still had a dad who cared about me.

It also made me hungry for pizza.

I tucked his letter and menu back into the envelope and walked it over to my cubby, then climbed back onto my bed. Jordana was in the shower, belting out a *Hamilton* song, and the Jaidas were visiting their camp sisters again, so I had the room to myself. When I broke open the envelope from Angel, two things came out—a white card with the Ramos Family Flowers logo stamped across the top and another sealed envelope. The second envelope said, *Read the card first.*

Dear Vic,

I took the flat mail thing as a personal challenge. I wanted to send you flowers, but I know that's not allowed, so my best attempt is inside the smaller envelope. Hope you like it.

See you soon,

Angel

I slid my finger under the flap to open it. There was no paper inside. I turned the envelope upside down and a shower of pink, white, and yellow flower petals—at least fifty of them!—rained down on my lap. The petals were different shapes and sizes, all dried and smooth and pressed flat. I scooped them up and let them fall again, watching them twist and turn as they fluttered like feathers back onto my lap.

It was the best flat mail I'd ever seen.

Day 44—Sunday

→→→·←←←

Sunday night dinner was always turkey with stuffing, green beans, potato rolls, and a red sauce that looked like a can of cranberry sauce had been dumped into a mix of cherry Jell-O. I had no idea what the sauce tasted like because I hadn't tried it in five summers and wasn't planning to break my streak anytime soon. Sunday dinner was my least favorite meal at camp. I ate one roll, then told Chieko I had a desperate need to go to the bathroom.

"Really? All of a sudden?" She doubted me instantly. "What are you, two?"

"Plus eleven, yes," I answered.

"You just did math—voluntarily," Chieko pointed out.

"Was it right?" I asked.

She stared me down, then said, "Go to the bathroom and hurry back so I don't get in trouble."

"Okay, but it might not be that quick, 'cause, you know, I have to—"

"That's enough information!" Chieko cut me off.

Jordana looked at me like she thought I might be up to something, which made sense—she would be the first one to recognize a sneaky plan. I just shrugged and said, "Be right back."

I stopped first at Vera's table to give her a quick hug and then headed to the door.

"Vic, wait a sec!"

I turned to see Eliza, the girl in Aster who used to ride with Carly, rushing toward me.

"Here," she said, and she reached her arms out and pulled me into a tight hug, squeezing me hard enough to lift me onto my toes. Then she let go and took a step back.

"Umm . . . ," I started.

"Oh, sorry! That was from Carly. I should have said that first," Eliza explained. "I got a letter from Carly yesterday, and she told me to give you a gigantic hug from her. So I just did. That was it."

I broke into a full grin. "Okay, thanks."

"She also said to tell you something about not letting any

butt-butt counselors force you into a freezing-cold lake at morning swim."

"Yeah," I laughed, "that sounds like Carly."

"Okay, see you later." And Eliza hurried back to her table.

As I closed the dining hall door behind me, I glanced at the head table where Brenda and Earl sat. They were eating dinner tonight with Holly and another horseback-riding counselor, laughing at something Holly was explaining with one hand in the air and the other hand lifting a saltshaker slowly over a basket of rolls. It was probably a riding story, and it looked like it involved jumping.

I jogged to the office to make a phone call.

"I only have a few minutes," I told Angel as soon as he answered.

"Where are you supposed to be?"

"In the dining hall. But I don't like this dinner and I knew I could get away," I explained.

"What would Eleanor Roosevelt say about you breaking rules and sneaking off? You seem to be channeling more of a D&D rogue than a former First Lady."

"What in the world is a D&D rogue?"

"D&D is Dungeons & Dragons. It's a role-playing game. Rogues are a specific class in the D&D world that are known for sneaking, stealth, and thievery."

"I'm not stealing anything."

"It's a slippery slope, Vic," Angel teased. "First you sneak away, then you break in, then you borrow, next comes stealing."

"Then I guess we just won't talk on the phone again till camp's over and I'm back home." It got quiet as I realized what I'd said. We had never talked about what would happen after camp ended.

"No, no, no," Angel backtracked. "I'm not saying that. It might be a good skill to have—the stealth abilities—you know, for emergencies and stuff. Rogues are hard to beat in the game. I could teach you how to play."

"Dungeons and Dragons?"

"Yeah. After camp, when you're home. We could FaceTime or Skype or something. It's a complicated game and it goes on forever, so we'd need a lot of time."

I smiled hard. I could already picture myself at my desk or stretched out on my floor, taking marathon phone calls from Angel while he talked me through his game world.

"Okay. So . . . do you want my cell number?"

"I was afraid if I asked for it you'd laugh in my face again."

"I promise the next time I laugh in your face it will be about something totally different."

"Wow. I'm really looking forward to that. Thanks for the heads-up, Vic."

"You're welcome," I said, and gave him my number. "I better get back to the dining hall."

"Okay. Don't get caught. And I'm going to name a rogue character in my campaign after you now."

"How flattering."

"You don't know D&D, so you have no idea what a huge compliment that is."

"If you say so. Bye, Angel."

I hung up and hurried back to my table in the dining hall. Dessert on Sunday nights was always chocolate pumpkin brownies, and I didn't want to miss them. Steven had to use canned pumpkin to make them, because you can't harvest pumpkins in the summer in New Hampshire. They were a fall crop. Thanks to farm, I knew facts like that now.

Day 46—Tuesday

→→→·←←←

"I'm doing a good deed so you'll let me skip tomorrow's social," I announced, bursting my way through the half-open door of the archery shack.

Chieko wasn't expecting me, or the box of archery supplies I was carrying, so she jumped when I came in. Something fell from her hands and clattered against the cement floor.

"Jeez, Vic, you scared the poop out of me!"

"Sorry." I peered around her and said, "But no, I didn't. There's no poop."

"Gross." Chieko sneered at me.

"You're the one who brought it up," I defended myself. "What were you doing in here anyway?"

And then I saw it. I saw what had flown out of her hands and hit the floor when I surprised her.

It was a cell phone.

Chieko saw me see it.

"Well, now I'll have to kill you," she said.

"But I brought you a package. Not flat." I held the box out to her and gave her my best angel face.

She took the box, set it on the one table in the cramped hut, and read the return address to herself. "I ordered these weeks ago. Great service, Arrowback Incorporated."

"So this is how you've been getting your technology fix all summer," I said, picking up her phone and looking for any damage. "No cracks."

"Hardly," she downplayed it. "There's no Wi-Fi here, just an outlet for charging. I use the phone and camera, and I can watch stuff I'd already downloaded. That's it."

"Pretty slick, counselor," I said, opening her Photo Gallery. "I won't tell."

The most recent photos on the scroll were of the archery range: pictures of the supply hut looking eerie in shadow, a close-up of a blade of grass glistening with morning dew, a purple finch resting on top of a target, which I could identify because it was New Hampshire's state bird and we learned all about them in the nature hut back in junior camp. Before that were photos of a bus depot and an airport, signs that said things like *Pickup Lane Only* and *Do Not Leave Bags Unattended*.

I kept scrolling backward in time through her picture collection while Chieko worked at unpeeling the packing tape on the box I'd given her.

I got to a picture of Chieko holding an orange-and-white cat in her arms, her face half-buried in the soft fluff of its fur. "You have a cat?" I asked, turning the phone so she could see the picture.

"No, that's Ramone. He lives in this bookstore I always go to."

"He's cute."

"He's fierce. He only lets, like, three people in the whole world touch him."

"And you're one of them, of course," I finished for her.

"Of course," she repeated.

I scrolled backward more.

"And who's this?" I asked, showing another photo. It was of Chieko and a girl with long brown hair, their arms around each other, smiling broadly in front of a wall of hay bales. They wore matching red team jerseys and had medals hanging from ribbons around their necks.

Chieko looked at the picture and quickly looked away. "That's Randy."

"Oh." I looked back at the photo. They were at an archery

competition and they both had placed, their medals reflecting glints of sun.

Chieko and her girlfriend. The girlfriend who broke her heart.

"She's pretty."

"I know," Chieko said. "And it's not especially helpful to point that out, thank you very much."

"And she's good at archery, like you?"

"Yeah, she's good." Chieko stopped working on the box to say, "But not as good as me."

I smiled at that. "Good. I like knowing you're the best."

"And I like knowing what's going on with my campers. You're different."

"I am?"

"You were all mopey at the beginning of camp, and now you're all . . . not-mopey," Chieko said.

"'Not-mopey' is the best you can do? Your vocabulary has failed you! This is insane."

"Inane," Chieko admitted.

"Well, I can be mopey again, if you want," I offered.

"No, you can't. You're not a performer. Only Jordana can pull that off."

"You're right." I handed her phone back to her. "I just had a lot of home stuff to deal with."

"So you dealt with it? It's done?" Chieko asked.

"No, it's not done," I admitted. "I'm just not afraid of it anymore."

"Nice. It's good to hear you're okay."

"I'm better than okay."

"Well, that's just braggy." Chieko plugged her phone back into the wall outlet and returned to her package.

"But I'm sorry for being mopey, you know, before," I added.

"No apology necessary. At least not to me. I'm the queen of mope." Chieko ripped the rest of the tape off the delivery box with the ferocity of a wild animal and opened the flaps. She dove both arms into the box, shuffled them around, and finally whipped out a long, narrow black case. She held it over her head in the air and declared, "Victory!"

She lowered the case, unclasped the end, and looked inside. "Are you kidding me?"

"What?" I asked.

"After all that? There aren't even a dozen arrows in here! Did I order from the most incompetent company in existence?" She pulled a few arrows out of the case.

I couldn't help it. I laughed.

"Good God, they don't even look new!" Chieko added, completely horrified.

I laughed harder.

"Ucchh," she groaned, and threw the case of defective arrows back into the box. "What. Ever."

Chieko collapsed into the wobbly plastic lawn chair that made up the only other piece of furniture in the hut. It squeaked under her weight, even though she couldn't have weighed more than a hundred pounds. I noticed three paperback books stacked on the floor under the chair, two of them with *Eleanor Roosevelt* in the title.

"You know, you're the best counselor I've ever had," I confided.

"You know, that *almost* makes up for my defective arrows," she said back, a sweet grin blooming across her face.

Day 46—Tuesday

-»»·«««-

Cheers of "We've got spirit, yes we do" rang out behind me as I walked down the hill from the dining hall to Yarrow. Brenda and Earl were passing a tray of Steven's homemade pizza around their table when I slipped out of dinner, complaining again of an emergency bathroom issue.

Jordana was definitely suspicious.

"Maybe I should go with you," she said, "in case you're sick or something. Maybe you shouldn't be alone."

"You're staying here," Chieko ordered. "And you"—she looked dead at me—"this is the last time."

I clutched my stomach, pushed in my chair, and ducked out. I knew Jordana would be able to see me if she looked out the windows on the back wall of the dining hall, so I had to pretend I really *was* going to the bathroom. I walked through the front door of Yarrow and then straight out the back so I could loop around behind senior camp and get back to the main office without being seen. I knew there was a back-door entrance to the office because I had seen Earl use it plenty of times when we were gardening.

I recited Angel's phone number in my head as I stepped over roots and rocks and moved quickly through any shadows I could find. I wasn't nervous at all this time. I almost felt like the stealthy rogue Angel had described.

By the time I reached Brenda and Earl's cabin, the only sounds in the air were the distant murmurs of campers talking and laughing in the dining hall. I walked by the garden and opened the cabin door to the office so I could surprise Angel with another phone call.

But the phone was gone.

The clunky old black phone wasn't sitting on the desk where it usually was. I scanned the shelves and looked high and low in the room but couldn't find it anywhere.

"Looking for something?"

I jumped at the sound of Earl's voice.

He stepped into the office from the short hallway beyond, his arms crossed over his white T-shirt, his blue bandanna hanging out of his front pocket.

My eyes shot right back to the empty space on the desk at his question.

"Aha," he said, then disappeared into the hallway and came back a second later with the phone in his arms. "That's what I thought."

There was no way out of this. I was definitely not a stealthy rogue.

I swallowed the lump that had formed in my throat and found my voice.

"How did you know?"

"I was born on a Sunday, but it wasn't *last* Sunday," Earl answered.

"I don't know what that means."

"It means I've got eyes, Vic. And I was young once, hard as that might be to believe. I know what's going on."

I stared at him and said nothing.

"You were gonna call Angel."

I didn't even blink.

"Again." He tilted his chin down and raised his eyebrows at me.

"Fine," I admitted. "Maybe. Yes."

Earl walked the phone back to the desk and plugged in the cord. He lifted the receiver to his ear to make sure it was working.

We both heard the dial tone fill the room. Then he hung up and said, "Angel's a good kid, comes from a nice family."

"You know his family?"

"'Course I do, known them for years. Think I'd let you go off with a stranger all these Saturdays? I'm responsible for you at the market. And where do you think Brenda's birthday flowers come from every July?"

My mouth dropped open.

"I wish I had a mirror—you should see the look on your face right now." Earl laughed to himself. He was truly enjoying this moment.

"All right. I'm busted. You busted me." Then I asked, "Any chance you'll still let me use the phone? Just for a few minutes?"

"Can't, you know that," he answered right away. "You'll make it till Saturday, Vic. I know you don't think you will, but you will. Trust me."

I sighed and accepted defeat.

Then I said, "I do trust you, Earl. Like, I trust that you won't tell anyone about me sneaking in here?" I crossed my fingers and held them up so he could see.

"I don't keep secrets from Brenda. But I won't tell anyone else. Just don't give me anything else to hide this summer. Deal?"

That seemed more than fair to me.

"Deal," I said.

Day 47—Wednesday

→»·«←

I picked Vera up from Chicory just as the rec hall's sound system began pumping out the first dance song of the evening. I was skipping the last social of the summer. Without Carly, socials were no fun for me. The Jaidas always spent the entire time dancing, and I don't dance. Jordana always spent the entire time flirting shamelessly with guys, and I don't do that, either. Tonight would be worse than usual with Jordana, since she knew her brother from Forest Lake would *not* be a chaperone.

So instead, Vera held my hand as we snuck into the woods. She held a bucket of chalk in her other hand and had a big manila envelope wedged between her arm and torso.

Once we got to the rock, she set her bin of chalk on the ground and held the flat package out to me like it was a tray of goodies. "For the Rocky project," she announced. "My research results."

"What Rocky project? And what research? There is literally no way to do research at camp."

"I have my ways," Vera said, raising both eyebrows. "I told you it's important to have resources."

I climbed up the rock and Vera climbed up next to me, scraping her knee on the way and muttering something about igneous rock texture as she rubbed the bump. Then she opened the envelope and pulled out a thick stack of paper.

"I wanted to know about the common varieties of chicory and yarrow and what they look like." She pointed at one large photo. "These ones are chicory."

A field of pale blue and lavender flowers stared back at me from the page. Each chicory flower had two layers of petals that spiraled around a small center, the stamens in the middle standing up straight like little yellow minions saluting the sun. They were plain but pretty, and according to the information on the sheet, they grew very quickly.

"I get it now, why they assigned Chicory to the youngest campers," Vera said. "Because we're the smallest, but we grow so fast."

"Could be," I acknowledged. "How did you get all this information?"

"My mom. I asked her in a letter," Vera explained. "I told her what to search and what to print. And she did it and mailed it all back to me. In this." She held out the now empty envelope to show me. "It's a flat package."

She really killed me. She couldn't climb a three-foot rock without hurting herself, but she could manage to make a thick packet of botanical information appear out of thin air. It was seriously possible that I was learning more from Vera than she was from me.

"Here's you," she said, thrusting a pile of papers at me. "These are all yarrow."

From the photos I saw that yarrow grew in shades of red, yellow, pink, lavender, white, and even orange. Individual yarrow flowers were tiny, but they grew in tight clusters. A cluster could be as small as a quarter or as large as a dinner plate. They were so beautiful that just looking at pictures of them made me appreciate the name of my bunk for the very first time.

"So how does this fit in with your project?" The light was slowly dimming. I had lost track of time and didn't know how much longer we could count on it.

"We're going to draw chicory and yarrow around the bottom of Rocky. On the side facing away from camp. The side facing camp should keep its natural camouflage."

I was touched by her plan to mark Rocky as ours, but there

was a major flaw. "Vera, the first time it rains, our drawings will be washed away."

"Nuh-uh!" Vera grabbed her chalk bucket and lifted the plastic lid off the top.

I looked inside. "Permanent markers?"

"They were in the arts-and-crafts shack. It's the end of the summer already, and no one was using them. They're practically brand-new," Vera claimed.

We worked side by side, using a marker until the tip dried out and then recapping it and continuing with another. Looking at all the flower photos and drawing my own versions of them onto the grainy rock made me think of Angel and all the flowers he and his dad displayed each week at the market. This Saturday would be my last market day of the summer, which meant it would be the last time I saw Angel until—until when? The thought dropped a weight in my stomach.

Vera started to hum as she drew, and I let her song pull me away from my thoughts about Angel and saying goodbye.

Once the sun decided to set, it went from dim to dark in the woods like the flick of a switch. We both knew we had to stop. Vera sealed all the markers in the watertight bucket. She wanted to store it under Rocky for our next visit.

"And we can leave it here until next summer even," she said, eyes wide with possibility. "And maybe other people will find it over the winter or spring, and they'll write on Rocky, too, and then we'll come back in June and find notes and pictures," she kept going.

"Maybe," I said.

"I want that to happen! We could meet uniquely interesting people!" she said, bouncing on her toes and clasping my hand again as we picked our way through the trees back to junior camp.

"That does seem to happen here," I had to admit.

Vera squeezed my hand. I squeezed back before letting go so she could run up the steps into Chicory.

I was halfway down the dirt path between flag and the dining hall when I noticed a shift in the air. It was like a buzz you could feel instead of hear. The rec hall stood in the distance, Meadow Wood girls and Forest Lake boys streaming out, standing in clumps outside the sliding doors. Counselors stood with arms stretched out like barricades, holding them in place.

What was going on?

I scanned the crowd for the Jaidas and Jordana, or Chieko, who was a social chaperone, a job she described as the true definition of cruel and unusual punishment.

I couldn't spot any of them.

As I got closer, I realized they were all looking toward the waterfront. I turned that way, too, and squinted to see.

A large mass of something stuck out of the water, leaning against the dock like a beached whale. It was too dark to see exactly what it was. Shadows of people huddled nearby.

I squinted harder.

As I got closer, I recognized Bella, Gabbi, two boys, and Simone, who was bent over, her hands on her knees.

A Marigold counselor was with them, her arms flailing. She grabbed Bella by the shoulders, but Bella kept her head down and her eyes fixed to the ground.

A figure emerged then, breaking out of the group, churning uphill at a pace that was fast but strained, forward but choppy.

I recognized him right away.

Earl was racing with something clutched to his chest.

And then it all came into focus, the way it does, first slowly, and then in an instant. Her legs swinging like broken pendulums, her head floppy as a balloon on a stick, her hair dripping a trail of wet behind her like ribbon unraveling.

Jordana.

Earl cradled her and ran toward clinic. His face was a mix of panic and effort, his shirt damp with lake water.

I ran toward him.

"What happened?" I didn't recognize the shrill in my voice.

"Get Brenda," he ordered without looking at me. "In the

dining hall. Get her car." Earl huffed out the words between short breaths. He switched directions then and turned from clinic toward the parking lot.

"Go," he shouted at me.

I sprinted to the dining hall and burst inside, banging my shoulder against the doorframe as I pushed my way in. Brenda looked up, a huge tray in her arms loaded with cookies for the social.

"Brenda!" I gasped.

She lowered the tray onto a table, a curtain of calm descending over her face even though I could see her hands tightening their grip on the metal tray handles, her knuckles pink.

"Earl needs you . . . drive . . . the hospital . . . Jordana . . ."

A ripple of worry crossed her face and then disappeared fast. She released the tray, clutched the walkie-talkie against her waist, and ran out the door so fast I felt a breeze hit me after she passed.

A kitchen staffer appeared from the back to ask what was going on, but I didn't stop to explain. I followed Brenda out the door and ran as fast as I could, scanning the ground in the dark to avoid tripping on the knobby roots and lumpy earth that made up the growing distance between Brenda and me.

When I reached the parking lot, Brenda was already in the

driver's seat, the engine revving, and Earl was sliding Jordana into the back seat.

He pulled the door closed and I watched him prop Jordana up against the headrest and buckle her into her seat belt. Then he collapsed beside her, his skin ashen under a sheen of sweat. Through the window I saw Jordana's eyes flutter open and Earl's slowly close. The car squealed out of the lot, kicking up gravel in its wake. I watched the car disappear down the road while music from the rec hall pulsed through the night, loud and heavy as my own pounding heart.

The rumors started immediately:

The boys boated the girls to the middle of the lake to smoke and then left them stranded there.

They all got drunk and stole Earl's cart and tried to drive it across the water to Forest Lake.

They were playing Truth or Dare, and one of the Asters dared Jordana to swan-dive off the dock near the shallow end and she did it. Or one of the Forest Lake boys dared her and she did it. Or no one dared her—she just stood up and announced, "Watch this," and did it herself.

But they were just rumors that grew and changed with each telling.

We all returned to our cabins that night with no idea of what had really happened and no idea if Jordana was going to be okay.

It was the longest night in the history of Meadow Wood.

Day 48—Thursday

->>>·<<<-

"She's back," Chieko announced, running into Yarrow to catch us between second and third period. "She's in clinic."

Chieko grabbed a stack of celebrity magazines from the top shelf of Jordana's cubby before clicking the cubby door shut.

The second we stepped into her room at clinic, Jordana's eyes welled up and she started to cry. She opened her mouth to speak but nothing came out, just silence to go with the tears streaming down her face. She had a bandage on the side of her head and she looked tired, but other than that, she just looked like Jordana.

"Shhh, it's okay," Jaida C soothed her, snuggling onto the bed beside her and stroking Jordana's long hair.

"We brought you supplies," Chieko announced, holding

the stack of magazines out in front of her.

At that exact moment, a nurse marched in and swooped the entire pile out of Chieko's hands. "No reading allowed. She has a concussion. All she's allowed to do is rest."

"No reading?" Chieko looked horrified.

"No TV, no writing, and certainly no reading," the nurse recited.

"Remind me to never get a concussion," Chieko muttered.

"And Jordana, honey, I just got off the phone with your parents," the nurse continued. "They've decided to have you come home on the bus on the last day, as usual."

Jordana's eyes crinkled like she couldn't believe what she was hearing.

"They said since camp is almost over, you might as well stay the last few days and leave with everyone else." I noticed that the nurse avoided eye contact with Jordana as she said this, and I couldn't blame her. Carly's parents couldn't get to her fast enough after her accident, but Jordana's parents didn't seem all that concerned.

The nurse refilled a water glass on the side table and flashed a light into Jordana's eyes, then scribbled something down on a chart. She turned to us to say, "Just a short visit now, girls. You can come back again later." Then she left.

"You scared us half to death!" Jaida A yelled at Jordana.

"You don't even want to know the stories people are making up," Jaida C said.

"What happened?" Chieko asked. "I remember seeing you by the speakers with Bella's group. You were dancing."

"When did you leave the rec hall?" I asked.

Jordana had stopped crying but was holding Jaida C's hand tightly in her lap. "During the slow song. They dim the lights so it's easy to slip out."

And then she told us everything.

The real story wasn't very exciting. It was just a bunch of dumb decisions in a row that ended up with Jordana hurt and everyone else in trouble.

There *was* alcohol. Gabbi and Bella convinced a kitchen staffer to slip them some beer, and they hid it by the waterfront right before the social. Eight of them snuck out of the dance—four girls and four boys—and chugged the beers fast, then decided to go swimming.

"Were you drunk?" Jaida C asked. Her tone was a mix of motherly scolding and genuine curiosity.

"No. I mean, maybe." Jordana tried to prop herself up in bed but winced, then sank back down against the pillows. "I don't know. I definitely felt different, but I thought I was fine."

Chieko nodded in a *been there, done that* kind of way.

"Then these two jerky guys"—Jordana sounded angry as

she continued—"they ran off and stole Earl's cart. They drove it right into the water, and I don't know, I guess we all thought it was funny at the time but—" she started to cry.

I saw the Jaidas exchange confused looks. Why was Earl's golf cart the upsetting part of the story?

"You got hit by the cart!" Chieko guessed.

Jordana shook her head.

I realized I saw the cart last night, flipped on its side by the dock, half under water. Those boys *were* jerks. Or else they were normal boys and the beer had turned them into jerks.

"So *what* then?" Jaida A asked. "How'd you get hurt?"

"I slipped," she said, wiping her tears away. "I hit my head on the dock and fell in the water, and I don't know, they pulled me out. I was unconscious."

"Who pulled you out?" Jaida C asked.

"The other two boys. The two not-jerks." Then she added, "So I'm told."

"And then Simone went to get help, right? I saw her by the lake—it looked like she had just run a sprint and was trying to catch her breath." I pieced together the rest of the story out loud. "So that means she got Earl and when he went to grab his keys, they weren't there because they were still in the ignition—that's how they stole his cart. So he ran to the dock and carried you all the way back to the parking lot. He could barely talk, he was running so hard."

And then Jordana burst into hard, body-shaking tears. As she cried, she pulled her knees up to her chest like she was trying to get smaller, like she was trying to disappear completely.

"Jordana, what is it?" Jaida C asked, fear on her face.

"Earl," was all she got out between heaves.

A sudden dizziness moved through me and my vision blurred. I'd noticed that Brenda wasn't at flag that morning—Holly had run it in her place—and that Earl wasn't in the dining hall at breakfast. I'd figured they were both busy dealing with the mess from last night, stuck on the phone with the parents of Aster girls and with the director of Forest Lake.

Jordana said each word carefully then. "I woke up in the car on the way to the hospital. He was next to me. His eyes were closed and he . . . didn't look right. Brenda's voice was all shaky. She was telling Earl how brave he was and how he was a hero for saving me. She told him how great he was taking care of everything at camp." Jordana took a deep breath and continued as fresh tears slid down her cheeks. "And then she started talking about their marriage and how he made everything beautiful, like the garden behind their cabin. How it would live forever."

My legs went numb and I started to sway on my feet. "Where's Earl?"

Jordana looked me in the eyes. "When we got to the hospital, she ran in for help and they took Earl first because he"—her voice cracked as she swallowed back another sob—"his heart stopped. He had a heart attack."

It happened quickly then. A wave of heat crept up my body and squeezed me until I couldn't feel my limbs and I couldn't feel my feet against the floor and I couldn't see. A bruised green color flashed behind my eyelids and my entire head tingled. I felt myself sink, my knees buckle and drop, and then everything went dark as the lake at night.

"You just couldn't let Jordana have all the attention, could you?" Chieko was standing over me, hands on her hips and a gleam in her eye.

"Huh?" I felt groggy, but nothing hurt. I was flat on my back on a cot just as hard as the one in my bunk. "What happened?"

"You fainted. Duh." Chieko crossed her eyes and stuck her tongue out at me. "You went down like a sack of beans."

"It's not funny," I said.

"It's a little funny." Chieko smirked. "Besides, you should be thanking me. I'm the reason you don't have a concussion."

"What?"

"I caught you before your skull crashed against the floor. Which wouldn't have been as hard as the dock Jordana hit, but still. I saved you from a head injury, which means you can read." She tossed the book she was holding at me. Chieko *always* had a book with her.

"Maybe later," I said, and put the book on the bare table beside me. I saw then that I was in my own room in clinic.

The door opened and Brenda stepped in. It all came rushing back then.

Earl.

Hospital.

Heart attack.

My stomach churned as I tried to read Brenda's face. Was that the face of someone who had just lost her husband?

My face must have been a cinch to read, though, because the first thing out of Brenda's mouth was, "He's okay."

Her face looked tired and paler than usual, but her hair was still pulled back into her tight bun and she was wearing her regular camp uniform, the walkie-talkie on her hip like always. Her clothes were wrinkled, though, so she must have spent the night at the hospital.

"Jordana said he had a heart attack" was all I could get out.

"He did. They took him into emergency surgery right away

and it went well. He's in recovery now." Her breath caught in her throat and she looked down at the floor for a moment. "He's got a long recovery ahead of him, but he's Earl. He'll be fine."

The invisible clamp that had been squeezing my chest released. I felt loose and light and okay. Better than okay. A whole lot better.

"How are you holding up, Brenda?" Chieko asked. "Is there anything I can do?"

"Yes, actually. There is." Then she turned to me. "Do you mind if I take Chieko? I have to get back to the hospital, and I have a lot of directions I need to go over first."

"Go ahead," I said, kicking a thin sheet off me. "And I can help, too. I feel fine. I don't need to be in here."

"Not your decision to make, Vic," Brenda scolded, sounding 110 percent like her regular camp director self again. "Wait for the nurse to discharge you. I'm sure it will be soon."

"And while you wait, you can read." Chieko pointed to the book beside me. "That's a different Eleanor book."

"You've been studying First Lady Roosevelt?" Brenda asked.

"No," I said quickly.

"Yes, you have," Chieko said.

"I haven't been studying her. I'm just reading some books about her," I explained.

"Same thing," Chieko replied.

"I hired an archery counselor who teaches American history on the side? I'm sure you don't get that at those fancy tech camps!" Brenda smiled, and some color returned to her face.

"It's true." Chieko shook her long bangs out of her eyes and lifted her chin regally. "I'm quite the find."

"Then can you *find* the nurse for me so I can get out of here?" I threw my skinny pillow at her.

"So uncouth." She tucked the pillow under her arm. "I'm prescribing you a dose of Eleanor, stat. Page one. Read."

I waited until they left and the door closed firmly behind them, but then the moment they did, I opened the book and started reading.

Day 49—Friday

>>>·<<<

Holly ran flag for the second day in a row. It was impossible not to notice the missing Aster girls. Bella and Gabbi were sent home because they were the ones responsible for the beer, but Simone was still here. Everyone knew by now that Simone was the one camper who hadn't drunk that night. She was also the only one with enough sense to go get help, the only one more worried about Jordana than about getting in trouble. As for the boys at Forest Lake, none of us knew what was happening to them.

Yarrow had been the smallest cabin at camp all summer, but now we barely even looked like a bunk. It was just me and the Jaidas standing on our patch of packed dirt, between the Clover girls and the Marigolds. Chieko wasn't at flag with us, hiding behind her dark sunglasses the way she usually did. She was in the dining hall, supervising the staff and filling in for the guy who'd been fired for giving the Asters beer.

She joined us at our table, though, when the pancakes came out.

"Drink some sunshine, darlings," she said, lifting a pitcher of orange juice and pouring it into our glasses one at a time.

"These pancakes taste like nothing," Jaida C said. "Where's the syrup? I need to drench them."

"They were so much better with blueberries. Remember that? At the beginning of the summer?" Jaida A asked, like it was a million years ago and not just seven weeks.

"Those blueberries were solid bombs of flavor," Chieko declared.

"Earl grew those," I heard myself say.

"We should make a flag of *that*!" Jaida C decided then. "We could paint blueberries all over it and write 'Earl's Berry Bombs.'"

"Do you wanna? For real?" Jaida A asked. "We have arts and crafts fourth period today, right after rest hour."

"Yes!" Jaida C said, then turned to me. "Vic, you have to help."

"Okay, I will," I agreed, "if I'm not in the garden."

But I already knew I wouldn't be in the arts-and-crafts shack with them. Brenda had promised me that Earl would be okay, but I felt antsy and anxious anyway, like every cell inside me was spinning in circles. There was only one place I could go to make myself feel better, and it wasn't Rocky. Rocky was where I went to think and zone out and do nothing, but right now I needed to do something. A lot of something. I needed to work. So I didn't go back to Yarrow with the Jaidas to change into my swimsuit for first-period swim.

I went straight to the garden instead.

It might have been my mind playing with me, or it might have been because the plants hadn't been watered in two days, but they all looked like they were drooping with sadness when I arrived that morning. I unwound the hose and got to work, giving each row and each bed the long drink it needed. I worked through first period and second period and third without anyone looking for me or telling me to get back to my scheduled activities.

I looked up once to find Brenda watching me through the window. She didn't say anything and she didn't wave. She looked like she was in a trance.

After lunch, where I swallowed about a gallon and a half of water, I went back to the garden. It was rest hour, but rest seemed impossible, and the hard work of carrying and bending and pulling helped, just like Eleanor said it would.

After tripping on the hose for the third time, I decided to coil it back on the wall hook, and that's when I saw it.

It had been rinsed and hung out to dry, the fabric thin and fading from the sun. I picked it up and ran the cool softness of it through my hands. Then I folded it into a long, thin band, the way Earl did, and put it back where I found it. Earl would need it when he returned to his farmwork, whenever that might be.

"Vic?" a small voice came from the side of the cabin.

I turned to find Vera watching me. She was shifting her weight from one foot to the other.

"Vera? Do your counselors know where you are?"

Vera nodded. "They said I could come."

I beckoned her over.

She started toward me with careful steps. She was carrying something, her hands cupped before her.

"What've you got?" I asked, guessing I was about to see another *Lithobates sylvaticus*.

But she wasn't holding a frog.

"For the garden," Vera said, and opened her hands to reveal two wet earthworms squiggling on top of each other. "For Earl."

"Worms?"

"*Lumbricus*," Vera said, then began her mini lecture on gardening science. "Earthworms are crucial for healthy soil construction. Their tunneling naturally tills the earth, creating air pockets and water space for plant roots. Earthworms also break down organic matter, fertilizing the soil so it's easier for plants to thrive."

"So . . . they're good for the garden," I summarized.

"They're great for the garden!" she expounded.

"Well, then, what are you waiting for?" I teased. "Get those babies in the ground."

Vera jogged over to the closest zucchini bed. "I can put them here where it's shady and they'll burrow down. Wanna see?"

"Sure."

I crouched down next to her, and we watched the worms snake and slide and push and turn into the soil until they disappeared entirely.

"I can get more," Vera offered. "I bet I can find a ton under the cabin."

"I bet you can't," I challenged her.

She grabbed a trowel, ran to the shaded side of the cabin, and started to joyfully hack at the ground.

I returned to my weeding by the tomato plants but was immediately interrupted by Vera shouting, "Bingo!"

She skipped to a different zucchini bed and gently placed two worms under a canopy of leaves, humming to herself as she watched them disappear into their damp, dark world. "Gardening is so much fun! Those tomatoes are part of the nightshade family. Did you know you get more nutrients from cooked tomatoes than you do from raw tomatoes? And these zucchinis are huge! My mom makes delicious zucchini bread. I usually eat it all summer long."

"We can send you home with a few zucchinis if you want, so your mom can bake for you," I suggested.

"Yes, please!" Vera ran back to the hole she'd made under the cabin. "I wish I was in senior camp so I could do farm all summer long. It's better than the nature hut."

"If you hadn't called me to Chicory that first week and made me miss sign-up, I wouldn't have known about farm," I told her. "So I owe you big-time."

"No, I owe you. You've been a superior camp sister. My canoe friend Jor—I mean my *friend* Jordyn's camp sister borrowed her only sunscreen and never gave it back and now Jordyn has a burn on her shoulders that's peeling and gross. You didn't do anything like that."

"Most camp sisters don't do anything like that."

"Well, I say you and me are even." Then she shouted, "Another one!" and lifted a long tan worm up from the ground.

"You are the worm whisperer, Vera."

She bowed. "You know, I was going to ask you if we could go to Rocky today, but I think I'd rather be here instead."

"To find worms?"

"Yes, or to just sit here and look at all the plants." She put her hands on her hips and took a deep breath. "It's very relaxing, you know."

I rested my dirty hands on my hips the same way and breathed in the scent of earth and water and sun.

"Yeah," I said back. "It really is."

Day 50–Saturday

→⟩⟩·⟨⟨←

Chieko shook me *gently* for the first time ever, rocking me awake in the dark while my bunkmates slept.

I sat up in bed, bleary-eyed and confused. "What's wrong?"

"Nothing's wrong," Chieko answered quietly. "It's market day. You have to get up."

I stared at her. "There's no market."

"Yes, there is."

"No, there isn't. Earl's in the—"

"Shush," Chieko cut me off. "You still have market. Hurry up. They're waiting for you." She pulled back my covers and swung my legs to the side of the bed in one motion. Then she pulled me to my feet and steered me toward the bathroom as if I were blindfolded.

Which I kind of was, because I was still half-asleep.

"Who's waiting?" I stumbled along, rubbing my eyes. "What are you talking about?"

"It's what Earl would be doing right now if he could, right?" she half asked, half told me. "You can't let all his hard work go to waste. Go sell his stuff. And take a minute to brush your nest of hair first, okay?"

The thought of being at the farmers' market without Earl filled me with sadness.

"Go," Chieko said, and gave me a push, then hurried back to her own bed.

I went through the motions of getting dressed, brushing my teeth, and even fixing my hair, which meant I ran a comb through it before pulling it into a high, tight ponytail at the back of my head.

When I was ready, I went to the counselor room and tried to explain it to her again. "There's nothing to sell, Chieko. I didn't pick much yesterday. I mostly watered and weeded all day. And it's too late now." I grabbed her wrist and turned it toward me so I could read her watch. "It's after six."

"It's already done," she said.

"What's already done?"

"The picking, or harvesting, whatever. They did it for you."

"Who's 'they'?" I demanded, now fully awake and fully confused.

"Some guy and his cutie-pie son. Just go outside already."
She hunkered down lower in her bed and kicked me toward the
door with her foot.

When I stepped outside, the dawning sun gleamed its
golden light into my eyes, and I swear I saw a vision of Angel
standing on Meadow Wood ground before me. I blinked several times and looked down at the packed dirt to refocus my
eyes. When I looked up again, Angel was still there, not a
vision but the actual person, and he was walking toward me.

"We heard. We're really sorry," he said.

He was wearing jeans and a dark blue sweatshirt with the
word *PEACE* printed across the chest. I kind of missed the
Ramos Family Flowers apron. He pulled me in for a hug and
my face rested for a perfect moment against his shoulder, the
soft blue cotton and the smell of his skin as reassuring as a
second chance.

"We did our best in the garden and have it all packed.
Brenda gave us the go-ahead," Angel's father said abruptly.
"Truck's ready to go if you are."

I was just about to thank him when we heard a high voice
in the distance yell, "Wait! Vic! Wait for me!"

We all turned toward the sound to find Vera running at us,
her hands fisted and swinging like maracas.

"Don't leave!" she shouted, panting her way toward us, so

light her feet made only the slightest sound each time they touched ground.

Angel and his dad both looked at me with bewilderment on their faces.

"Vera, what are you doing?" I bent down to her eye level once she stopped in front of me, panting for breath.

"I want to go with you. I want to go to the market. Please take me," she begged as she patted down her bedhead hair and straightened her rumpled nightshirt.

"I don't think I can. I'd need permission," I told her.

The door to Yarrow creaked open and Chieko appeared. "I can take care of that," she informed us. "Just give me five."

An hour later we were all set up, our tables covered in the glory of Meadow Wood's fresh August produce: green squash, red and yellow bell peppers, and tomatoes. The morning air smelled like ice water and the market was already busy, shoppers flowing up and down the aisle in a steady stream, pushing strollers and walking dogs, some singing along to songs pumping through earbuds.

Angel's dad napped in the truck while the three of us ran the stand, making change and bagging groceries and accepting warm wishes from the people who had heard about Earl's heart attack. Every time his name was mentioned my eyes welled up a tiny bit, and even though Angel was busy bagging food or counting out fives and ones, he'd find a way to bump me lightly with his hip or his shoulder to let me know he was there.

Vera single-handedly changed the name of the whole operation by shouting at every shopper, "Earl's Produce, grown with love, picked by hand. Get your Earl's Produce, here and only here!"

And it worked, too. People couldn't pass by a precocious seven-year-old with tangled hair and sleep still in her eyes. She made a ton of sales.

She also made the most of the opportunity to discuss the health benefits of plant foods with customers. She told more people than I could count about "the common misconception that orange juice is the best way to get vitamin C when it is fully understood by nutritionists that red bell peppers provide more per unit."

As the hours passed and the sun grew higher and hotter, Angel peeled off his sweatshirt to reveal a Ramos Family Flowers T-shirt underneath.

I watched Vera read it, then tap Angel on the arm to ask, "Are you a Ramos?"

"I am," he answered. "Angel William Ramos, at your service."

Vera stared at him. "Is William because you were named

after the flower sweet William?"

"Yes, exactly." He broke into a grin. "My mom picked it."

"Where's your flower stand?" Vera switched topics.

"We didn't set up today. We wanted to do this instead." His eyes met mine and I felt a spark between us, a quick moment of something shared.

"Your business can withstand a day without market income?" she inquired, her arms crossed in front of her chest like a tiny investment banker.

Angel cracked a smile. "We'll be okay," he assured her.

"What kind of flowers do you sell? Do you sell sweet Williams?"

"Of course."

"Do you sell chicory?"

"No."

"It's a member of the daisy family," Vera said. "It's an herbaceous plant. You can eat the leaves and you can use the roots to make coffee, *non*-caffeinated, which is an important alternative to have. You should consider it."

"Do you drink coffee?"

"No," she answered immediately. "I'm *seven*!"

"It's easy to forget that," Angel replied, shooting me a look over Vera's head.

"What about yarrow?" she asked.

"As a dried flower, sure. It's great for cutting and drying."

"And then it keeps forever, right?"

"Right."

"Vic is a Yarrow," Vera said. "So, symbolically speaking, you could keep her forever."

"Vera," I snapped at her, a blush exploding on my cheeks.

Angel blushed, too.

I quickly changed the subject. "What's your top seller? Roses?"

"Always roses." Angel nodded. "Which I hate working with, 'cause of the thorns. But that's what everyone wants."

"I'm not surprised," I said, feeling a wave of Chieko wisdom pass through me. "Roses are classic and thorns don't lie."

"And a rose petal is meaningless without a thorn beside it. The beauty is in the contrast. One has no impact without the other." Vera shared this insight like she was just listing what she ate for breakfast.

"Are you, like, the smartest kid in the world?" Angel asked her, a look of awe on his face.

"I highly doubt it," she answered, "although I do like to think I'd give that kid a run for their money."

Angel and I cracked up and Vera raised her arms in question, like she couldn't figure out what was so funny.

I stopped laughing to sell three bell peppers to a woman

with a baby strapped across her chest and then, as if on cue, my stomach grumbled like an animal trapped in a well.

"Feeding time," Angel declared. "I'll be right back."

He returned ten minutes later with a bag of steaming doughnuts and a jug of peach cider. We pushed all the produce we had left to the front of the table like a wall and then sat in the folding chairs behind the stand. We poured paper cups full of cider almost too sweet to drink and took our time chewing our way through the warm cinnamon goodness of Hoefel's special recipe, letting the cake melt in our mouths like a gift from the doughnut god.

When the stand beside us began to pack up, we realized it was almost noon. They broke down their tent, folded up their table, and swept their space like a choreographed dance, but I wasn't ready yet to go.

I had Vera sitting on my left, her legs swinging aimlessly, still not long enough to reach the pavement but getting close. She was licking the sugar off her fingers while carefully observing the shoppers strolling by.

I had Angel to my right, his legs stretched out in front of him, his feet planted on the ground. I watched him take another sip of his drink and realized how well we matched, as far as calloused hands and farmer tans and split-up parents were concerned. There was something special between us because of all we had in common, and it felt good knowing that no matter what happened after camp ended, we would always be connected that way.

I imagined what the three of us looked like sitting in a row in the parking lot under the Meadow Wood tent—Angel with his piercing green eyes and crew cut next to me with my frizzy high ponytail and dirt-lined fingernails next to Vera with her doughnut-crumbed face and butterfly nightshirt tucked into shorts. We were as mixed and random as a meadow of wildflowers.

Earl would have gotten a big kick out of it, I was sure.

"Vic," Angel said, and broke me out of my thoughts.

He reached for my hand, his warm clasp familiar and soothing to me.

He didn't say anything else.

He just held my hand and I held his back and we watched the market slow and empty until the lot was almost bare.

Day 50—Saturday evening

→»·«←

I knocked on Brenda's cabin door, a thick stack of cash in my hand and a small lump in my throat. I heard shuffling and footsteps and then the inner door opened. Her eyes looked puffy and her hair was down. I knew immediately that I had woken her up.

"I'm so sorry. I didn't know you were sleeping."

"It's okay, I'm glad you knocked." Brenda rubbed some of the tired off her face. "I didn't mean to nod off but, well, it's been an exhausting few days."

"I just wanted to give you this." I held out my hand even though there was still a screen between us. "It's from the market."

Brenda pushed open the screen door and pulled me to her in a big hug. "Thank you, dear." When she let go, she said, "Come on in."

She placed the money on her desk and looked out the window to the garden. "Earl loves working the farm with you, Vic."

The lump in my throat doubled in size, and my eyes started that prickly feeling they get right before tears come.

Brenda sighed and then smiled with every inch of her face. "He loves the garden and he loves the market. He'll be so pleased you went today. I'll tell him first thing."

Everything I was holding inside about the night of the social spilled out at once.

"I'm so sorry, Brenda. It shouldn't have happened. What if I was at the social? Maybe I could have stopped it. What if I'd stayed with Jordana? What if I saw those boys get into Earl's cart? What if I—"

"Stop," Brenda cut me off. "I've got a whole closet full of what-ifs, Vic. You know what I can do with them?"

I shook my head.

"Absolutely nothing." Her words dropped like a hammer.

She paused for a moment, then continued, "*What if* is a waste of time. *What now* is the question we should be asking." She lowered herself into the wooden rocking chair by the window. "That's the question we can do something with. *What now?*"

The room was quiet outside of the creak of the chair.

"I don't know," I said.

"I don't know, either," she said, "but I'll figure it out. There are three days of camp left. Then I have Holly and some kitchen staff staying to help close up. The last two weeks of August are for cleaning and maintenance and reminiscing about the season. Earl can only help with the reminiscing, I guess." Brenda smiled.

I scanned the worn floor, the frayed edges of the throw rug, the stains that were probably older than me. And an idea popped into my head. It was crazy, but I said it anyway. "Let me stay."

"What?"

"Let me stay here, with you. If I don't leave camp on Tuesday with everyone else, I could help with all the Earl jobs. And my brother, Freddy, could help, too, if you'd let him. He's a really good worker for an eight-year-old."

"I don't think so, Vic," she said, shaking her head.

"Freddy and I could live in Yarrow together and eat in the dining hall and we'd just go from cabin to cabin, or however you do it, and help you clean and pack things away."

"Not all the work is appropriate for kids."

"But some of it is," I gambled. "And what about the garden? I know more about that than anyone. Someone has to take care of it." I was gaining momentum, my plan growing the more I talked. "I could even get another Saturday in at the market. Maybe two, if you'll drive me. It would help not to have all that food go to waste, 'cause you won't have any campers to feed it to. Please? I want to help. I want to stay."

It would be like doing work to pull oneself out of the depths, I thought. Good, helpful, important work. It was one of the best things I had learned all summer.

"You can ask your mom," Brenda said. "I'd love your company, of course, and it's a generous offer, but I doubt she'll go for it."

"She'll go for it." I could convince my mom. She was the one who wanted Freddy and me gone in the first place. I was certain I could get another week or two out of her.

"I can't believe you just turned my words on me. *What if* your mom lets you stay? That's a good what-if. That's one I *can* do something with."

"I think there are a lot of good what-ifs out there," I said.

"Just don't let me see a *What If* flag on the pole tomorrow morning, okay? I've had enough surprises."

"I didn't even think of that. You're thinking like an Aster," I pointed out.

"Dear, I was a camper for years before I was a director. And the camper in you . . ." She looked across the room at the bookshelf lined with Meadow Wood yearbooks. A soft smile spread across her face. "The camper in you never dies."

Day 51—Sunday

->>>·<<<-

I found Chieko in the archery hut after dinner. She sat tilted back in a chair, so the two front legs didn't touch the ground, a book in her hands and her eyes glued to the page.

I knocked on the half-open door, so I wouldn't scare her.

She didn't even look up at the sound. She just held out her hand in a *wait* gesture while she got to a good stopping point in her book. She was like Carly that way, and Jamie, too. I realized right then that I seemed to really like people who really liked books. I wondered what that said about me. Maybe I should try reading more.

"For the record," Chieko said when she was done, closing the book around her finger, "you found me busily cleaning arrows and organizing equipment."

"I did?" I asked.

"Yes, you did. I was so focused on my archery work I didn't realize you were standing there waiting for me." Then she leaned toward me and coaxed, "Right?"

I caught on. "Yes. Right. So focused. The hut's never looked better." Which was a gigantic lie. The shelves were stuffed with mismatched arrows and torn boxes and broken pieces of bows. There were wrist guards, rolled-up paper targets, and safety booklets piled on top of each other like a trash monument that just needed one quick puff to send it toppling over. The table was still littered with the box and packaging materials that came last week, and the one window was caked in layers of smudges and handprints. The hut was a disgrace, and Chieko had only one full day left to get it into shape.

"So," she said, "to what do I owe the great honor of your presence?"

"I need your ankle," I answered.

"What?"

"Just give me your ankle a sec." I walked toward her and reached out for it.

"Not without a trade," she countered. "Give me an elbow."

"Chieko," I groaned. "C'mon. Give it."

She stuck her leg out at me—she was wearing sneakers but no socks—and returned to her book.

I pulled a black Sharpie out of my pocket and told her, "Now don't move."

"Good God," she replied, but she held still for me.

I hunched over her ankle and carefully drew a fancy capital *E* in front of the *R* that was already on her skin, trying to size and space it just right so it would match. I moved beneath the letters then to ink something else, my hand shaking a bit as I tried to control the thick tip of the marker. I moved back to see how it looked from a distance, then leaned in again to add to the *E* so it would look more like calligraphy. Then I let go of her leg.

"Okay, I'm done." I sighed heavily, hope brewing in my gut. "What do you think?"

Chieko closed her book slowly, slid it onto the crowded tabletop, and pulled her leg into her chest to get a close look.

"E R?" she read.

"Uh-huh." I nodded enthusiastically.

"Emergency Room?" she asked incredulously. "That's a terrible tattoo. And why is there a skinny pointer finger underneath it?"

"That's not a finger."

"It looks like a finger," Chieko said.

"It's a candle."

"It looks like a really creepy finger." Chieko shuddered.

"It's not a finger!" I yelled. "I'm not a professional artist, you know."

"Clearly." Chieko showed no mercy.

"And it's not Emergency Room. The *ER* stands for Eleanor Roosevelt, and the candle is for something cool Brenda mentioned when we were talking about Eleanor," I explained. "Apparently she's a real fan of hers, too."

"Everyone should be a fan of Eleanor," Chieko replied. "What did Brenda say?"

"She said that, at Eleanor's funeral or something, a good friend of Eleanor's described her as someone who would rather light candles than curse the darkness."

"Hmmm." Chieko twisted her ankle from side to side as she examined the new design, tossing her long blue-black bangs out of her eyes with a quick flick of her head. She straightened her leg back out and examined it from there, biting her bottom lip and not saying a word.

I waited.

After a full minute of silence, she said, "So, since I can't undo my tattoo, I should change it into something else? That's what you're saying?"

"Yeah." I explained, "It works perfectly. You said Eleanor Roosevelt is your soul sister, and half her initials are already on you. Add the candle—a good candle, by an actual artist—and it will be like the spirit of Eleanor is with you all the time."

"Say it again," Chieko said.

"The kind of person who would rather light a candle than curse the darkness," I repeated.

"Of course. Definitely." She looked at her ankle again and squinted a bit, maybe imagining a professional version of what I'd tried to draw. "So . . . try to do something good instead of wallowing in the bad that already happened," Chieko thought aloud.

"That you can't undo," I added, thinking of Earl and of my parents, of the darkness that had already happened and the new beginning—the light—we'd have to make now.

"Huh," she said with one quick bob of her head.

"Yeah." I copied her bob.

"Well." Chieko stood up from her chair and pushed it back against the wall, then faced me. "My work here is done, young one. The student has become the master."

"Huh?"

"You're brilliant. I'll do it—your idea. It works."

A smile hijacked my face and I felt seriously proud.

"Although we all still need our small moments of cursing the darkness. It's a great release—the cursing," Chieko assured me.

"Okay, fine," I relented, "but *after* the cursing—"

"Yes, *after*, then it's candle-lighting time."

I folded my arms in front of my chest in satisfaction and said, "Words to live by."

"No—words to *cheer* by!" Chieko became suddenly animated. "Where's *that* cheer, huh? Instead of bananas and screaming over who has more spirit, we should have candle-lighting Eleanor cheers."

"Yeah, good luck with that, Chieko."

"What? If there were Eleanor cheers, I would actually join in and scream along with the rest of you bozos."

"No, you wouldn't," I told her.

"No, I wouldn't," she agreed.

I turned toward the door. "Gotta go to Brenda's real quick and then visit Vera."

"Wait, there's something I have to tell you." Chieko straightened her posture.

"Yeah?"

"I'm going back on the archery team. When school starts again, my junior year. I'm gonna compete."

"Yay! What made you change your mind?" And then I smiled and answered my question before she could. "Wait, I know: 'You must do the thing you think you cannot do,' right?"

"Wrong," she shot back at me. "I'm just crazy skilled at archery. It would be cruel to deny the team my excellence."

I smiled even bigger and then she did too, her eyes bright and happy.

I walked straight to Brenda's cabin from the archery range. She had scheduled this time for me to call my mom to ask for two more weeks at camp. If anyone had told me back in June that I'd want extra time at Meadow Wood, I would have laughed in their face.

I figured the biggest problem with staying at camp would be figuring out how to get home. The bus ride on Tuesday was already arranged and prepaid, so once we missed that, I didn't know what the options were. I knew Holly was driving herself back to Vermont and the kitchen staff would be flying back to England. Brenda lived at camp year-round, so she was already home. I'd meant to have a solution ready before I called my mom, but I still didn't have one.

Brenda swung open the screen door just as I lifted my hand to knock.

"I need to meet with the girls in Aster, so I'll be gone about a half hour. The office is yours. Good luck."

"Thanks."

"But only call your mom. And your dad, too, if you need his permission. But not Angel."

I hadn't thought about trying to call Angel even once since Earl caught me.

"I know," I said. "I wasn't going to—"

"Good luck," Brenda said again, and walked out.

I lowered myself into Brenda's chair and pulled it all the way into the desk so my stomach was pressed against the smooth wood and I was forced to sit up straight and tall. I gazed at the phone. My palms felt clammy. *You must do the thing you think you cannot do.*

I picked up the phone, dialed, and held my breath as it rang.

"Hello?"

I let my breath go. "Hi, Mom."

"Vic. Honey, how are you?" Her voice changed and she asked, "Is everything okay?"

"Everything's fine. I'm fine."

"Good." She let out a sigh.

"How are you?" I asked.

It was quiet for a heartbeat, and then Mom started to cry. Really cry. High-pitched sobs and short gasps for air flooded my ear from miles away. I pictured her at our kitchen table, a cup of tea gone cold in front of her, tissues balled up and dropped to the floor. She sounded so sad. And alone.

"Mom—" I started.

"I'm so sorry," she interrupted me, her voice crumpling. "I really messed up, Vicky. I messed up everything."

My mom hadn't called me Vicky in years, not since I turned eight years old and told her I wanted to be Vic and only Vic from then on.

I swallowed, then asked, "With Darrin?"

"With everything." She blew her nose. "And Darrin—he was a mistake. And he's over. That's over."

"So Dad's back?" The words were out of my mouth in a flash.

"No, honey. It's not that simple."

I felt stupid for sounding so eager, for sounding like a little kid.

"We still have a lot to figure out, your dad and me. We're having a hard time. But we'll work something out, okay?" my mom said. "I promise."

I nodded even though I knew she couldn't see me.

"And I'm so proud of you, honey. All the farming you've been doing with Earl—he told me how helpful you've been. And the money you sent—thank you, but it's your money. We'll open a savings account for you once you get home. You should always have your own money. For emergencies."

"Carly has one. Because of babysitting."

"You'll have one, too. You deserve it."

"Mom, I wanted to ask you something."

After I explained the situation to her, all she wanted to know was if I *really wanted to stay* and if it *really meant a lot to me*. When I said yes to both, she agreed she'd try to make it work. She needed to talk to Freddy first, because he shouldn't have to stay unless he wanted to. She was right about that. She also needed to figure out the logistics of getting me, or us, back home.

Then she said something that really surprised me.

"Who knows? Maybe I could drive up for the last day or two and join you. Maybe that would be good for me, for the three of us, to spend the time together."

It didn't make sense. A few months ago, my mom couldn't wait to get rid of us, but now she was talking about leaving her home to do dirty unpaid work with Freddy and me at Meadow Wood?

I didn't believe it.

I knew she wouldn't come.

But maybe it was enough that she thought of it. It showed that she was trying.

And right now, maybe trying was enough.

Day 52—Monday

>>> · <<<

"This is bizarro," Chieko announced, walking into our room with a stack of letters in her hands. "You each got mail with the same handwriting, and they all say 'BUS LETTER' all over the envelope."

"Carly!" Jaida A and Jaida C screamed at the same time, then rushed at Chieko.

"What's a bus letter?" Chieko asked as the Jaidas grabbed the mail out of her hands.

"I forgot about the letters!" Jordana said. She had moved out of clinic and back into our cabin yesterday but still wasn't allowed to do much. "And I'm not allowed to read. And I'm not allowed to write," she reminded herself aloud, panic rising in her voice.

"What's a bus letter?" Chieko asked again.

"We'll help you. Don't worry," Jaida C said right away.

"But you're not on my bus, so you won't be able to read to me. And you can't help me write my bus letter to *you*." Jordana was becoming distraught.

"You can get anyone on your bus to read to you," Jaida C said. "And Jaida A will help you write my letter and I'll help you write Jaida A's and Vic's and Chieko's."

"Carly's not even here and she still did this—she's the best!" Jaida A said, clutching her letter to her chest.

"WHAT ON GOD'S GREEN EARTH IS A BUS LETTER?" Chieko shouted.

The room went silent as we stopped in our tracks and stared at our counselor, her arms raised in total frustration.

Jordana took center stage by answering in a clear, calm voice, "It's a letter. That you read. On a bus."

Chieko's arms dropped to her sides in total surrender. "Good God," she muttered.

"Except for Vic," Jaida C said, turning to me. "You're gonna read your bus letters here, right? After we're gone?"

I had told them about the after-camp-close-up plan. "Maybe I'll bed-hop. I'll read your letters on each of your beds, to make it more . . . authentic." I looked at Chieko so she would note the use of a higher vocabulary word.

"You guys are total ding-a-lings," Chieko said. "I've got

more mail duty. I'll be back." She rolled her eyes at us and left the bunk.

When she returned a half hour later, she found us all sitting on our beds bent over stationery, furiously scribbling six-, eight-, ten-page letters to each other. And to other friends outside our bunk. And to favorite counselors. And to camp sisters.

"It's your last rest hour of the entire summer and this is how you're spending it?" Chieko couldn't believe what she was seeing. "You look like you're all cramming for midterms."

No one even looked up.

The letters had to get done.

But I had to admit, the bus letter tradition always confused me.

A stack of bus letters from your closest, dearest friends was definitely fun to whip out and read when you were stuck on a boring, hot, hours-long bus ride. In the letters, we retold private jokes and memories and went on about how much we would miss each other until next June, and we wrote our phone numbers and addresses in huge print to remind each other to use them. But writing them was a complete drag. Instead of spending our last day enjoying each other's company, we all spent the day alone, isolated like little islands of deep thought, writing until our hands cramped and our fingers went numb.

It kind of made no sense.

"So, you're wasting your last bit of time together by writing about how much you're going to miss your time together?" Chieko summarized, pity clouding her voice.

It obviously made no sense to her, either.

But still, I was going to write her one.

"How about the last Roses and Thorns? Is everyone's thorn writing these endless letters right now?" Chieko prompted.

"Yeah," we all answered in unison without lifting our heads from our papers.

"And your roses?" Chieko continued. "Would that be knowing you're all getting a special stack of letters tomorrow?"

"Yeah," we all echoed back again.

"Fantastic," Chieko said. "The last Roses and Thorns of the season—done." She made a big check mark in the air and left the room, shaking her head at us.

But that night, when the lights were out, and I was trying to close my mind to sleep, I saw Chieko at work on something under her covers with the light of her cell phone, which I guessed she felt she didn't need to hide anymore. There was too much of a steady scratch sound for her to be reading a book. I was pretty sure she was writing a bus letter.

And I was pretty sure that it was for me.

Day 53—Tuesday

-»»·«-

For the first time all summer, I woke up before the bugle all on my own. I dressed and brushed my teeth and made my bed, knowing I was the only one in the cabin who would have to do that this morning. Everyone else would be ripping off their blankets and pillows and stuffing them into their duffel bags for the trip home. I had heard from Brenda, who had heard from my mom, that Freddy couldn't wait to move into a "real" cabin at Meadow Wood, which he probably considered a luxury hotel compared to his tent at Forest Lake.

I opened my cubby and pulled out a black Sharpie marker. On the inside of my cubby door, I wrote *Vic was here* and drew a candle next to it, which came out a lot better than the one I drew on Chieko's leg. Then I closed the cubby door and left the marker out for my friends to use.

I left the cabin without a sound. The chill of the morning was already fading, the sun inching skyward. I walked up the hill and rounded the corner behind Brenda's cabin to check on the garden.

There were tomatoes ready, so I picked them carefully. I helped myself to Earl's bandanna, which was hanging by the hose right where I left it, and wrapped the tomatoes inside. I put them on the windowsill where I knew Brenda would find them, and then walked back over to a row of raised beds. I sat on the edge of one, careful the splintering wood wouldn't stick me through my shorts, and watched the plants wake up with the sun.

I noticed the tomato plants by the back of the garden, how they weren't growing as well as the others because the berry bushes blocked some of their sun. Earl said it was a mistake he wouldn't make again next summer. He had never grown tomatoes before, so he didn't realize how much direct sun they needed. He said it was trial and error and that making mistakes and learning from them, adjusting to the results, was usually an okay way to go.

I thought about mistakes. I thought about glaring monumental mistakes, and I thought about smaller ones that build on each other, like beads on a string.

I thought about Earl and knew he would never consider

what he did a mistake, running for Jordana, carrying her to help. He made that choice and I was certain, beyond any doubt, that he would make it again.

I thought about my mom and how, when I first saw that email, I thought Darrin was the mistake she was making, but now I knew I was wrong. The mistakes came first, between her and my dad. As much as it bothered me to consider it, maybe the mess with Darrin would turn out to be part of the solution.

I thought about Chieko and the mistake she got printed into her skin, and the way she planned to fix it.

I thought about Brenda and her closet full of what-ifs—the what-ifs she could do something with and the what-ifs that she couldn't. And I thought about how smart she was to realize that *what now* was sometimes the better question.

I thought about Jordana and the mistakes she'd made this summer, always trying to be older, cooler, to get the attention of the Aster girls. I hoped the time she spent resting in clinic gave her a chance to sort them out. And learn from them. And adjust.

If there was one thing I had learned from my mom and dad, it was that you were never too old to make mistakes. I knew I still had plenty of mistakes ahead of me, big and little. I knew I'd get stuck and I knew I would need help.

But I had resources now.

I was crazy rich with resources.

I could read Eleanor.

Or I could do research like Vera.

Or I could call Chieko.

Or I could find some ground and dig deep like Earl, turning the soil until it sparkled like a mine of gems, shining its possibilities up at me.

And then I'd go from there.

Acknowledgments

A giant thank you goes to my wonderful and talented agent, Joan Rosen, for your constant support, dedication, and expertise. I appreciate everything you've done to keep the good squidgy alive!

I also want to thank everyone at HarperCollins Children's Books, especially Cat San Juan, Liz Byer, Valerie Shea, Erin Fitzsimmons, Erin Wallace, Vaishali Nayak, and Mitchell Thorpe for all your hard work poking and prodding this book into shape.

A huge thank you goes to my smart and exacting editor, Jessica MacLeish, and a heartfelt thank you to the very attentive, professional, and supportive Courtney Stevenson for holding my hand across the finish line.

I am in love with Jane Newland's art and am eternally grateful for her gorgeous cover illustration.

I want to thank indie booksellers everywhere for working passionately to match books with readers every single day. A giant shout-out to Julie, Jen, Sarah, and Basia at Inkwood Books in

New Jersey. You are all bookselling queens!

I also want to thank my fun and very supportive book-nerd family at the Haddonfield Public Library. Work doesn't feel like work with you.

Thank you to my mom for bringing me one hundred home-made chocolate chip cookies every single summer on Visiting Day, (plus another hundred for Gayle, plus another hundred for Jan), and thank you to my dad for introducing me to the very unique world that is sleepaway camp.

My deepest thanks go to Jeffrey, Nina, and Mike. I love you more than anything in the whole wide world. Thank you for always being there for me. You are my everything.

And to all the campers who know what it's like to be ripped out of a glorious night's sleep by the sound of a bugle screeching over a lousy PA system—this book is for you.